Eric Mota

Twitch - EricMotinha

In the twelve cycles of souls
We only remember the things
That really marked us

Table of Contents:

Prologue

"Hello there, I am writing this in an attempt to regain my sanity, most likely no one will ever get to read this, but if someone ever does, please know, hell is real. "

Charles, a jobless Brazilian, has been plotting ways to pay his bills when he suddenly comes across a frightening figure who offers him a job, one that is too good to be true, and this is how his newfound adventure begins, how he comes to discover life as it really is, delicate, fleeting, incredible, supernatural, and strange.

Lacking any choice, Charles ultimately accepts a five hundred year contract with Hell, a contract which grants him some benefits. but little did Charles know that this would bring forth the intervention that would alter the existence of mankind as we know it today.

Deep Web, torture chambers, dream world, lucid dreamers, reincarnation, and the seven leaders of hell. The following story takes place in the 21st century, nowadays, and the various characters, monsters, and entities described can be found in various different cultures described in different ways and forms. But this story is not just a historical legend; you may or may not believe it; but this is a story based on true accounts, but to find out more about it, you need to pay close attention to the story and the many details I am about to share with you.

The Damned Pop-Up

Hello there, I am writing this in an attempt to regain my sanity, most likely no one will ever get to read this, but if someone ever does, please know, hell is real.

My name is Charles, I always had a quiet and fairly normal life, but everything suddenly changed, and this all thanks to the internet.

It was a day like any other, I was sitting in my room listening to some "good music" - not the crap they are making these days - and watching some nonsense on the Internet.

I lit up a joint and pondered on how to get a job to pay my bills, but was unable to come up with one - last month's rent was already hard enough to pay - I could maybe call my parents and ask to borrow some money, but they would certainly not be able to help - just like they have said all my life.

Actually, it wasn't just any day, on this day I got tired of listening to the same songs and not even the random setting could fix the issue - it messed up the "flow" - so I started looking for a new and fresh playlist.

I had a look at the Youtube recommendations, but even then I had no luck - nothing appealed to me - then I had the damned idea to look for one of those pirate radio stations you find through suspicious links on the internet.

After some time going through some forums - which I regularly use - I found a link posted by the user "Cirfelu". The link redirected me to a radio station with songs from the "80s", the audio quality was kind of bad - but at least the songs were good - and sometimes the connection even went down for a few milliseconds - making it seem like one of those small town radios.

Probably hardly anyone still accesses this kind of link and listens to music of this quality anymore. I wondered what kind of audience would access this kind of pirate radio stations - besides the difficulty to find the link the sound quality was awful - plus the high chance of getting a virus on your computer, with the countless pop-ups that keep opening after each song, all for the sake of listening to something different.

And it all started thanks to one of these annoying pop-ups.

I had come to terms with it, and left the 80's radio playing, went to the sofa to chill with the Bong in hand, but when the first song - The Police/Every Breath You Take - was playing, the "phantom" radio stopped.

I had to get up and grab my wireless keyboard and mouse - I always plugged my notebook into the television in my room - I moved the mouse and saw it was another pop-up, but quite unlike any I had ever seen.

The climax was gone - everything was going wrong that day - the bong was almost fulfilling its purpose - getting me "high" - but having to get up and mess with the computer woke me up and made me curious to know what was going on - even more so since I am involved with IT.

I touched the mouse and the screen was no longer dark, this time I didn't see anything to stop the music from playing, I exclaimed -

what the hell is this? - And coincidentally, or not, the pop-up appeared out of nowhere.

Very flashy, with background music - Kansas/Dust In The Wind - I liked the music so I decided not to close it right away. While listening to the song I began to stare at it - it was very strange - full of colors, symbols and strange messages - it was in a strange kind of language - and at the same time it was psychedelic, it was also very "dark". I noticed that in the center there was a digital stopwatch - showing eight hours and some seconds and counting down - very interesting, and scary at the same time - further making me curious about it.

I put some of my computer skills to good use and with a few tweaks to adjust brightness, contrast and colors I could see that at the bottom of the pop-up there was something written and as I read it, my spine froze.

- "We found you".

As soon as I read that, the music stopped, the ad disappeared and the radio station that was previously playing went back to playing the "80's" songs.

I spent some more time examining the computer, rebooted, formatted, turned it back on and off, I was a bit shocked wondering if I was too stoned and if all this had really happened.

Finally, I had a few laughs - alone - and told myself that it was most likely all in my enormous imagination.

I decided to make myself something to eat - I was feeling really baked - so I grabbed a bite and watched some Netflix until I fell asleep.

It was about ten to three in the morning when I woke up, still on the sofa, the computer light was on, although I remember turning it off, I had the impression of hearing a quiet sound coming from the TV, however, it was loud enough to disturb me and not let me go back to sleep unless I went over there.

- Why do these things only happen to me! - I exclaimed aloud.

The TV was still on, I switched from Netflix to the computer screen and as soon as the picture was switched I got a big shock, the sound of the music suddenly increased and as I reached for the remote to turn it down the TV went back to mute - even then I turned the volume down - the brightness of the computer screen was still high thanks to the adjustments I had made earlier to investigate the pop-up, so I readjusted the brightness and just as I was about to turn off the computer and go back to sleep, I noticed something minimized in the left corner of the screen.

It was the pop-up.

I considered for a brief moment whether to shut down the computer and go to sleep, or whether to maximize it to check if it was the same pop-up as before. I maximized it - my curiosity was louder than sleep - I found out that it was the same one as before, although it wasn't exactly the one, this time not as colorful, as if the chronometer - now marking five minutes to zero - was sucking the color out of the pop-up.

I tried to close it, but no command on the computer worked, the only thing that still seemed to work was the chronometer slowly decreasing its counter.

I was now in a dilemma - to wait for the timer to reach zero or not? - Since there were only five minutes left, I decided to wait.

I was not sure why, but a strong emotion began to take over me, and the closer the timer got to zero, the greater my curiosity to find out what would happen when the timer ran out.

I wished it was only a dream, but unfortunately the silence of the dawn seemed too real and deafening for it to be one.

There was now only one minute left, and as soon as the stopwatch hand made the transition from minutes to seconds, the damn thing began to make sounds, the volume was very low, so the sounds that were emitted by the decrease of each second were mingled, with the most distinctive and clear one being the sound of a ticking clock dictating a countdown in the background - tick-tock, tick-tock, tick-tock, tick-tock, tick-tock, tick-tock - the closer the clock got to its final seconds, the louder the sounds seemed to get and even though the volume was set to zero on the TV and computer, the sounds didn't stop and now another sound began to stand out in the background along with the other sounds, it was the sound of people screaming.

Slowly it got closer and closer to zero, things got weirder by the second, even with the sound volume at zero, the hollow sounds of the changing seconds were getting louder throughout the room - or inside my head - and the previously "colorful" shades of color in my room seemed to be sucked in by the stopwatch.

I pictured on my mind that at any moment I would wake up sweaty on my bed or on the couch with Netflix on, but when the stopwatch reached zero, a deafening alarm rang at the same instant, it was so loud I had to put my hands to my ears, covering them and also closing my eyes, as the whole house seemed to vibrate with the sound of the alarm, I even thought that I would explode with the noise, a few seconds later, I noticed the noise and all the vibration had passed, I pulled myself together but bumped into the glass that was on the table in front of me and instead of falling, the glass with a little water floated off the table, as if the time around me stopped.

- What is this? - I asked myself.

The noise of the street, of cars passing by and dogs barking - which almost never ceased - had stopped, but this lasted only for a brief moment, as seconds later I caught a glimpse of a figure passing by, as I turned to face the figure I heard the dogs howling and then realized that there was someone sitting on the sofa.

There was a "man" sitting elegantly cross-legged on my couch, he was wearing an elegant suit, along with a black top hat - with odd-looking white trimmings - his skin was very pale and contrasted with his long, wavy black hair.

The hair and the top hat did a perfect job of hiding his face, maybe that's why I didn't get scared and kept calm, assuming it was a dream.

- You are calm, maybe that is the reason I am here, many would be scared to death and I feel no fear coming from you, only suspicion, nice to meet you Charles. Yes, I know your name, even though you don't know me, I heard that you are in need of a job and I have the perfect job to offer you, but first I will grant you the right to three questions, feel free to ask them," said the figure smiling, showing his bright white teeth.

It was by far the strangest "dream" I ever experienced - and also one of the most interesting, so I decided to play along.

- What is your name, where are you from, and what do you want with me? - I asked.

- Straight to the point, you asked all three questions at once, I remember when I was also as immature as you. I went by several names, but my real name is Oliver, I was born in London, but nowadays I don't come from anywhere, and what I want with you is the same thing they wanted with me five hundred years ago.

- Five hundred years ago, what the hell is this? - I asked him.

- No more questions, I said I would answer three questions and you have asked them all at the same time. Now shut up, I will explain to you what I am doing here and don't think there is any easy or simple way out of this situation, you will only have one hour to make up your mind, but in the meantime I will tell you a story.

Part of me was enjoying all of this, so I just stood there and didn't show any reaction.

He spoke again.

Young Oliver

I was a young Englishman, age 18, who believed in neither heaven nor hell, my family had a good status, being close to Queen Mary I, and so I grew up spoiled and overprotected, being allowed to stay during my childhood and teenage years only on the outskirts of the castle.

At that age the teenagers and servants of the castle did not get so close to women, other than the fat, old women of the castle - things were much stricter in the old times.

On some of the better days, I would cross paths with the princess or go to the village market with my father and do some groceries for the castle, other days were pretty much the same, I would wake up early to fetch the bread that the baker had left in a basket and take it to the castle kitchen, where my mother and Aunt Evelyn, both cooks, prepared the royalty's breakfast.

After stealing some breadcrumbs and drinking the leftover glasses of milk, it was time for the part-time job they had arranged for me with the excuse that it would help me in the future. I was assigned to help the elder who took care of the scrolls and the healer who treated the sick.

They both had the same speech about payment, my payment was the knowledge that I acquired in the presence of the two babbling old men, but the truth was that I witnessed many bizarre things that the two did with their patients in the search for self-knowledge, while one experimented the other wrote down in the scrolls what worked.

After organizing the scrolls and feeding the sick, it was time to help at home with my household chores, and at the end of the night I often had to go with my father - the palace guard - to learn how to patrol.

In the beginning he even taught me a few things, but now most of the nights that he called me to patrol with him, it was because he wanted to sleep, so he let me do his routes and watch the castle while he slept.

That was basically my life, until I had a great idea while thinking with the wrong head.

It was only days before my eighteenth birthday and since I had never been with a woman - and I couldn't stand it any longer - I decided to come up with a plan to quench some curiosity.

Basically, the plan was as follows, stop being a boy and become a man, by going to a whorehouse in the village, it was a brothel with a good reputation - Madame Blade's brothel - which was a little far from the center of the village, it was a place I had heard the guards speak well of several times.

I planned it all in my head - I told no one - the idea was, after my parents went to sleep, I would climb out of my bedroom window and go with my savings to Madam Blade's brothel.

So that's what I did. On my birthday, around eleven twenty at night, when the castle was not very busy and my parents had already gone to bed, I began to carry out the plan.

I took three sheets, tied them together, secured them to the bed's headboard and threw them out the window of my room - like a rope - after holding on for a few moments I managed to accomplish the task quietly and with little effort.

Euphoria took over me and I didn't even realize the risk I had taken, I could have broken my neck, but it was all for my big day. It was a long walk from the castle to the brothel, and since electricity had not yet been invented, I hid a lantern during the day near the exit so that I could see the way from the castle to the village.

I kept following the plan, went towards the village and after half an hour of a hard walk I saw the first street lamps of the village.

Unfortunately my destination was still on the other side of the village, so I had to cross it. I kept walking, but as I got further away from home the feeling that something was going to go wrong began to grow, but on the other hand the desire to get to the brothel didn't diminish.

I reached the center of the village and it was already practically empty, but there were still some open taverns, full of people warming their bodies with drinks, women, fireplaces and other types of narcotics.

I kept my head down, hoping not to bump into anyone and to get to the brothel as soon as possible.

Less than two kilometers to go, I decided to take a shortcut to narrow the path and arrive even faster, it was then I noticed on one of the alleys I left behind, two men, they spotted me and decided to stalk me.

As I tightened my steps, so did they, I tried to get away by turning in some alleys and crouching down quietly, trying to lose them, but even so they were getting closer and closer, so I thought about running - home or to the brothel - but as I was trying to decide they shouted.

- Hey kid, we know you're still here, where are you going in such a hurry, huh? - said one of the men.

I said nothing, the brothel was about three hundred meters from me and so far the plan was working, there were only a few more corners left, so I got up and ran.

- Hey kid, are you deaf?

I felt a blow behind my head, followed by a hollow noise and the next thing I knew I was down - the two guys caught up to me - I looked at the ground and saw a bloody rock, I put my hands on my head and could feel something wet, it was my own blood.

They had thrown a rock at me and hit me straight on, I got a little dizzy and collapsed to the ground. One of them approached me and seemed very drunk and a little scared.

I tried to say something, but was interrupted by the other guy.

- Give me everything you have – said the other guy.

I couldn't move properly and before I could even understand or react, he took my coat, shoes, money, and watch - everything I had of value.

The other guy looked worried about me, but when he saw his "friend" robbing me he did the same.

I tried to scream for help, but when they realized that I was going to scream, one of them - I couldn't identify which one - covered my mouth and stabbed me in the back with a knife.

As I felt a horrible pain in my spine I could no longer react, I remained motionless on the cold ground while the thieves went away and left me waiting for death to come.

I began to wonder how my parents and the people in the castle would receive the news.

"Young dead boy found near the alley of the most renowned brothel in town. Dead and still a virgin!". This misfortune would be remembered and laughed at by the palace guards for a long time to come.

But even there, about to die, I was still thinking about what would happen later, even though I didn't believe there was any later.

They always say that in our last moments time passes differently, and this is true, they just don't say that it is different for each person.

Not much time had passed since the thieves had left me there and for me time had already begun to pass in a different way - slowly - until a figure appeared out of the dark and slowly approached me - at first I thought it was death itself coming to get me - my eyes were blurred, I struggled to see and recognize that the figure was a woman and that in her hands were two heads, the heads of the thieves who had attacked and robbed me.

She threw the two heads against the wall with such force that they were blown off, then walked slowly towards me, crouched down beside me and threw my stolen belongings over.

I couldn't speak and my attempts to ask for help were in vain, but she realized this and spoke up.

- So much potential. I have been watching you since your ingenious escape from the castle. There are very few things in this world that can hold my attention, but the scent of your desire managed to excite me. I know what you intended to do,- at that moment she touched my blood with her finger and put it in her mouth, then kept on speaking,- I know of your "silliest" and deepest desires, I know that for you many of them seem sinful, but to see a young man like you, who doesn't know anything yet, have his life sucked away like this, by drunks, who wouldn't even mind spending their money on the whores you intended to "meet". This makes me very angry, don't you feel the same? - said the figure that turned out to be a beautiful woman.

Saying it all helped to reignite some of the flame inside me that was about to go out, it was everything I was thinking and those words fueled my anger, anguish and all the feelings inside me, and with a lot of effort I managed to say something.

- Damn them! - I said to her.

The cut had clotted and the puddle of blood - warm - was keeping me somewhat heated, yet I was beginning to feel as if one of those butcher's hooks that hold the pigs in the freezers, had entered my spine, so a strange cold, which I had never felt before, was beginning to run up my spine and I could no longer feel my feet.

- Calm down! You can't die yet, I need to show myself to you. - she said.

She stood up and let her big overcoat fall down.

She had the palest skin I had ever seen, and also the most beautiful pair of breasts - perfectly round - more perfect than I had imagined in my dreams and "sinful" thoughts.

- Even like this and after losing so much blood, do you still feel this? This feeling makes me crazy - she said, looking at the bulge in my pants.

Without reason or explanation she began to kiss me, smoothing me and it was the strangest and most pleasurable sensation I had ever felt in my life, I fought to remain lucid and survive a few more minutes to not die a virgin, at the same time I fought with the thought of not wanting to die yet.

Even though my body was sore and my wound was bleeding again, I surrendered to the moment when she started sucking me. A short time later she was on top of me, and I no longer felt cold, in fact I couldn't feel any part of my body, I could only feel two things, fear and pleasure.

Her motions were perfect and as the cold went up my spine and intensified, her moves also increased, so that after a few minutes I couldn't hold on any longer.

I came, and it was at this moment that my time seemed to be up, I was in the abyss on the brink of death, completely paralyzed with my vision darkening little by little, the only thing I could feel now were the weak beats of my heart, second by second, getting weaker.

She stood up, got dressed and approached me whispering something in my ear.

- It was the best first time I have ever witnessed, I wonder what is going through your head now? How did it feel to ejaculate whilst on the verge of death? Funny how my curiosity about you only increases by the second, I also have many other curiosities about mortality and free will, too bad we don't have more time. At least not now, you still have a minute to decide, so listen carefully. As I said, I have been watching you, but I was not looking for you, it was a happy accident for you to have me watching you, I could not resist and ended up interfering in the life of those bandits and in their cold and lonely deaths. A ship will set sail in 1519, commanded by the Portuguese Ferdinand Magellan, and you will have to serve in America and carry out some missions - which in the future will influence the world - this new continent is to become one of the most important and strongest continents in the world. You will remain there until we meet again and I give you new orders, I know this must not make any sense to you now, but I am offering you immortality, you will only have to submit to our orders and do everything you are told for the next 500 years, that is the contract. You don't have much time, I need a sign, blink twice fast to accept or stand still and die like a man after having at least fulfilled your most sinful mortal desire.

- The worst thing about being human is that we always want to survive - said Oliver finishing his tale.

Back in the room with the stranger

With each passing minute it got increasingly stranger, he resumed speaking, therefore I didn't interrupt.

- As you may guess, I didn't have much choice and here I am, five hundred years later, about to get rid of this "contract", but first I was charged with this last mission. That's where you come in, I have a job to "offer" you, and I won't take no for an answer - said Oliver.

After talking for a long time he finally took a break, put his hands in his pocket, took out a cigarette and lit it, took a long drag, I thought about saying something, but before I could think of anything he spoke again.

- Here's the thing, you have two choices, the first you don't accept the job, it's not something I would recommend, since the refusal of such offer would imply your death, and I'm not talking about just any kind of death, I'm talking about you being found tomorrow in a way that is not pleasant for your family, "poor depressive kid, he committed suicide with medication and a high dosage of heroin" - said Oliver taking another long drag on the cigarette and a slight smile.

- The alternative would be to accept the "job" - along with its benefits and curses - you could even continue living your life normally for a while - which was denied to me - but only until your mid-forties, after that you would be better off moving, changing your name, city, and having no more contact with acquaintances, since you will stop aging at thirty-three - ironic, right? Being the age of Christ's death - so you could probably only disguise yourself without raising many suspicions until around forty-something, since you will then be immortal and no longer age, it is better if people don't ask questions. There are also curses to deal with, seeing your whole family, passions and sometimes even children die, being left behind, besides all this, you will get to know things that you never thought existed, such as monsters, hell, purgatory, paradise, etc. The validity of the contract is "only" five hundred years, after which you can die as a mortal. There, now you can talk! - said Oliver, snapping his fingers and reaching into his pocket for another cigarette.

Could it be that I couldn't talk? I thought about it for a while and the fact that he snapped his fingers seemed to me to be far more than a mere gesture, for until then I thought I wasn't talking because I simply didn't want to interrupt, but after he snapped his fingers I felt something different and this time I really felt like talking.

- This is the strangest dream I've ever had, the only answer is that, I don't need to answer anything, I'll wake up soon anyway - I stated trying to keep calm and under control during the dream.

It had to be a dream, I would never have the courage to speak to a strange and frightening figure in such a loud and mocking voice as I just did.

- You really have the nerve to talk like that in this situation, but I was already expecting an answer similar to this, since I also thought I was dreaming or hallucinating in my time. So you think all this is a dream? Good, then get up and go to your desk, there is a box of medicines I brought for you, take them all, don't you disobey me! - said

Oliver, snapping his fingers again and flashing his evil, devilishly bright white smile.

Suddenly I couldn't control my body any longer, I had no idea what I was doing, I couldn't control my movements, so I stood up and did exactly what he asked, I took the medicine box, put them all in my mouth, and to help it go down I took the whiskey that was in the glass next to the medicine.

After swallowing the pills I regained control over my body, but still couldn't believe what had happened, I picked up the medicine box to check what I had swallowed, but couldn't understand a fucking thing, the words were all eastern.

A couple seconds later, I started to feel dizzy, a huge pain and burning in my stomach going up my throat. I tried to get up, but my legs felt weak, so I sat down again.

- The meds are in, all that's missing is the heroin, waiting in the drawer next to you. Anyway, you only have a few more minutes before the medicine kills you, so I think the heroin overdose can wait a little longer, maybe you will change your mind - Oliver said.

With all the burning and pain I really started to believe this was not a dream.

- Why me? - I asked him.

- Nope, your three questions are already over, you could have asked me anything, today I was "clear" to answer them, but this hasty youth never pays attention to details - Oliver answered.

– But how can you offer me something and not give me time to respond? How can I think with all this pain? Besides, you haven't even told me enough, so I won't have to worry about some things, but what about money? What will I have to do? In your story you had choices, that woman didn't threaten to kill you. Is there any other curse? What else should I know? Who is your boss? These powers you're using on me, am I going to get them too? I can't think straight with this pain - I told him with my mouth already foaming.

- I told you, no more questions. You only have three more minutes, the pain will get much worse, but in the meantime I think I can tell you a little more about the "position". As I told you before, you won't have to worry about several things, and money is one of them, you will always get more than you can spend, I have already done several crazy things and even so, I haven't managed to run out of money, it's as if you were getting an infinite amount, I don't know exactly how this part works, I only know that you don't have to worry about it - said Oliver.

The pain increased every second, he kept talking, started to narrate some adventures he had had, how he spent about two million dollars in one night in Las Vegas, the stories seemed interesting, but at a certain point I couldn't think about anything else but the pain and this whole arrangement.

- This proposal was too good to be true, I want to "wake up" soon - I started to repeat it over and over.

- ... that's why you shouldn't trust redheads. Are you still with me? Do you already feel the bad taste in your mouth, as if your internal organs were rotting? - Oliver asked.

My vision darkened and I awoke again to Oliver kneeling beside me, slapping me across the face.

- Hey, don't die yet, you haven't even answered, last chance. So, do you accept it or not? - Oliver asked again.

- I accept - I replied, wanting it all to end soon.

Oliver got up from the couch, came over to where I was lying, put his hands on me, spoke some strange words that after being said made all pain and convulsions stop.

Again he crouched down beside me and whispered in my ear.

- Don't go crazy, try to have fun and we'll see you around - Oliver said.

I passed out and woke up the next day being absolutely sure that everything was just a dream or a bad trip. Too bad this certainty did not last long, because after getting up in a state of total denial and taking a long time in the shower, I decided to get my wallet to buy something in the bakery, but when I found the wallet it was next to a box of "Chinese" medicine - was it all real? - At this moment in shock I lost my hunger and gave up going to the bakery.

"How could all that be real?"

I went to the kitchen, got some water, added sugar and put it to boil - I needed a coffee urgently - more than a coffee, I needed a good explanation for everything that happened.

"How was all that not a dream?"

I sat down in front of the computer - already with a cup of coffee in hand - I needed to do some research on the internet and find something that made sense.

Even after searching a lot and trying to use my IT knowledge, I found nothing, and I kind of expected it, but I left some symbols and partial stories on some forums, so that maybe someone had seen those symbols before, or had been through something similar.

I had my coffee and gave up on looking it up on the internet, I kept thinking about some crazy things.

"Does this immortality business work?"

"Has the money already dropped into my account?"

"Do I have powers?"

"Does hell exist?"

"Was it all real?"

I thought of a few ways to answer any of these questions, until I made the decision to check the easiest one, went to the kitchen, got a knife and made a cut on my arm.

The worst that could happen to me would be a scar and a much calmer mind about that whole "dream" - I really wish that everything that happened was a lie.

The blood started gushing and I felt the normal pain, I rushed to the bathroom to get a bandage - with a smile on my face - but as soon as I put my arm in the water to clean the blood before bandaging it, the blood and pain were gone and the wound was closed - I am like "Wolverine", but clawless.

I was happy that the pain had passed, but I would be even happier to find out that all of that stuff from yesterday was just a hallucination or strange dream.

"What now? What should I do?"

Nice way to start the week.

Leaving the bathroom and coming back into the living room, I heard a noise which I knew was coming from the computer - there I go again, isn't that sort of how it all started?

I moved the mouse and I could see an icon on the home screen that was not there before, it was an icon with a letter design and on it was the number one in red, I double clicked on it and a message opened.

"Hello it is a pleasure to have you with us. Your first payment has already been credited to your account, buy whatever you want, but don't draw too much attention, at least not during your "first life". Wait to be contacted, we can send your missions by e-mail, or through someone. If you have questions, you can ask one question each year, but since you are still a newbie you don't have the right to an initial question, so think carefully what you will ask next time. Good day and knock knock."

Just as I finished reading the email, there was someone knocking on my door - damn " knock knock knock" - it was my friend Bill.

My Friend Bill

I met Bill years ago at my previous job.

It used to be at one of those big multinational companies that suck the souls out of millions and millions of employees, where the machine twists and turns mercilessly, grinding away dreams and taking precious hours of life from the poorest of the poor, without even giving them what is rightfully theirs - dignity.

I was the manager responsible for the IT area of the company and there was an internship offer, which I was in charge of interviewing and selecting a candidate to teach him a few things about the company and what the IT team did.

After the trauma of interviewing every applicant, each one crazier and stranger than the other, I was left with two choices, the hot girl who would give HR problems or Bill.

I chose the one that I thought would be less bad for my job and would fit my profile and industry, despite the temptation to have a harassment suit with the hot one.

My job was already automated for two years, so I went to the office just as a formality - and to avoid suspicion, of course.

With time I ended up liking him, he was a quick learner, and his inexperience allowed me to make him do the more "manual" work during the first month, where I led him to believe that our mission was to automate some processes and tasks - that were already automated by me years ago.

As time went by I managed to "corrupt" him and we automated the rest of the tasks without telling anyone, so we had more time to spend with other things - in the first months I even taught the kid a thing or two about advanced programming.

But it was work, not friendship.

By this time I had a rule not to make friends with people from work, I even made some jokes and went out to happy hours with them, but it always was merely a relationship among co-workers.

Even on my birthday I was forced to work overtime, they needed me to fix some mess that the shitheads from the other sector couldn't, yet another Friday working while I should be having fun. I called everyone whom I invited to cancel the celebration, I tried to reschedule with some of them for Saturday, but the majority had commitments, therefore most of them would go to the bar and wait for me as long as they could.

It was already eleven o'clock at night and I was still there - stuck - I couldn't find the problem, nor think of a solution for that damn code, my programming was a little rusty in that outdated language they used and the anger and frustration didn't help at all.

I heard a noise, it was someone coming into the room from the hallway - alone in that place any tiny noise is easy to notice - when I glanced to see who it was, I saw Bill.

- Do you need some help there Boss? - said Bill

- I told you not to call me that, on the day I become your boss you will have to salute. How did you get in here? You know you can't be here at this time, right? If people say you're working after hours, it could be a big mess for the company - I told him.

- Relax, I was at the happy hour in the pub Babaloo around the corner with the fellas, I looked for you and someone said you were here, so I decided to drop by and give you something.

It was a small box wrapped in gift paper.

I took the wrapping and opened it, to my surprise what was inside the little box was some Lemon Haze, my favorite delicacy.

I had my suspicions about Bill hacking into my computer - he always denied it - but I think that this is how he found out I liked this kind of stuff and it was thanks to this that our friendship began.

I was so happy to get it that I forgot to play dumb and tell him how it was dangerous and all the morality chatter we have to keep up in the workplace when you have a position with a high degree of authority.

- Geez, those are my favorites, but wait a minute, how could you know that? I don't smoke cigarettes, how would you know that? You hacked my computer, you son of a bitch - I asked him.

- I just knew. I didn't hack it, I swear! - replied Bill.

- You must have, but since it's a gift I won't mind, but don't ever try to hack into my computer again. These herbs are hard to get, thank you very much. We have to go to the terrace to try them, I need to squeeze one now to relax - I told him.

We went upstairs talking about how much it sucked to work on our own birthdays. After rolling a joint and enjoying it on the terrace, we went back downstairs. Bill offered to help me with the problem, but I refused and told him to get the hell out of there before someone came along and reported us.

- Okay, I'm going, but if you finish this, stop by the PUB. - Bill said, walking away and leaving me there alone.

Now not only more relaxed, but stoned, I went back to the computer and a few minutes later, I was able to identify and solve the code problem and correctly generate all the steps and reports.

After the matter was resolved, I closed the office and went to the Babaloo pub which was where my friends and Bill were waiting for me.

The night was fantastic, with lots of drinks, friends and my favorite drug, all thanks to Bill, so I broke my coworker rule and thus Bill and I remain friends to this day, even though we are both unemployed, because of one another.

And as jobless people have nothing to do, he would always show up here at home, so we could eat a few things, take some freelance jobs that came up, to chat, play video games and smoke some weed - sometimes he would even come more than I would like him to, but I didn't care much, after all I know how boring and unbearable it can be to live with the crazy parents we all have.

Money

Knock Knock Knock.

Bill was still knocking on the door, so I went over to open the door for him.

- Where is your key? Did you lose it again? - I said.

- No, I must have left it here yesterday. You don't look so good and it seems you're not in a good mood either. What do we have to eat? - said Bill as he walked through the house to the kitchen.

- My night was terrible, I couldn't finish my freelance work for the extra money and I didn't sleep well. Will you go to the bakery and get us some bread and bologna? There's nothing to eat here and I'm already feeling sick, I haven't eaten anything since yesterday - I told him.

- Give me the cash and I'll go fetch it. Also that Lemon Haze acquaintance is back, if you have some money we could go get some - said Bill.

- Really? Maybe later we will, I got a new "job" that pays very well, but it's confidential, I can't tell you about it - I told him.

- Is it for the government? - Bill asked, virtually picturing a conspiracy theory in his paranoid head.

- I can't tell you about it - I told him, which made him even more curious.

- Seriously, if you don't want to tell the truth, you don't have to make up stories, I know that you wouldn't work for the government, plus they would never hire you, either - answered Bill.

We went into the living room and turned on the video game, before he left to buy things, we played a match and of course I won - it wasn't going to be after immortality that the apprentice would surpass the master.

I handed Bill the bank card so he could go to the bakery to buy supplies for our craving.

- Bring the things we always buy and if you find anything else that looks tasty for us to bite you can bring that too.

- Now I feel confident, you've got some cash, punk! - said Bill, taking the card and leaving to go to the bakery.

I wasn't sure if there was any money in the card I gave him to buy the stuff - since before everything happened I was penniless - but as I needed to test if they had deposited the money from the "new job", I took a chance and didn't tell Bill, because I knew that if I told him about having doubts about whether or not I had money, he wouldn't go for it.

I continued playing while Bill was at the bakery and minutes later he returned full of bags.

- Holy crap, man! What did you buy? - I asked him.

- Since I know us, and to avoid having to go back there again and again, I bought everything I know we can eat a lot when you have money. Nutella, ice cream, snacks, chocolate, cake, soda, potato, mozzarella cheese, ham, bagels, and the rest of the things you asked for - Bill said, leaving the bags on the kitchen table.

- You did well, kid - I told him, happy to have money in the card for so much.

Thank goodness there was enough on the account, for if there wasn't I bet he would be so embarrassed and spit fire at me for asking him to buy something without any credit.

After putting things away in the fridge, we smoked and played a few more games to pass the time.

I could not forget or get out of my head everything that happened the night before, also could not tell Bill anything, so I decided to leave him playing and go out for a walk, I told him I needed to sort some things out and come back later, he did not mind, in fact he liked to feel in charge of the house when he was alone.

I was very curious to know how much money I had in my account and I needed to find something "good" so when the shit hit the fan, so I could see at least one good side about working for hell.

I got to the bank and went to the ATM, took out the account statement, but the balance that should appear in numbers was with some strange symbols that I had never seen before.

I tried to withdraw the ATM withdrawal limit - R$5,000 - and all that money came out without any problem.

It was really happening and working.

I took all that money, left the bank trying to keep myself cool and do as they recommended - "don't draw attention" - but it was too late, when I realized I had already picked up my old car and was on my way to a dealership.

I left there with a black Veloster, trying not to be too flashy, not to call so much attention - since there were more expensive cars - at least I was satisfied with my new acquisition. I also stopped by the mall and bought some new clothes - I had never carried so many bags of clothes.

I tried not to overdo it on the shopping, but I was a little doubtful if I had succeeded, since not even when I was working as a coordinator in a multinational company, could I have enough money to do this kind of thing, on the other hand, I could very well have gotten the best car, shopped at the most expensive stores and I didn't do that. I kept my style and in the end I came to the conclusion that I didn't overdo it - too much - I just bought the things that I lacked and would normally buy if I had a fair salary.

Halfway home I remembered that my parents would come to visit me this weekend - tomorrow - and it would be even more difficult to explain about the car, but now it was no use to keep thinking and torturing myself about it, I had already bought it, what I needed was to think of a good explanation - make one up - about a normal IT job for them to believe.

The "dream" job - or not!

II drove home honking and burning some rubber in my new car to get Bill's attention. It worked, he looked out the window trying to see who it was and almost didn't believe it when he saw me. He immediately ran outside as if he couldn't trust his own eyes. He came in with some bullshit about a party that was coming up this weekend and how we should go to it - I bet that if it wasn't for the car, the bastard would never have told me about this party - after calming him down and explaining several times that I wasn't going to tell him how much I was earning at my new job, we went inside and I asked him if anyone had shown up there while I was gone, and if anything strange had happened with the computer - he found the question a little strange - but until then, according to him, everything was normal.

He told me that nothing was out of the ordinary, he played games, smoked and ate junk food in the living room, no one came by, but he said that there were some calls on my cell phone, which I forgot among the sofa cushions when I left distracted.

- Your parents called, I didn't answer, I just dropped it on voicemail. Other than that, you haven't received any important messages, except for the call from Paty saying that last night was terrible and that she never wants to see your face again," said Bill.

- Did Paty really say that? You didn't tell her I asked you to answer it because I didn't want to talk to her, did you? Like when you said the same to Raissa and I only found out a few weeks later, when she asked me why I hated her, don't give me that crap again, you bastard, I told you I won't forgive you next time - I said to him.

- Relax, I'm kidding. Paty didn't say that, nor did I say anything, I only said that you weren't home and I'd let you know that she called. And you know that with Raissa I got you off one, she didn't like you and she didn't like anything we like to do either, you should thank me for that - Bill said before insisting again that I talk about my new job.

In a way Bill was right about Raissa, I didn't like her and she didn't like me, she was a pain in the ass, but beautiful as hell.

He insisted a little more about telling him what my new job was, but I gave him a look as if I wasn't going to say anything and it was starting to get annoying, he seemed to understand.

I picked up my cell phone to check the message my mother had left.

"Charles my son, we won't be able to come visit you tomorrow anymore, next holiday you can come here or we can visit, your uncle decided to come for a visit this weekend, so we decided to stay, call me later, take care and God be with you, I love you."

It was great news, I was missing them, but due to the circumstances it was great. I called them and took the opportunity to tell them about the job, I made up something important and that the salary was good. I told them more than once that it was the "dream job", and since they didn't understand much about my work, they just said they were happy that I was "happy".

The ordinary life in a different way

A few weeks had passed and nothing happened and no "work" showed up.

The money was still "infinite" and I was beginning to like it all - it is easy to get used to wealth and immortality - time seemed to fly and nothing bad happened.

I ended up with the false impression that now things were going to be normal again, only in a different way.

For a long time I avoided my friends, I spent time on the internet looking for answers about everything that had happened - without any success - but hiding at home for too long could arouse suspicion, so I had to go back to hanging out with my friends, drinking, chatting and having fun. That was all I could do, and it was also all I needed at that moment.

I made three phone calls and arranged with some of the best people - Bill, Luana, Giovane and Thaiz - to meet at the bar downtown, good drinks, some pool and karaoke that went on until the early hours of the morning.

After a few rounds of beer and a few games of pool, we ended up mingling with another group who was around, and before we knew it, the groups turned into one.

The night seemed to drag on forever, until someone suggested we go to another bar, this time a better looking one with great live music and room to talk. In this bar we ran into other acquaintances and in the end we numbered about fifteen people together.

The live music ended early and so we decided to switch to yet another place, the bar was named nightcap, where usually everyone in town went at the end of the night to finish their partying hours before going home.

We arrived there and everyone was already very excited, so we joined the people standing outside the bar, since it was already crowded inside, therefore, everyone who couldn't fit in stayed outside the bar, drinking and chatting with each other.

Meanwhile, I showed Bill a table inside the bar with three beautiful girls. I needed someone excited to go there with me and at least find out the name of one of them. He agreed and we went there anyway. We made some small talk about Bill believing that he knew one of the girls and that her name was Juliana, but none of them were named that, so after some laughs and apologies, they gave us an opening so we ended up staying with them at the table to chat.

Ana Paula, Lorrayne and Nathalia were their names and the one that caught my attention the most was Lorrayne, with colorful hair.

Chatting away, things seemed to be heading towards a happy ending for all of us, but suddenly a "freak" arrived saying that one of the girls was his girlfriend and started putting his hands on me - quickly stressing out everyone at the place.

I already had a few - too many - beers and the girl was worth the urge to impress, so I didn't think twice, I closed my right hand and sent a cross punch straight into the guy's face, with just one punch he dropped like a sack of potatoes to the floor and everyone in the bar stopped doing what they were doing to stare at me - not drawing attention, was not working.

We left before the security guards arrived and Lorrayne wanted to accompany us, leaving the jerk on the floor without any remorse, it seemed that she felt obliged to explain the whole boyfriend thing to me, so on the way out she explained that they had recently broken up and that the guy didn't take it very well.

My hand was hurting, it was the hardest punch I ever landed on anyone, the pain didn't last long - immortality baby - that's when I started thinking and noticing that there were some different things happening to me. I was physically stronger and also more resistant to drinks and drugs, but I could only realize that now, everything took longer to take effect and needed a much larger dose to kick in.

I found it strange and at the same time impressive that Lorrayne didn't care one bit about her ex-boyfriend, she just left with me and my friends from the bar, we kept on talking, walking through the empty streets at dawn, as if nothing had happened to us and as if the sun was no longer threatening to rise.

We passed by an almost empty square whose only residents seemed to be the homeless and young people who bought cheap drinks and stayed there drinking all night and throughout the early hours of the morning.

I invited Bill and the girls to finish the night at my place, since we were near there - the party of the party - after some charm on their part, I believe on account of everyone having just met, they ended up accepting.

When we got there I went to the kitchen to get some glasses and beers, went back to the living room and when I got there Bill had already gone into the guest room with the two girls, so in the living room there was only Lorrayne waiting for me, a little embarrassed.

We kept talking about all kinds of subjects but the chat didn't last long, I approached and took a seat next to her, she slowly moved towards me until we kissed and started to make out right there in the living room, when things started to heat up, I suggested we go to the bedroom, Lorrayne accepted, but asked to go to the bathroom first.

I suggested the bathroom in my room, but as I also wanted to go to the bathroom I said I would use the bathroom downstairs while she used the one in my room, when I got back to the room, Lorrayne had already left the bathroom and was waiting for me almost naked in bed, I hopped on top of her and we had sex for almost an hour, until someone knocked on the bedroom door, it was her friends telling Lorrayne to go home with them, they couldn't sleep outside and one of them was working the following day.

I called an Uber for them and minutes later they were already in the car heading to the house of one of the girls, I got Lorrayne's phone number, but we never spoke again.

My first sex as an immortal, I also noticed another change - I could go all night if I wanted to.

Deep Web - The first job

Another couple weeks went by and the lack of news from work started to bother me, something might not be right, but at the same time I wished everything would go on forever like that - enjoying life rich, immortal and without drawing too much attention - but close to the fourth month of "employment" something happened.

During this time many things had changed, I replaced almost all the furniture in the house, bought new high-end household appliances, wore better clothes, and was going out more in these last few months than I had in my last ten years.

I had to keep my mind busy, as the lack of information about what was going on, and the amount of questions about the strange things that had happened, made me dangerously anxious for explanations or for something to happen.

And if that wasn't enough, during the last week I had started to have horrible nightmares during the night.

During one of these dreams my soul left my body - like an astral projection - and started flying around, it didn't seem scary at first, but after a while I started to realize that my soul seemed to be attracted - like a magnet - to some specific place and no matter how much I resisted or tried to fly away, but ultimately I was always attracted in the same direction. Every moment I resisted, the stronger the pull seemed to get, so after a while I gave up fighting it and just let myself go.

I traversed the whole city flying over the houses and buildings, people could not see me, nor hear me, in a short time I had already moved away from the city - drawn by something or some place - now there were no more buildings, stores and shopping malls, but rather just a few houses, and the more I flew in that direction, the farther apart the houses became.

I arrived in a place where the surrounding buildings were only a big house and a barn at the end, and the force that was pulling me seemed to come from the house, I moved further until I got so close that I could go through the walls of the house.

Suddenly I felt the speed increase and the fear of crashing into the walls made me close my eyes for a brief moment and when I opened them again I felt as if a bubble of soap burst and now I could no longer fly and so, I was thrown with force against a wall, which I could no longer go through, rather I felt as if my whole body had been broken.

Thankfully, in the dream I was also immortal, so I got up groaning in pain and gradually regenerating myself.

The place was a kind of combination of basement and cave, but the weird thing was the fact that there were no stairs to get in or out, the only thing besides rocks around me was a red door on the ground with several strange writings around it.

As I approached the door it opened, I looked inside and couldn't see anything, I stepped forward - being an immortal - trying to get a better view, and in the darkness I could see an arm pulling me, I ended up falling into the door, and as I went through it, the door shut.

It was a big fall until I hit the ground again, I couldn't see anything inside, I only heard a noise coming towards me, I closed my eyes trying to focus on the noise trying to figure out where it was coming from and what that sound was. It sounded like breathing and it was getting closer, I opened my eyes wide open when I began to get used to the darkness of that place, I could see a figure, I wasn't agile enough to dodge it, so it grabbed my arm and suddenly there was a flash of blue light, emerging from the figure's eyes. The light illuminated the whole place at once, thus revealing a huge cave, full of specters wandering in the dark, all holding unlit candles, marching towards me.

Beside me one of these specters held my arm, causing his candle to light up again, as he squeezed my arm, he whispered something into my ear which I can't remember, but right at that moment I woke up to a loud deafening noise coming from the living room, my computer, which appeared to have turned itself on.

I approached the computer and the icon of the letter had a number one, I was afraid to click, but it was no use being in denial and curiosity was also speaking loudly.

I clicked and the following message opened.

Following is your first assignment, attached are two files. File I labeled as life and File II labeled as afterlife. You must produce a video edit and a report with the purpose of popularization (attracting interest). Caution! As this is your first assignment, after watching the attachment II you will realize some things that you could not see before, the content of the file causes this, you will begin to see the supernatural. Your deadline is three days to complete this task, when it is finished, attach it to this e-mail and answer it, this will post the video directly on our LLEHTorture forum in the Deep Web, if you want, search for free content on the website, this way you can have a base or copy the style of the latest works, this is up to you, but remember after this task, your work will be evaluated and depending on your performance you may get different tasks in the future, good luck, we hope you do well.

The weirdest thing was that the e-mail actually seemed similar to one of the corporate e-mails I used to receive from the companies I worked for, another interesting fact was the Deep Web quote, years ago I had a phase where I was obsessed with surfing there - the place on the internet that most people do not know about.

Using a few programs and the right knowledge it is possible to access a part of the internet that is "invisible" to the rest, and the most interesting thing is that this invisible part makes up the biggest part of the internet, all the content and files on the internet that most people know or know exists, is just the tip of the iceberg.

In the Deep Web you can find everything - really everything - from cannibalism, aliens, murder, books about magic, black market, organ selling, but it was also possible to find good and interesting things like natural medicine, banned books, reports of after death experiences, stories about other worlds, drugs and several tutorials about anything you would need to learn.

I never imagined that the "job" would have any involvement with this and the deadline would be short for someone who had never entered the Deep Web or did not know how to edit a video - which was not my case - so they knew I have been there before and was capable of doing something worthwhile.

I decided to start right away - I was excited and at the same time curious, I opened File I and inside it there were two more files, a video file and a text file, I opened the text file first.

The file contained the data of a person with a photo, his name was Carlos Edualves Bolnaro and that huge file contained basically all the information of his life, some information drew more attention, such as a graph called "Purgatory / Hell", it showed a percentage of eighty-seven percent "Hell" and thirteen percent "Purgatory". Next to this chart there was also a listing of things that raised the Hell percentage and things that raised the Purgatory percentage.

Hell - corrupt politician, directly ruined the lives of seven thousand families, responsible for the deaths of one hundred and ninety-five people, unfaithful husband, no belief or faith, greedy, liar - and several other things as the list was very long.

Purgatory - helped a few people in need (with dirty money), was a good father, loved his daughter, repented in the end and accepted the Christian God before death.

Verdict? Hell!

From what I understood, that was a form containing some information to identify the person who was in the video and that I should extract as much information as possible to create a report with the intention of spreading this content in the Deep Web, that is, to sell in the Deep Web how tortures are performed in hell.

The second file in the first folder was a video, I clicked on it, maximized the screen and played it.

The video started with a countdown - five, four, three.... - it was exactly like a movie tape, there are three people in a room - a woman, a priest standing next to an old man lying in bed - a typical farewell scene for an old man - the priest is saying his last words to the dying man.

The woman was crying a lot - she was a beautiful blonde - I figured she must be the daughter of the old man lying on the bed who was barely able to open his eyes.

- If you accept Christ and ask forgiveness for all your sins, say amen - said the priest.

The damned old man could barely open his eyes, but he managed to say amen and die right after that.

Another countdown appeared on the video, counting down, and another scene started.

In this scene the old man who died peacefully in the previous scene was younger, it took me a while to recognize him, he seemed to be in an amusement park with a little blonde haired girl - who I presume to be the blonde woman from the previous scene - in this scene she was in his arms with a huge cotton candy and they both appeared to be having a great time - this was probably the best day of that little girl's life - you could tell by the way she looked at him that to her, he was the best father in the world.

Another countdown and another scene, this time he was even younger than the previous scene, he was on a plane sitting next to a pregnant woman.

- Carlos, are you sure they won't find us? - the woman asks.

- Rest assured, we are safe, just remember the information I gave you and remember to memorize our new names on the passport. Trust me, we will start our lives from scratch and be very happy.

I was getting tired of the countdowns, another one and a new scene.

In this scene Carlos was in a room full of people, he was signing some papers and after signing, many people in the room stood up and started to applaud and shout Carlos' name.

After a few nods he stands up and begins to speak about the maintenance contract for the dam which he just signed, the applause continues and minutes later he gets into one of the cars of his entourage and leaves the place.

Inside the car he picks up his cell phone and calls someone.

- I just signed the papers, starting today we will start the inspection and maintenance of the three tailings dams with our ghost company, that idea of hiring a smaller company to take care of the dam and overprice the contract with labor, materials and equipment was brilliant dad, it seems strange how easy it was to win the bid using our political influence, after all being a senator does have its advantages - said Carlos on the phone while bragging and celebrating.

This time the scene didn't change and there wasn't another countdown timer either, but as soon as he turned off the cell phone, the camera approached Carlos until it froze, focusing on his face and suddenly flashing with disturbing images and sounds, of the desperate cries of the people who suffered with the dams breaking and hitting the small town of Anairam. The images of families, animals and destruction, of people not knowing if their acquaintances, relatives and family members were alive.

The video kept bringing up the actions during Carlos' life that led him to go to hell, it was virtually a summary of his entire life and lasted about an hour.

After seeing all that, I really needed to take a break. In the e-mail they said that the next file was "heavier" and had "side effects".

I lit a cigar and opened a beer, turned on a soccer match that was on TV, but I wasn't paying attention, I lay down on the couch by the window and stared at the stars, listening to the game in the background, but wondering if I had ever done anything bad enough to end up in hell.

Eventually I fell asleep.

By the time I woke up it was midnight, I had not slept this much in a long time. I got up and went to the kitchen to prepare sandwiches and after eating them, I went straight to the computer to check the last remaining file.

I opened the folder and there was only one video file in it, as I played the file the house lights flashed three times before the video started.

No countdowns this time. In this video Carlos looked to be about thirty-three years old, he was in a bedroom sleeping and suddenly got up apparently after having had quite the nightmare, he sat up in bed, put his hands on his head and stood up in the direction of the bathroom. There he began to prepare himself for a bath, while the sound of the water filling the tub filled the place, another noise seemed to begin to bother Carlos, a noisy dripping that came from the faucet in front of the mirror.

As he moved in front of the mirror Carlos admired himself for a couple of seconds and as he approached the noisy sink to close it and put an end to the disturbing noise, he realized that there was something strange about the water coming out of the faucet, It was dark - almost black - and had a different viscosity and stench, so the sink started to get clogged, causing the black water to overflow, and even with all Carlos' efforts to unclog it, nothing worked, all his attempts to close the faucet were in vain.

The dark liquid began to clog the bathroom floor drain, and now his bathtub was also overflowing with the viscous liquid.

Carlos tried to get out of the bathroom, but the door was locked, he was trapped, and at this moment he realized that something strange was going on, there were no windows, the drains were gone, the corners of the walls were leaking the viscous liquid and making the bathroom fill up like an aquarium.

He exhaustively tried to open the door in every way he could think of, he didn't seem to understand what was going on, but finally he gave up on the door and started trying to make that dark water stop rising, without success either, at this point the dark water was hitting his thighs.

Carlos couldn't understand what was happening and the desperation in his eyes was clear, he tried everything with the door, taps and the drains, but still nothing worked.

The water kept rising higher and faster - it was already up to his waist - now he was tired from all his attempts and started to scream again - desperately - for help.

Just as there seemed to be no way out and he was beginning to accept his fate - with the water up to his chest - he heard a voice on the other side of the door.

- Daddy, are you in the bathroom? - it was a little girl's voice.

It sounded like his daughter and as soon as she started calling him the black water began to rise even faster and now had a mud-like viscosity.

Carlos climbed up on the toilet and answered.

- Daughter, open the door for Daddy - Carlos asked with water on his neck.

The little girl stopped responding and the flow of mud continued to rise rapidly, the bathroom now resembling an aquarium about to overflow.

There were only about two feet to go before it was completely full, Carlos struggled to jump up from the toilet and grabbed the shower-head as his last gamble.

- Open the damn door Joana - he desperately shouted.

- But we are the ones who locked you in there daddy - it was a different voice than before, now it was strange, distorted and terrifying.

And as soon as he heard that voice Carlos instantly changed his expression and began to scream desperately, disturbed - insane - it was as if hearing the voice had reminded him of something and it affected him so much that it drove him crazy.

The water just filled the entire bathroom space, killing Carlos in agony underneath the liquid unable to breathe.

For a moment the computer screen went black and after a few seconds it came back on again, showing another scene.

Carlos woke up again, frightened from another dream he had had, but this time he coughed as if he was choking or couldn't breathe, after he pulled himself together and managed to breathe his way back to reality, he looked to the side and realized that he was sitting in a bus, but didn't seem to remember getting there, he looked around once more and only then realized that everyone there was wearing the same clothes - inmates' uniforms - and that the bus was on its way to the prison.

The trip was not long and before Carlos could do anything the bus stopped and the guards began to unload everyone in rows, it appeared to be a federal prison - huge - it was surrounded on all sides by armed guards and endless wire fences.

As Carlos entered, he passed near the courtyard where the inmates were sunbathing and exercising - they were divided by a huge wire fence - so, the inmates who noticed the new arrivals began to approach the fence to observe the fresh meat that was arriving, some of them even dared to say some funny things and make provocative comments, things like, see you later, funny things, but they were soon reprimanded by the guards who were leading the line of new prisoners.

Carlos, who up until then just followed the line with his head down - distraught - said nothing and seemed to be in a state of shock.

All the newcomers were taken inside the prison and went through a sort of search, where everyone left their belongings, received their uniforms and were taken to their cells, where they would meet their fellow cellmates.

After Carlos went through the entire search process he was taken to his cell, where he met his fellow cellmate, a grumpy old man who didn't give a damn about him, so the waiter showed him to his bed - the top one - and showed him the pot to do his needs that was at the bottom of the cell in a stinky hole in the floor.

After the guard left them there, Carlos tried to introduce himself and get the old man's name, but to no avail, he was ignored as if he didn't exist, the old man just looked at him for a brief moment and then turned the other way. Carlos then climbed onto his bed and there he found a pillow, when he picked up the pillow he found a picture of a blonde woman inside it, after a while he recognized her and murmured - Joana - it was his daughter, but this made no sense since Carlos seemed to be almost the same age as the woman in the picture.

Something had changed, if until then he had kept an apathetic appearance and was quiet - even too quiet - now, after having recognized the person in the photo, he was desperate, agitated, and shouting throughout his cell.

- This is another dream, it has to be. How did I get here? I'm innocent, I want to talk to my lawyer. I want to wake up, I want to wake up, somebody wake me up! - he screamed hysterically non-stop, attracting a lot of attention.

- Shut your mouth man, do you want to get off on the wrong foot here? - said his cellmate, before turning to the side and pretending to be asleep.

Carlos went on, his desperate screams were so loud that they drew the attention of the guards who immediately went over to his cell. The other prisoners were silently watching this whole outcome, the guards arrived and immediately tried to silence him with rubber bullets, kicks and punches, Carlos didn't have a chance to defend himself as they beat him until he fainted.

With Carlos lying unconscious on the floor, the guards looked at his cellmate who remained motionless facing the side of the wall - pretending to be asleep - one of the guards then picked up the unconscious Carlos from the floor and threw him into the top bunk.

Carlos woke up in the middle of the night, but the most he could do was move a little and moan, the next day first thing in the morning the guards entered the cell again and with a stretcher. placed Carlos in it and took him to the infirmary.

Most of his body had purple bruises, after some dressings by the nurse, he was released and the guards took him to the yard, where the inmates were sunbathing and exercising.

He was walking awkwardly and with some difficulty - his leg was almost broken during the beating last night - and this made him attract even more attention from the other inmates, when he arrived in the yard everyone knew who it was that caused the scandal last night, and as a result of the scandal all the guards were in a bad mood, which meant a bad day for all the inmates, so the attention of everyone in the yard fell on Carlos.

Carlos spotted some benches with no one around at the back of the courtyard, the benches were near the sports field that until then was totally empty, as far as he could get from the other inmates, so limping he walked slowly over to the benches and sat down.

It was hard to imagine that he would be alone for long in that hostile environment, but this became even clearer when he just sat down and minutes later all the empty seats around him and the sports court filled up instantly.

Not a single friendly glance, everyone passed by and looked at Carlos in a subtle way, he always looked away - down - and mumbled to himself in a quiet voice.

- How did I get here? What is happening? Is this a dream? Another dream? - Carlos rambled on in his thoughts, muttering quietly, until he was interrupted.

- So you were the little girl screaming last night? - said a guy who looked about two meters tall, white, bald, tattooed on his neck, and surrounded by two other guys who looked a lot like him, only skinnier, so I figured he might be the leader of a prison gang.

Carlos didn't answer, he didn't seem to know what to say, and before he could think of something to answer, another gang approached them and interrupted.

This time there were three black guys, and they were also very strong, but still nowhere near the height of the other leader - the one with the tattoo on his neck - of the white man's gang.

The rival gangs argued for a while over who gets the fresh meat, and after some pushing and shoving, frowning, cursing, and the first signs of trouble, they got along, so once it was decided who "won"

Carlos, the leader of the winning group - the tattooed white guy - looked at the "prize" and as he left said grinning.

- See you later, scandalous bitch! - said the tattooed white man.

As the groups dispersed, the other inmates scattered from there and the guards approached, for the sunbathing period had passed, they blew their whistles for the inmates to be taken to the huge sheds, where the prisoners were separated into work groups, and left in the sheds to do manual labor, tasks for the prison and for a small community consisting of the nearby residents.

Carlos took the line that was routed to the prison laundry, a few minutes after arriving, the guards showed the newbies how to do laundry work, once they got the hang of it the guards spread out, only sometimes doing patrols inside the shed.

The groups that finished their tasks were directed to the shared bathrooms, where the detainees had a break to do their needs and take a shower, and this is how Carlos met up again with the tattooed white guy and it all happened right there.

The tattooed man's accomplices surrounded Carlos and kept watch in the hallway in case the cops showed up.

Carlos, who was already bruised, didn't stand a chance against them all, so the white man and his accomplices took turns raping him until he couldn't take it anymore and died.

This caused him to wake up once more startled, but this time something was different, from the very beginning he had that expression of when he discovered it was all a dream, he was also in a room strapped to a stretcher with something in his eyes that wouldn't let him close them, he had some kind of ball strapped to his mouth - preventing him from speaking or screaming.

This was not a normal room, the walls were on fire and yet the flames did not spread or burn the place, so I immediately figured that this place must be somewhere in hell.

He was naked and immobilized in front of a large old television set, which appeared to be turned off, as soon as he woke up he began to roll his eyes from side to side incessantly - as if looking for something or someone - he remained like that for a long time, until the door to the room opened, hearing the door creak open made Carlos start trying to make some sound with the ball in his mouth, but the only thing he could do was grunt and get agitated.

I was curious to know what or who entered the room, I imagined several different scary shapes, but however, whoever entered the room seemed to be a normal nurse like any other, he entered the room holding a clipboard and proceeded to leaf through it and talk.

- You shouldn't be awake, it looks like your last "journey" was quite intense - said the nurse as he turned on the television that was facing Carlos.

The TV began to make noise and show static - those tiny gray, white and black squiggly dots - Carlos was positioned to stare at the TV without being able to move.

The nurse took from the pocket of the white coat he was wearing a syringe containing a shimmering green liquid and immediately applied it to Carlos, causing his pupils to nearly explode and his eyes to go totally black, then after that the TV returned to playing images and stopped with the annoying sound it was making before.

On TV there were some images of Carlos with his daughter Joana, holding her in his arms for the first time, changing her diapers, supporting her in her first steps and always beside her on her birthday.

- Holy shit! - I thought to myself.

He seemed like a really good father, if it wasn't for his other crimes that ruined other lives, maybe he wouldn't be there, suffering through all of this, but who was I to judge, as it turns out, everyone gets the ending they deserve.

The TV suddenly flickered on and off, and then it went back to static and white noise.

Carlos, who up until then remained motionless and with black eyes, returned to his senses and his eyes returned to normal soon after. Another injection was taken from the nurse's coat and applied to him again - only this time the color of the liquid applied was blue.

Once again Carlos' pupils expanded, but this time his eyes were completely white and yet again the TV's static stopped and pictures started to appear.

Once again Carlos' daughter, but now she appeared to be about twenty-five years old and was walking normally on the sidewalk when suddenly a van stopped beside her, inside of which some hooded people got out and pulled her into the car.

It was a kidnapping and the first tears started to roll down Carlos' eyes - paralyzed in front of the TV.

The masked men in the van injected some drugs into his daughter, causing her to remain unconscious, a while later she regained her senses. As soon as she woke up a phone started ringing and one of the men who captured her answered it, kept talking but we couldn't hear what he was saying, a few minutes later he hung up and waved to the other two men in the room.

They immediately stripped her clothes off, she was awake, and screaming trying to stop them, so they had to put her to sleep again to quickly finish completely undressing her.

She was left tied on top of some kind of table with only her panties, bra, and a heart-shaped necklace that lay at breast height - all the men in the room took her clothes and left.

A few minutes later, when she regained consciousness once again, another man, identical to Carlos - in his mid-thirties - entered the room and approached the table removing the gag that Joana had in her mouth and as soon as he did she began to beg.

- Get me out of here, please? Who are you? Why are you doing this to me? - asked Joana unaware of what was happening.

Carlos didn't answer immediately, he just stared at her with a strange smile on his face, as he fixed his eyes on her body.

- I know you're not her, I have to do this! They promised that if I do the dreams will stop - Carlos said, changing his expression again and taking a pair of pliers that were on the side of the table and with a simple squeeze of the pliers, pulling off one of Joana's toes.

She began to scream loudly, which caused him to take the gag and again put it in her mouth.

- Does this seem like a dream to you? Because for me, everything has been like a dream, an eternal dream! But this time I will pass the test, this time I talked to him and he will get me out of here, he said, I just need to have fun - Carlos said without really making any sense and torturing his own daughter, non-stop and not realizing what he was doing.

There was no strength left in either of them, Carlos was extremely insane, and numb, Joana had already lost two fingers and had several cuts all over her body, causing her to lose a lot of blood.

Carlos approached her with a pair of scissors near her eyes, she started to cry again, and just as he seemed about to finish the whole thing by piercing one of her eyes, a tear reflected from the spotlight for a brief moment and ran down Joana's neck, causing Carlos to look and notice for the first time the necklace she was wearing, and without a second thought, he tore it off her neck with a single pull.

With the necklace in his hands he gazed down upon it, and the look on his face began to change again. The sound of the click of the heart necklace opening and revealing the picture of him with his daughter did the final job. Now he was Joana's father again.

Without much thought he took the pliers he had in his hands and cut the restraints that held her, took her clothes and handed them to her, shouting

- Go! Run away! Get out of here! - said Carlos encouraging her to get out of there.

As soon as he released her, she looked at him saying.

- It's time to wake up Daddy - said Joana, waking Carlos up.

The TV went back to static and the clipboard nurse spoke again.

- You just had to do what you were told, but you decided to be nice, something you had never been before, and now you are going to stand there wondering what happened to her, wondering a thousand things. Did it really happen? Was it a dream? Was she really your daughter? Did she manage to escape? Did she survive? Did you ever leave this room? I think it's time for you to dream again - said the nurse, cutting Carlos' throat with a scalpel.

Which caused him to desperately wake up in another situation that would probably lead him to another gruesome death.

The video ended and there was so much psychological torment.

I took advantage of all this still fresh in my mind and made a report very similar to the one I'm giving you, edited all the video with the "best" parts and in a bizarre and disturbing way, the video was better than I expected, I regret to brag about it, but it was really "better" than it should be.

So I opened the email, and sent the report and video to them, as I was told.

The whole thing had me exhausted and I couldn't wait to get back into bed and try to digest everything that just happened. I turned off the computer and went straight to my room, but before I went to sleep, I needed a good shower. I grabbed some clean clothes and went straight to the bathroom, put the bathtub on to fill while I brushed my teeth and waited for it to fill enough to relax in.

Already inside the bathtub I closed my eyes, I thought to myself - that's enough for today - but it wasn't, with my eyes still closed I heard a noise and as soon as I opened my eyes I saw something moving in the darkness of my room.

I left the bathroom door open, since the door led to my room and I lived alone, but I was so exhausted that I decided to let it go, I didn't get up - fuck it, I'm immortal! - I took my shower and only afterwards I went to see what the hell it was.

As soon as I finished my long shower I wrapped myself in my towel and slowly got out, trying to see if there was really something there or if it was just my imagination.

The Supernatural

There was no way it was my imagination, something was really there, a woman with her back against the wall, very pale skin, and wearing only a white transparent sweater. I put my hand on her shoulder to ask if everything was okay, trying to figure out what she was doing there, but as I did so she turned to me, and her face was in a monstrous and frightening shape, which scared the hell out of me - I reacted by punching her in the face with a loud punch.

- Hey, what are you doing dude? Wait a minute, you see me, how could you hit me? - said the woman, turning back to a normal, sympathetic face.

- Who and what are you? What are you doing in my room? You've messed with the wrong person, go away, I'm tired, my day has been full enough - he said to her, a bit rudely, considering he just punched her in the face.

- First of all this is my room, or at least it was when I was still alive. - cough, cough - Pleased to meet you, my name is Lucía, I don't even remember how long I've been dead, I lost my way and got stuck in this house. The life of a ghost is not an easy thing, I managed to cope in the beginning, but with the isolation and seeing "living" people invading my old space, I couldn't keep my sanity in check for long, and like most lonely ghosts, I ended up losing my sense of time and space, turning into one of those vengeful spirits, but you managed to punch me and I was able to regain consciousness - said Lucía, the very chatty ghost I had just met.

I no longer knew what was stranger, whether it was the fact that I had managed to hit a ghost or the fact that she was standing there telling me I helped her.

- Sorry about the punch. It is just how I respond when I am startled or surprised - I told her.

- Okay, I didn't mean to scare you, only to rip your guts out and bathe in your blood, HAHAHA, just kidding, but I can't understand how you can see me, talk to me, and punch me. I've never seen it happen before - said Lucía.

– I could try to explain right now, but I'm really tired and since it's your house after all, make yourself at home, don't bother with me, you can stay wherever you want and tomorrow we can talk more, in case you're not a hallucination or something, I'm so exhausted right now that I just want to lie on my bed and sleep - I told her.

- Okay, I'll take the armchair over there then, that's where I used to sit when you and the others couldn't see me, good night to you - she said, sitting down in the armchair and not saying anything else for a while.

It was strange the way she looked at me, but I lay down anyway and a few minutes later I was starting to fall asleep, but before I could, I heard her say something.

- Did you say something? I couldn't understand - I asked her.

- Oh, it's nothing, just a silly idea, but please go back to sleep, you were almost there, I promise not to disturb you anymore - said Lucía.

- Idea? What was your idea? Go ahead, we can talk while I'm lying down, it's hard to fall asleep anyway - I lied to her.

She got up from the chair without me noticing and was already beside me on the bed when I turned around to realize she was reaching her hand into my underwear.

- Earlier, when you couldn't see me, I watched what you did to relax and sleep. Don't you want a little help? - she said.

This couldn't be happening, that night kept getting weirder.

I didn't stop her - despite her cold hands - I stared into her eyes and she made a signal for me to stay still and quiet.

It was very strange, her touch was unlike that of a living person, but it seemed wet, slippery, and sometimes even better than a living person. At first I was in conflict with myself, wondering what was going on, that none of it made sense, lying to myself once again saying that it was a dream, and while thinking about it all I still couldn't let go, but then she whispered in my ear.

- I want to try something else - Lucía said.

And with unusual strength for a woman her size, she ripped off my pajamas and rolled me over on the bed at once, reaching up and taking off her clothes, which vanished onto the floor in a shimmering blue as she threw them off.

That's why people say that men only think with their bottom head, how could I allow this to happen? To have sex with a ghost and forget about all the fatigue I left behind, with just a ghostly massage with a happy ending.

I was a little timid, paralyzed by what was happening, but still tolerant.

This time I was submissive, a spectator, contrary to all the other times, she was the one who took the lead and acted.

She embraced me and for a few moments, she lifted me up wrapped in her arms, turning me around, grabbing me, and moving me into any position she wanted.

Very carelessly, she sat on top of me and put it inside her in a way that once it was done, we both emitted an involuntary moan of pleasure. As she increased the pace, a few blue sparks fluttered around us, causing her body to start getting increasingly warmer.

The heat and the blue sparks intensified until we came, after which I only remember waking up the next day.

The following morning there was no one beside me, but as my dreams were never really dreams, I had no doubt it really happened, and as I heard a noise that seemed to come from the kitchen I was reminded about Lucía and last night.

I calmly got up - completely naked - put on a shirt and shorts, walked towards the kitchen and when I went through the door to see what was going on I was greeted by Lucía, she had suddenly appeared in front of me shoving a knife in my chest - she was again in her spooky ghostly form.

I felt the knife lodging between one of my ribs and the taste of blood coming out of my mouth, it wasn't a good feeling, so at the same instant I ended up spitting a ball of blood in Lucía's face and pulled the knife out of my own chest - good thing I was immortal.

Once I removed the knife the wounds began to heal on their own.

- What the hell are you doing, Lucía? - I asked her.

She didn't answer and jumped on me again, but now I could react and punched her in the middle of her face again, thus bringing her back to consciousness and returning to her normal form.

- Goodness! What have I done? - said Lucía, worried at the sight of blood.

She the blood all over the kitchen and was very worried, thinking I was going to die, I took some time to explain the whole immortality thing to her and after a few minutes I managed to calm her down again.

Once I was done explaining everything to her, I asked why she had gone back to her creepy self and attacked me, she swore she had no idea, only saying that it happened after she went into the kitchen to make me a cup of coffee, so at first I didn't understand what was going on, but I figured if she felt lonely, sad or other things like that, she could turn into her ghostly form again, which means I now had a ghost to take care of.

She showed me a breakfast she prepared, scrambled eggs, bacon, coffee and chopped fruit, while I ate she watched, at first I was a little uncomfortable eating in front of her, but she insisted that I eat everything and enjoy it for her, as she couldn't eat anything anymore, but enjoyed watching people eat.

- Don't you smell things? - I asked her.

- I feel something, but I have no memory of the smells from when I was alive, so I can't say whether it matches with what I feel now.

I couldn't quite understand it, but I figured it made sense to her.

- Can you see other ghosts? Are there others like you here in the house? Why did you get stuck here? - I asked her.

- I can't tell if I am able to see others like me, if there are others, I have never met them, but I don't think there is anyone else, I missed my way to the afterlife when I died, I saw a tunnel above my body that was sucking out my soul, but I remember looking into the tunnel and seeing my grandmother, she seemed to be at peace and I was climbing towards her, but as I thought about my mother, I remembered that she would find me dead and murdered and this made me feel as if I had something unfinished, a sense of revenge for having the rest of my life stolen from me, so with these feelings I felt heavy and stopped climbing up the tunnel towards my grandmother, so I returned to the ground until the tunnel was completely closed.

- I remember to this day my grandmother's smile closing in on me. - Lucía said tearfully as she told me.

- Were you murdered? - I asked her, insisting on the subject.

- Yes, this house where you live alone used to be a women's group home, we lived in three, over the years this structure has changed a fair amount, previously this house had three smaller rooms. The residents were Maria, Aparecida and myself, up until the arrival of the murderer... - Lucía went on, I refused to interrupt her.

Lucía's murder

A long time ago there was a college in this neighborhood, it was close to "our" house - I don't even know if it still exists - and at that time the three of us - Maria, Aparecida and I - were students there.

Maria was studying nursing, Aparecida was into fashion, and I was in law school.

The three of us were very close and had all been born in the same small town, so we had always known each other, and even planned to go to the same college and live together.

It was our second year attending the college, we were already getting acquainted with the house, the town, and the people.

During the first year, as we knew virtually no one in the city, the three of us mostly stayed at home, getting used to our new life in the big city, so our routine was basically from home to school, from school to home. Almost every weekend or school break we would go spend time with our relatives in our city, so the feeling of going back to school became increasingly a feeling of having our freedom back.

It was at the beginning of our second year, right after carnival, that everything began to change from the previous year, after Aparecida met Humberto - a playboy and medicine student - and they started dating.

As a result, most of the time Maria and I would join her for outings, and this is how the three of us learned more about the places and people of our age in the city. Now we often went to discos, bars, and parties around town, so we started to be noticed more both in college and in our neighborhood.

With this new popularity in college our new friends always asked if there would be the party in our house, since only the three of us lived there, but I always stopped the girls, I can't tell if it was a bad feeling or if it was just the fact I didn't like these kinds of parties very much, the rooms would always turn into a mess and nobody respected and cared about the rules of the place, besides there were always those who went overboard on drinks, throwing up and destroying things in the house.

For most of the year I managed to convince them not to throw any parties in our house, but with Halloween coming up and being the one holiday that I particularly loved, the two of them joined forces against me, so this time I couldn't convince them, instead they convinced me, but with a few conditions. We would have a costume party, decorate the whole house, but the party would be in our backyard, so only people we knew very well or wanted to use the bathroom would be allowed into the house.

We planned everything in advance, but five days before the party, the news reported about several murder victims throughout the city, but since we youth do not care about these things, nobody paid any mind, and by the day of the party the backyard was full of people.

Many of them did not know us, but the majority of them were from our college.

We placed a few tables and chairs in the backyard for up to fifteen people, but there were already almost thirty, so the majority of people were standing and wandering all over the place.

Aparecida's boyfriend - Humberto - was the one who brought most of the guests, and he was usually away from his girlfriend, which annoyed Aparecida a lot from the very beginning of the party.

Most of the time the three of us stayed together - in the girls' group - and most of the men stayed in the backyard near the freezers and the barbecue grill.

We had access to the bathroom in the house and the boys had access to the bathroom in the backyard.

With the neighborhood decorated, the night had a great atmosphere of mystery due to the costumes - you didn't ask, but I was dressed as Wednesday from the Adams family.

Inside the house the gossip was running wild among us, we split up the girls' group around the house, some in the hallways, some in the kitchen, mixing alcoholic drinks, and others in the bathrooms looking at themselves in the mirror and touching up their make-up.

I managed to get over the anxiety from the first half hour of the party, now I could start to get into the mood a little more, it seemed as if everyone had already arrived and when "we all" left the house, the backyard was crowded with all boys holding glasses in their hands, standing still, as if waiting for us to come dance to the music.

We passed by and everyone stood there looking at us with their silly faces, thinking that they were the ones to choose.

Werewolves, lots of hair.

Vampires, but none manly enough.

Pirates, literally wooden-legged drunks.

I tried to see some different costume that would catch my attention, but they were all so cliche.

The Hawaiian, Batman, Super Man, Spiderman, Jason, Scream, I looked around until I spotted someone from afar wearing a Jack Skellington costume - from The Nightmare Before Christmas costume.

He was wearing a beat-up black turtleneck blazer, with his head tucked into a pumpkin painted white, making his eyes completely black, just like in the cartoon.

Just as I thought about going over there to see if I could find out who was inside that pumpkin, Maria put on Stayin' Alive by the Bee Gees and turned off the lights on the balcony, turning on the globe of lights and making almost everyone go to the "dance floor".

The party was getting more and more fun, people seemed to replace each other, some would leave and others would arrive, making the place always busy and with different people.

After a while dancing, the lights came back on and gradually people began to spread out again. I managed to get Aparecida to sit next to Humberto to put an end to the mood from the beginning of the party, although during the dance the two of them had kind of made up, at least with their kisses and playful hands.

It was time for the picture, but my camera was inside the house.

Aparecida, Maria and I, respectively Vilma Flintstone, Green Witch of Oz and Wednesday Adams.

I got up and went to the house - the camera was in my room - when I got to the living room it appeared as if there was no one in the house, I went upstairs to my room, I heard a noise coming from Maria's room, I glanced up and thought I saw the person dressed as Jack,who had vanished before when the lights went out.

The door was open so I went over.

- Hello, the bathroom is not there - that's what I said when I entered.

It startled me a little, since I entered the room and there was no one there. I looked quickly inside the wardrobe, under the bed, and even behind the curtains, but nothing, there was no one there, it must have been my imagination - I told myself.

I turned my attention back to the camera that was a few meters away, but when I went towards my room I was surprised by something or someone that hit me from behind and from that moment on I only remember falling to the floor unconscious with my eyes blurred.

I woke up in my bed, the party was still going on and it didn't seem that much time had passed since I passed out, I felt a little strange, I got out of bed and my body felt as if it wasn't mine anymore, my vision was way above my head, it was as if I was seeing myself, to this day I still don't know how to explain it, but I remember looking around hoping that the person responsible for knocking me down was around there, but I didn't find anyone, so I walked with great difficulty, practically dragging myself carefully down the stairs.

I felt a growing discomfort, my heart was pounding and racing, making me sweat a lot. I just wanted to get to one of the girls so they could help me and take me to the hospital.

I thought to myself, Maria will know what to do, she is a nurse.

I managed after a lot of struggle to get out of the house so I went through the tables, but I couldn't carry on since before I even got to the girls' table, I tripped over something, falling in the middle of everybody.

I saw people coming over to see what was happening and try to help me, but at that moment, I was no longer the person lying on the ground, I was floating and I saw them carrying me into the house, I watched as they freaked out when my body started shaking and struggling with foam coming out of my mouth and it was at that moment that the tunnel I told you about appeared, above my body and that thing with my grandmother happened, the feeling of revenge didn't let me follow the tunnel, which turned me into this vengeful ghost that kept wandering around unseen, at least until I met you, Charles.

Can Bill see Lucía?

- I said enough already, but to wrap it up. After I became a ghost and didn't go through the tunnel, I followed the girls living here for a long time, and during this time I found out that I was murdered by a serial killer, he drugged his victims and fled the scene, he often attacked at young people's parties, so this scenario often confused the police, they couldn't tell if they were overdose cases or if it was the Overdose Killer, that was the name the newspapers gave him - concluded Lucía.

- And did they get the guy? - I asked her.

- So, I remember that after a while the girls moved out, and since I couldn't interact with anyone, not having any friendly faces around, I ended up losing my sense of self and became what you saw when you found me, but as far as I remember, up until the moment the girls were here, they hadn't found the person responsible for the murders - Lucía finished with a look of dissatisfaction.

I considered asking her if she has gotten over her death after all these years, but it seemed like a stupid question, seeing what she turned into when she was by herself.

To lighten the mood I complimented the breakfast she prepared, which was really good, and went into the living room.

I sat on the couch and thought about everything that had happened, the job, immortality, hell, ghosts. It all went by so fast, Lucía was in the living room with me and after telling her whole story she wasn't so vocal anymore, so I turned on the TV and that appeared to amuse and distract her.

While she watched TV I was wondering about her always being there and only being to interact with things after i saw her - brewing coffee, picking up a knife and striking me - would anyone be able to see her now? If I had another person in, would she be able to become visible or interact with something? Or can she only be visible and interact with things when everyone around watched something from hell?

Anyway, why was I thinking about that?

While we were distracted by the TV, I asked her if she remembered being able to touch anyone or anything since she became a ghost, but she said that up until the moment I gave her the first punch, she was never able to do anything like that, at most she could make the lights flicker a few times.

I asked her if she was willing to do some tests and she agreed, so I asked her to go to my room and get an object from there and bring it to the living room, as soon as I finished explaining she floated out through the walls, reached the room, got a picture frame and came back up the stairs.

- I almost broke the picture frame! - said Lucía.

- What happened? - I asked her.

- I took the first object I saw, but when I went to go through the wall it got stuck, the object didn't go through, I had to go back and go through the door - said Lucía.

Simple physics, I thought. It made perfect sense that she couldn't get an object through the walls, as she was the only one who could de-materialize.

I wanted to run more tests, so I asked her to stay in the living room while I took a shower and went out to buy some things at the supermarket, I wanted to see how long it would take for her to get her ghostly form back on her own.

She agreed. I took a shower and went to the market, it took me about two hours, and when I came back she was looking pretty normal, watching TV.

- Yeah, I guess it didn't work - said Lucía.

- Could it be because of the TV? What are you watching? - I asked her.

- I don't know, but I liked it, and I didn't even notice the time passing by watching this show - answered Lucía.

There was a program that mixed cooking recipes with daily news, and the hosts were a woman and a parrot - a puppet - who assisted with good humor.

Maybe she needed to be alone, with no interaction or distractions to get back into that form, or maybe the longer I interacted with her the longer it would take her to get that way.

I didn't want to make her sad or feel lonely, so I let her watch TV and explained how the remote control worked, if she wanted to change the channel.

One question kept running through my mind: would Bill be able to see Lucía?

While Lucía was distracted with the TV, I went to my room and called Bill.

- Hey, kid, what's up? Are you home now? Stop whatever you're doing, I'll stop by to pick you up and show you something that will blow your mind! - I said to him without giving too much explanation, I just wanted to make sure he was home.

I stopped by Bill's house, honked my horn to avoid entering and in a few seconds he was already outside, getting into my car.

- Come on, dude. What's so important that you came all the way out here? - said Bill, already burning with curiosity.

I didn't even know where to start, I couldn't just tell him the whole story, so I started the car and told him I had something in the house that would blow his mind.

Our relationship of not talking too much about personal things always worked with each other, but I decided to take it to another level when I tried to test whether Bill could see the ghost in my house watching television.

In the car Bill turned on the stereo, I told him that we were going to stop by our "pal" first to pick up some fine spices, before we went to my place.

The music was playing and I was thinking how I had managed to resist the temptation to tell my best friend about what was going on with me, even though he was bugging me every single day asking what I was working on and if I couldn't fit him "into the mix".

We arrived at our "pal", I gave Bill two thousand reais and asked him to fetch about fifty grams of any kind of weed they had there.

He didn't believe me and asked again.

- Man, you need to tell me what you are getting yourself into and where this money comes from. Which kinds do I get? - asked Bill.

- Whatever you want, just have fun and don't take too long - I replied.

Bill entered our "pal's" house, so I got right back into my previous thoughts.

I began to think about why all this was happening to me, the real reason they needed to post something on the Deep Web and what they would get in return, besides money with bitcoins.

I already scoured the regular Internet and the Deep Web about these reports - who had done it before? - I managed to come up with a few theories, at that moment the one that seemed to me the most plausible, was that there was a market based on demand and popularization, and now maybe all the evil in the world would even begin to make sense, someone is profiting from hell and making hell on earth.

And how did this market work? You must be wondering, but after much searching around the Deep Web, I managed to break some levels and go even deeper. I used the money they gave me and got to a place where I had to spend almost five million reais to access, but since money doesn't matter, I paid it anyways, the link directed me to a page with information to deposit more bitcoins and some symbols similar to the ones I seen on the fateful night I met Oliver.

I came across this link through a story in which powerful people were donating unbelievable amounts of bitcoins to that account and receiving links to see something from hell for a few minutes, thus gaining certain abilities and seeing the supernatural, and in the same story, it was said that there were commissions to see the punishments of some "famous" people such as Osama Bin Laden, Adolf Hitler, Josef Stalin and many others who were suffering in hell.

Bill left the house and walked back to the car with a wide smile on his face, like a child leaving a candy store.

- I took five kinds, 10 grams each. Wow, I've never seen so many delicacies together, where did you meet this guy? - asked Bill.

- I met him on the Deep Web and luckily he lived in town - I replied, starting the car and driving home.

Bill was already prepping a joint.

- Tangerine dream - he yelled, playing Tangerine by Led Zeppelin.

We arrived home. I purposely left my wallet in the car and when I got to the door I slapped my hand in my pocket as if I didn't realize.

- I forgot my wallet in the car, get it for me - I asked Bill.

He complained a little, but asked for the car key and went to get it.

I rushed into the house and looked everywhere for Lucía, but she was neither in the kitchen nor in the living room.

The TV was on a channel talking about politics.

Bill came back faster than I thought and asked me if I was looking for something - showing me my wallet.

I thanked him for bringing the wallet.

- Thanks, now stay there and play for a while. I need to go to the bathroom to take a shit, when I get back I'll show you the news that will blow your mind - I told him as I went to my room to look for Lucía.

I went upstairs wondering if I should have even brought him at that exciting moment. I hadn't even thought about how to explain to him about a ghost and all the rest.

I arrived at the bedroom and as I went through the door I saw Lucía in her ghostly form, so I decided to throw something at her, threw my shoe at her and as soon as it hit her right on the head, she went back to being a friendly ghost.

- That friend of yours is down there, my other form thought of a hundred and forty-five ways she would kill or fuck him, while all I could think of was that I would love to have sex with you again - Lucía said in such a sexy way that I had to restrain myself from getting into bed at that moment.

I told her my idea, and of course she agreed, saying that she was open to any new experience - again chanting in a teasing way, making it evident how naughty that ghost was.

I went back to the living room and the first test would be to see if Lucía would be visible to Bill. He was facing the TV, so he didn't see when we sneaked in, but as soon as Lucía crossed the room, he could see her and was startled, squealing so funny we started laughing at him.

- What the fuck is this? Why are you laughing? I got fucking scared, what the fuck, what is this? A hologram? - said Bill trying to recover and understand what was happening.

I didn't expect him to be able to see her on the first test, I wanted to make her move objects around - I was gonna say I gained some kind of power and trick him, but now I had to figure out what I was going to tell him.

- She's a ghost - I told him as Lucía introduced herself.

- Hi, nice to meet you Bill, my name is Lucía and I've known you for a long time, but we've never talked. - I don't know how, but at the end of the sentence she was already on Bill's lap.

Bill unresponsively let her sit on his lap and from what I know, he was already enjoying this even though he was still trying to figure out what was going on.

- It is not a hologram, but how am I able to feel her sitting on my lap and caressing me? Man, what the fuck is this? - said Bill.

Before I could respond, something happened, and Lucía, who was previously on Bill's lap, ran out and up the stairs at such incredible speed I hardly could see her, so when I looked at Bill, he was paralyzed and motionless.

Hell's Cave

I didn't understand what happened, I looked around and only then noticed Oliver - sitting again on my sofa - with a cigarette in his hand, a bright smile and hair covering his face.

–What do you think you are doing? Mortals can't handle this kind of knowledge and now this fellow is going to start seeing certain things that can make him stop being the person you know, my bet is that he will either die or go crazy - Oliver said while everything around us remained "frozen".

- I trust him, besides, what are you doing here? Some new assignment? - I asked him.

- You don't have the right to ask questions anymore, remember? I was in the neighborhood and decided to stop by, see how things were going. Apparently my visit came in handy, I just dropped you off for a while and looked at how things are going already - Oliver said as he stood up.

In one sudden movement, Oliver the skinny white man grabbed us by the shirt and said something - I couldn't understand it - so he threw us up with such terrific strength, I only realized we hadn't hit the ceiling of the house when I looked around and there was no ceiling, no floor, and even less my house.

We kept ascending, but we were apparently falling down.

I looked at Bill and he was still paralyzed - with a very funny face - and after a few seconds - which felt like minutes - things started to slow down and out of nowhere, the three of us arrived someplace.

Bill - still frozen, being held by Oliver.

Oliver - appearing to be amused by the situation holding his top hat on one hand and Bill's shirt collar on the other.

Me - not confused by everything happening and badly injured, squashed on the floor.

The crash was tremendous, I fell with my knees on the ground breaking both legs, Bill was protected by Oliver, holding him by the collar of his shirt and Oliver who masterfully landed and couldn't keep his sadistic smile off his face.

I felt dizzy as if the "world" was spinning like a slot machine. Bill started moving again, dropped to his knees and began to vomit. I leaned on the walls as my two broken legs regenerated, then I also began to vomit.

The nausea took a while to wear off, and only then did I realize where were we, brought to a dark place which appeared to be a cave, there was also a strange noise that kept repeating itself from time to time.

- Urgh, what happened? Where are we? - asked Bill when he stopped vomiting, he just now realized he was no longer in the living room with Lucía on his lap.

- Who is this guy? And what is he laughing at? Am I high? What was in those herbs? - Bill was nervous, and when he gets like this he becomes more paranoid.

- Shut the hell up Bill, this guy is from my work, he brought us here - I said explained.

Oliver ignored us, so I decided to ignore him as well, since I couldn't ask him anything anyways, I decided to let him do the talking this time, as he was the one who had taken us there. I looked around the place and approached Bill, told him to be calm, and whispered to him that we needed to stay alert and ready for anything.

I kept looking around and concluded that we were in a cave, and given the length of our fall and also the trouble breathing, that cave could be part of hell.

Oliver began to walk and looked at us as if telling us to follow him, the cave was dark and without knowing where we were, thus we decided to stay close to him, a few minutes of walking later, we reached a hole in the ground, the hole was so dark that it was impossible to determine the bottom, so, when I approached it, I purposely let some small stones fall into the hole, so we could see if the stones would reach a shallow bottom, but instead of hearing the noise of the stones, what we heard was the same noise we heard earlier.

However, now, standing right next to the hole and focusing on the noise of the rocks, I could hear better and identify that the wind came with screaming noises, which were shouting together for help.

- Could it have been the stones? - asked Oliver laughing.

I looked at him and his white teeth shone in his sarcastic smile, before I could say anything I looked at Bill - who looked completely stunned - I didn't know whether to pray, ask a question or light up a joint.

- Bill, chill out, this guy is Oliver I already know him - I told Bill, but was interrupted by Oliver.

- Hey, this is no fun, you wanted to get a mortal involved, we should have some fun - Oliver said, tossing his top hat on the floor and evaporating into it like a lamp genie.

I picked up the hat and there was no hole in the ground, and no miniature Oliver.

I looked at Bill and he looked as if he had seen a macabre magic trick that melted his brain.

If that wasn't enough, now the screams from the hole came even more frequently and emitted a deafening sound of joint cries for help and rescue.

Bill tried to say something, but was always interrupted by the screaming, so I signaled for him to keep quiet, he seemed to understand and calmed down.

After a few minutes of silence, the screams coming from the hole began to decrease in frequency and strength, we could finally hear better and realize that there was another noise coming from the direction we were standing.

Our eyes were beginning to get used to the darkness of the cave, so with our field of vision increased we could see what was approaching us from the way we had come with Oliver.

Even though we could now see, we couldn't tell what all these things were, several creatures - defective - crawling along the floor, side walls and ceiling - like an anthill - and it was approaching us.

I was the first to see them, yet I couldn't believe my eyes, when I turned around to see if Bill noticed them, he quickly started screaming, which caused the cries from the hole to come back and only then I realized that the wind from the crying hole was keeping the wretched creatures away us.

Considering talking wasn't so easy near the hole, we moved away to the other side, where there were no creatures to be seen.

- Bill, stay here, I'm going over where the creatures are to get a better look at them, and check if there's a way out from that side - I told him, already a little farther away from the hole.

I headed towards the defective creatures, and upon approaching them, they attempted to grab and bite me, but they posed little danger, as some had only their heads and arms attached to them, and others had no heads at all, consisting only of legs with eyes and mouths that crawled around grotesquely like zombies.

I went back to Bill and said we'd better head that way, so unaware of where we were going we headed away, leaving the hole behind and hoping that the creatures wouldn't chase us.

We moved on until we reached a spot in the cave with three passages, each one had different symbols on top, which I was not familiar with and had no idea what they meant.

I stared for a while at the symbols hoping that somehow one of them would start to make sense, but it didn't, so I asked Bill for his opinion.

- What should we do, which one do we choose? - I asked him.

Bill wanted to understand everything that was going on, he needed an explanation, I needed to get that doubtful look off his face, he probably thought he was dreaming, but self-inflicted slaps and pinches were not waking him up.

- What the fuck is going on? This is a dream, this is a dream, this is a dream! - repeated Bill.

- Stay calm, I'll tell you everything I know, but don't go crazy, I need you to help me get us out of here - I told the whole story that had happened to me up to this moment, from back when I met Oliver up to now, I explained everything to him about immortality, but I didn't talk about the infinite money, I only said that they paid well.

He didn't seem to believe it all, but the explanation at least managed to calm him down a little, and helped make sense of it all so Bill wouldn't go crazy, he no longer thought he was in a dream at least.

- This must be a game for Oliver, and if it is a game, we have to win, otherwise we will be left here, help me and together we can get out of this place - I told him, changing the mood.

- Do you have your lighter with you? - I asked him, and he responded by handing me the lighter.

I could use my "experience" - from movies and series - so I took the lighter and turned it on at the entrance of each passage.

On the first passage the fire from the lighter turned on and continued to burn with no change. The second one, the fire came on, flickered and went out, a sign of air flow, just as I was about to check the third passage Bill interrupted me.

- Found a joint in my pocket, hand me the lighter again - he said.

- Are you sure this is a good time? - I asked him.

- You drag me into this weird otherworldly stuff and you want to keep me away from my weed? Give me that lighter, before I take it by force, if I'm going to die or be stuck here forever, I'd rather do it stoned - said Bill, coming back to his former self.

There was no better argument than that, I passed him the lighter and said I also wanted a few puffs.

Once the cigarette ended - maybe the last one of our lives - we smoke it until our fingertips burned, I took the still burning cigarette and threw it in the third passageway, where I was going to test it with the lighter, I just didn't expect that as soon as the cigarette entered the third passageway the place would catch fire.

Almost like a dragon's breath, a gigantic flame rose from within the passage, causing the entire cave we were in to become hot and bright.

- Damn, I'm glad you didn't try the lighter the first time - Bill said, looking at me and starting to laugh.

Not because it was funny, or maybe it was, but I think it was more likely the effect of the marijuana, as I also started laughing along with him.

With the third passage now on fire it was soon discarded.

Two passages remained for us to decide which one to go on, I decided to choose the second one based still on my logic from movies and series, I figured that because the flame flickered and went out, it meant that there was an exit in this passage.

- Are you still here? - said an ominous voice coming from the third burning passage.

We looked into the passage and even though it was very bright because of the flames, we still couldn't see much.

- I will help you - the same voice spoke and the flames began to be sucked into the cave passage as if they were being swallowed by the voice that continued to speak as it approached us.

With all the flames now having been sucked in, the thing started to come out of the passage, we were not sure what it was.

It had six arms, no legs, and crawled like a slug to get around, its head looked like a buffalo's, and instead of hair there was smoke that turned into flames when the thing spoke.

- Are you seeing this? - asked Bill.

- Yes, I see it! It's not the weed, run! - I answered him and ran to the second entrance.

As soon as I said that Bill ran in as well, screaming.

- Run, let's get out of this place! - yelled Bill as he rushed.

I had no reason to disagree, I ran along trying to stay close in case I needed to protect him.

Out of nowhere the demonic buffalo came out of a fire, saying he would help us, only in the movies would people stand still or believe such things. Bill and I were sure that we wouldn't want to find out how he would help us.

We arrived at a rather spacious place that appeared to have no exit, as soon as we entered, the passage through which we had come collapsed.

- At least Boitatá was left behind. Where is that damned exit that you talked about, movie and series experience my ass, you son of a bitch, we are going to be stuck here forever, why did you have to show me that ghost - Bill was beginning to give in to despair.

– Boitatá? HAHAHAHA – I laughed.

- I told you to calm down, let me think, you wretch, look at the size of this place, there must be some way out - I answered him still laughing about the nickname he came up with for the thing, but deep down I was beginning to think that I really shouldn't have shown or told him anything.

There had to be some way out of there, maybe the right passage was the first one, a place with nothing made no sense, not even something scary, so I waited, I was sure something was going to happen or there was something we didn't see yet.

Not much time passed and while we were searching the cave the collapsed passage began to spew smoke and light shone through it - the rocks seemed to be melting - that is, Boitatá was coming to us.

- I found something - I told Bill pointing to something on the ceiling.

It was another symbol, and as such, Bill couldn't see it, I climbed up there with Bill's help and when I got very close to the symbol, it didn't look strange to me, although I was sure I had never seen anything like it before in my life.

- Do you see it? What does it mean? - asked Bill.

I stared at the symbol and without really knowing what I was doing some words just came out of my mouth, without even knowing what they meant.

- Ман ҳар касро даъват менамоям, назди ман биёед! - The words came out of my mouth.

As soon as I did, the whole cave began to shake, turning the place upside down and revealing several tunnels opening everywhere, we assumed it was our way out, but the tunnels were filled with creatures that began to come out and attack us.

Out of the first tunnel some bald dog-like creatures with large spines on their backs came out, they had gray skin and a horrible smell, their dental arches were unlike any creature we had ever seen before, and they moved really fast.

Before we could think of how to defend ourselves against the dogs, other creatures started coming out of the other tunnels and each one was weirder and more unusual than the last.

The next thing we knew we were surrounded by several creatures, a snake with bat wings, which had two heads, one on top and the other at the end of its tail.

A black antelope the size of a boar, with large horns that moved in any direction.

Several child-sized creatures connected by umbilical cords, their bodies were mottled and had elongated body parts of disproportionate size, their heads were so large that the creatures screamed in pain as they moved, they were horrifying creatures.

A kind of deformed man with his head turned backwards, his arms, fingers, nose, mouth and ears were twisted and he walked on only one leg as his other leg appeared to have been amputated.

A woman who looked like a witch with gray hair, a hunchback disproportionate to her body, crooked teeth, lice, she had something that in addition to all these other things made her especially unpleasant, her eyeballs were hanging down only by the optic nerve making her dry, continuous laughter send shivers down anyone's spine.

I dodged a frog that had a greenish beard and long hair, its body was covered with seaweed and its skin had black fish scales, and it reeked.

It all seemed like a nightmare I couldn't explain, there were so many creatures I would never even imagine existed, and then there was the demon of fire - the boitatá - which was still melting the passage we came through.

I forgot about Bill for a moment and as my attention turned back to him I realized just how much trouble he was in. I don't know exactly what had happened, but all I could see was a large piece of cloth - looking like a huge white bandage - flying towards him and wrapping itself around his face, causing Bill to fall and squirm on the ground.

When he stood up, the cloth was wrapped around his face and his eyes were - yellow and red - his behavior was different as if he was possessed by a spirit.

If all this wasn't enough, "Boitatá" managed to melt the rock all the way through with an explosion, he finally reached us.

I feared that "Boitatá" would arrive and lead all those dozens of creatures that were scattered around the place, but as he entered the cave some creatures began to attack him too, thus forming an endless war of the monsters among themselves and among us.

Bill, possessed, attacked other monsters and even me if I tried to get close, for a while I was paralyzed, had no idea what to do, getting rid of some monsters while they were attacking me, thinking of a way to get us out of there and meanwhile several other creatures arrived and ran through the cave that was on fire everywhere due to the fireballs "Boitatá" was throwing.

At least someone seemed to be having fun, "Boitatá" laughed a lot, threw fireballs from his mouth and his six arms, taking turns throwing balls and fighting with the creatures that managed to get close to him.

- This doesn't make sense, do you hear me Oliver? What are you trying to prove? I already understood how dangerous the underworld is for mortals - I yelled hoping that he would listen to me while all the confusion was going on.

- You don't think introducing the supernatural to your friend is fun anymore? Why don't we introduce all of it at once? HAHAHAHAHAHA! - Oliver's voice came out of his hat that was lying next to Bill.

I approached the hat and picked it up, put my ear to the hole in the hat to try to hear if he was going to say anything else, but as soon as I did a hand pulled me into the hat and again in seconds I was thrown - teleported - to another place, a huge dark empty space, there was an armchair in which Oliver was sitting with a cigarette in his hand and a TV that was showing everything happening to us in the cave.

I looked around for Bill and he wasn't there with us.

- You son of a bitch, what are you doing? And what's going on? Where's Bill? - I said furiously to him, he remained calm, sitting still with his crooked smile.

- Have you ever stopped to think that you are too angry and stressed out for someone immortal? Your friend was only caught because he was drugged, the ITTAN-MOMEN love unconscious, drunk and drugged-out numb people - said Oliver.

- We need to go back there and save him, you were all this time watching what was happening to us from here and did nothing to help us? - I asked him, but was interrupted by the change in Oliver's expression that for the first time changed his calm demeanor.

- Help you? Who do you think I am, your fairy godmother? Where was my help five hundred years ago? You should be ashamed of yourself, whining for help, you're the one who got your friend involved in all of this - Oliver said, blurting out and returning to his usual expression.

He was not at all wrong, if something happened to Bill I would be the culprit, but the one who had brought us to that cave full of creatures was not me.

- I get it and I feel like shit, is this how you wanted me to feel? What can I do to help him? - I said, begging for help.

- Nothing! You would never really find your way out, I won't let you help him, his soul will be consumed by one of those creatures and he will probably go to that hole where the screams came from, suffering eternally until he becomes one of those creatures, and all this thanks to you - Oliver said laughing and teasing me.

- Thanks to me? I already admitted that I am partly to blame, but who brought us here? - I questioned him.

I couldn't take it anymore. I went after him with all my speed and newly acquired strength. It was time to enjoy immortality and stop being afraid of this guy, I needed to teach him a good lesson.

I was right next to him and as he didn't expect, I managed to surprise him and throw a punch, he remained motionless as if nothing had happened, then I grabbed the collar of his shirt and with his hair down over his face, I shook him, and saw his mouth and he was smiling.

- You've got some nerve - he said, snapping his fingers and throwing me out of the hat again.

Back to the cave with Bill and the monsters.

When I returned it didn't seem like any time had passed since I had entered Oliver's hat, it was as if I had never been out of there, and the creatures were still causing trouble.

I put the top hat on my head and ran to where Bill was, he was still possessed and as I tried to get closer several creatures, including Bill, tried to attack me, I didn't mind and had the impression of being more agile, so I could easily dodge the monsters.

I reached over to Bill, grabbed the ITTAN-MOMEN - the bandage from hell - and with one motion using all the strength I had, pulled it off Bill, who began to spin around like a pawn until the entire bandage was unwrapped from his head.

I reached over to Bill, grabbed the ITTAN-MOMEN - the bandage from hell - and with one motion using all the strength I had, pulled it off Bill, who began to spin around like a pawn until the entire bandage was unwrapped from his head.

While all this was going on, the other battle continued, the creatures and "Boitatá", fireballs, screams, witchcraft, hellhounds and ghosts, were everywhere, many had already been destroyed in the middle of the battle.

"Boitatá" was still going strong, and the new creatures that kept coming from the other tunnels were attacking everything in their path.

I had to see if there was still a way out of there, since Oliver mentioned that we couldn't find it, there was certainly one.

I decided to go back through the passage that "Boitatá" reopened and try the first tunnel, but for this we would need to pass by the monsters and also "Boitatá".

I ran past some approaching monsters and headed for the passage, where the wretched "Boitatá" saw us and launched fireballs at us.

Since I still had Bill on my back my speed was hampered, and I couldn't dodge all the fireballs, so in order to keep Bill from getting hurt, I absorbed the fire with my body, which started to burn, except for Oliver's top hat, which got hit, but was still intact.

- Ugh! It hurts, didn't you say you would help us "Boitatá"? What are you, anyway, and what do you want? - I asked him, unable to resist calling him by the nickname we had given.

- What did you call me? Respect Kagutsuchi - he said, throwing several more fireballs, which this time had no effect, for I had already moved away with Bill and none of them reached us, although they hit several creatures that were trying to get close to him.

- I want to help them, sucking their souls to burn forever in me - said "Boitatá", all excited.

- Thank you very much, but we are not available - I answered him while I waited for the burns from the fireball to stop hurting.

I couldn't leave Bill unconscious on the floor, otherwise another creature could take advantage of this, but I also couldn't go through "Boitatá" with Bill on my back.

I needed to act up and approach the tunnel, but to do so I needed to kill the monsters in the whole area around us, I put Bill on my back again and approached a certain point where the fireballs that the "Boitatá" threw wouldn't threaten us and most of the creatures wouldn't approach because of the danger of being hit by them.

Even though we were safer, I had to keep on being careful with the fireballs that continued to be thrown from all sides by "Boitatá" and also with the few monsters that dared to approach, most of which were flying monsters.

Some kind of snakes with bat wings were getting very close to us, so I jumped to push and throw them away, but I misjudged the strength of the jump, because of how pressured I felt, the strength I had acquired seemed to have increased even more, so when I jumped, I got much higher than I thought I would, so I went straight through the snakes and from up there, I could see two passages with strange writing like the previous ones.

I fell back to the ground and managed to capture the approaching bat-winged snakes.

"Boitatá" slowly crawled to us and now the balls he threw were becoming too dangerous for us to stand there.

I picked Bill up again on my back and started walking towards the two passages I had seen, so I gave up the previous plan of going through "Boitatá" and now needed to improvise.

We weren't that far from the entrance, but with Bill on my back it certainly wouldn't be possible to make the jump to get where the two passages were, so I decided to test my agility, so with Bill on my back I ran in circles to get used to his weight.

A while later, having gotten used to its weight, I decided to throw him up to the passages and then climb up to protect him in case there were monsters around.

We were a few meters from the entrance and "Boitatá" seemed to realize my plan and with his speed he couldn't catch up with us, so as soon as I threw Bill with all my strength to the top of the cave where the passages were, "Boitatá" started to make some kind of noise, as if he was clearing his throat and as soon as he started to do this the monsters ran away, back to the holes where they came from.

At first I didn't understand what was going on, but I knew it wasn't good.

- Boitatá, you disgusting thing, didn't your mother teach you any manners? - I said to him, yelling and taking advantage of the fact that the monsters were returning to their dens, so I jumped up to where Bill was standing.

"Boitatá" got even more angry and red at what I said, the noise increased in frequency and as soon as we were a few steps away from the two entrances the noise suddenly stopped and when I looked back all I saw was an explosion along with laughter.

- HaHaHaHa we will see each other again some day - said "Boitatá" exploding the whole cave.

The flames were approaching fast and so I didn't have much time to choose which of the two passages we were going into, I just picked Bill up off the ground and jumped into one of them with him on my back, carefully so that the fire wouldn't get him.

I fell to the ground with half my body in flames, the passage we had entered collapsed and now we were in a different place, it was not a cave, it had power cables and lights on the walls illuminating the place.

The place seemed to pose no threat, I left Bill on the ground and stood for a few minutes regenerating myself feeling a horrible pain. I never thought that an immortal could feel so much pain, my body was slow to regenerate and my burned flesh smelled like barbecue.

I eventually fell asleep and was woken up by Bill who was already conscious and poking me to see if I was still alive.

- Hey man, are you okay? Where are we? - Bill asked.

I noticed I wasn't burned anymore, except for my clothes that were burned up where the fire started.

- Yes, I am, and how are you? I managed to get us out of that place, we've gone up a level by the looks of it - I told him not really sure what I was talking about.

- Level? This isn't a fucking game, you have this regenerating thing going on, but I'm standing here shitting myself that could be killed at any moment - said Bill exaggerating and desperate as always.

- I carried you on my back against a thousand fucking monsters, and we're here now safely, you are welcome. It was you who said, "you need to get me involved", "tell me about your job", "you can count on me, get me a job there" - I told him, remembering the times he insisted I told him everything.

He was annoyed, but thought about it rationally and then asked.

- How are we going to get out of here? Where is the guy who brought us here? - asked Bill.

- As far as I know he is over there - I said to him, pointing to the top hat that was tied around his waist.

He didn't understand, but still didn't take the top hat off his waist.

- It looks like we are somewhere underground, this place now even has lights - I pointed, showing the wires that connected the lights to each other.

We follow the lights and walk for a few meters until we reach a corridor with several side doors.

The torture chambers

The place seemed familiar, but I was reluctant to believe that this was where we were. The doors were identical to the door from where Carlos - the guy from the Deep Web video - was, and while I trying to be sure, Bill tried to open door after door, but they all appeared to be locked. He kept trying until he found one of the doors unlocked, he opened it and went inside.

We went inside and there was a person tied to a stretcher like they did with Carlos, the person seemed to be on drugs and a few meters away there was a television showing something.

I wondered whether to tell Bill that I have seen a place like this before, but just as I thought about opening my mouth, he interrupted by saying.

- Look, the guy tied up is on TV - Bill said, pointing at the TV.

I gave up telling Bill about the room and focused my attention on the TV, already knowing roughly what was supposed to be happening.

The guy on the stretcher appeared to be at a party and at this party there were many young people, everyone was drinking, talking and dancing. After some time, the guy goes to the bathroom and stays there for a long time, rinses his face with water, stares at himself in the mirror, until another guy comes through the bathroom door and goes to one of the stalls, enters it and closes the door. Meanwhile the guy on the stretcher stared at himself in the mirror a little longer and left the bathroom.

The TV kept showing the bathroom mirror, and a few minutes later we heard the sound of the toilet flushing and the boy from before coming out of the stall and going to the faucet to wash his hands, fix his hair and leave.

The TV kept following the boy out of the bathroom, he walked towards the party, until then he was surprised by someone who immobilized him and got him unconscious with a cloth with some kind of liquid on it.

It was the guy on the stretcher, who carried the boy carefully to avoid being seen, lifted him into a room and took some pills from his pocket and forced the boy, who was still half unconscious, to swallow them.

Everything happened so fast, that as soon as the boy swallowed the pills the guy on the stretcher left and returned to the party.

Bill and I looked at this without comprehending what was happening. I expected something bad to happen to the guy on the stretcher, as it did to Carlos in his experiments, but this was not what seemed to happen.

We kept watching and the TV started to show the guy on the stretcher coming back to the party as if nothing had happened, he sat further away from everyone, picked up his glass and started drinking again.

Minutes later some of the boy's friends found him unconscious and brought him to the party, they tried to wake him up and when they finally did, he woke up and said something pointing to where the guy on the stretcher was.

- It was him - said the boy pointing to the guy on the stretcher.

As soon as he noticed, he tried to run away, but it was too late, he was surrounded by several people who started to pull him to where the boy was.

When they got there everyone present formed a circle around the guy on the stretcher and yelled together.

- Murderer. Murderer. Murderer! - everyone yelled.

The boy approached the guy on the stretcher, held his head and started vomiting into his mouth, causing him to start choking until he died and thus woke up in another hellish nightmare.

Bill was shocked and looked at me trying to understand what was going on. It was the cue I needed to tell him about my first job and where I thought we were.

I summarized for him the story of Carlos and what happened to him on TV while he was tied up on the stretcher, and also told him that I had put this story and video on the Deep Web.

- Now at least something is starting to make sense, so we are in hell and this guy tied up is suffering his punishment - he said strangely calm.

- Yes, I think that's it. That's what I deduced too - I answered him.

- And all those doors are people, are we close to the exit? - Bill asked.

- I have no idea, I saw a similar place on the video, but I didn't imagine that there were so many doors or even those horrible creatures, until then I had only gained immortality, started seeing ghosts and having lots of money - I answered, coming clean with him.

Bill nodded and looked around the room we were in. I felt obliged to reassure him that we could get out of there.

I opened the door and looked down the hall to check that there was no one there, everything was very quiet after the chaos in the cave with the monsters.

There wasn't much besides us, the stretcher, the TV, and the guy tied up in the room.

Bill got tired of looking and went back to watching the TV.

I kept standing in the doorway making sure no freaks or monsters came looking for us.

- Hey Charles, isn't that Lucía? - asked Bill, pointing at the TV.

- What? - I exclaimed as I approached the TV, leaving the door open with no one watching.

On the TV I could see perfectly and it was Lucía, yes, we were watching on TV the costume party that Lucía had described to me earlier, the party where she had been murdered, but this time we were seeing it from the perspective of the killer - the guy on the stretcher.

I told Bill about how Lucía was killed and that this was probably the guy who killed her. Bill, who by then was too quiet to believe, picked up the TV and before I could do anything, threw it at the guy on the stretcher, causing it to explode and waking up the killer.

- Why did you do that? - I asked him.

- I don't want to see her die - replied Bill.

- You moron, you didn't hear what I said, he killed Lucía and is suffering in hell, the TV would probably show a way for him to die suffering and then he would wake up in another dream.

He realized how he screwed up, but we soon stopped the bickering when we realized that the guy on the stretcher was conscious and was already free.

- Who are you? Where am I? Is this another dream? - the guy on the stretcher asked, heading for the door.

I went towards him with my increased speed and managed to catch him easily.

I held him down and pushed him back to the stretcher and as soon as he realized his disadvantage he started his little theatrics.

- I didn't do anything wrong, why are you doing this to me? - he said, almost in tears.

Before I could respond, Bill said.

- Oh, innocent boy, we were watching your innocence on TV and we know a ghost that you killed - said Bill, not taking any crap from the killer.

- A what? Who are you? - the guy on the stretcher had already changed his innocent face and now appeared to be a calm, cold and thoughtful person who all the time was evaluating the situation trying to find a way out.

- A Halloween party, a Jack Skellington costume, and yet another victim killed by "overdose"! - I asked him ironically.

- A beautiful job, wasn't it? - he replied, in an aggressive tone and with his eyes fixed on us.

I looked at him with enough desire to kill him at that moment, but I thought to myself what this could lead to, and so I did nothing.

- How could a guy like you, who has nothing special, not be caught by the police quickly? You don't even look like a serial killer, look how skinny you are, how dumb you look, and you don't seem to have any talent at all - I said to him teasingly.

- Did that friend of yours tell you how I touched her while she was unconscious? - he kept his offensive posture, even though he was in shock after hearing my words, yet he still didn't know who we were.

- You don't even have to tell us, as we saw on TV one of your self-esteem problems that made you want to poison young people at parties was because at one of your parties a girl took you to her room and when you pulled down your pants she started to laugh - Bill said, I didn't even know if this had really happened, as I hadn't paid as much attention to the TV as he had.

This upset the guy, and he went after Bill, wanting to fight, but before the two of them could get into a fight I punched the guy really hard and he fell unconscious to the floor.

- I could handle this piece of shit - said Bill.

- I'm not going to risk your mortal ass, and you don't even know Lucía well enough to want revenge - I told him.

- It doesn't matter, you told me her story and from what you told me she stayed on earth to get her revenge - said Bill back at me.

It was true, I also wished that she could find him for revenge, but we had to find a way out of there first.

I always had the habit of repeating people's names three times when I wanted them to be with me at the moment, and Bill, already knowing this habit of mine, repeated it along with me when I said it for the first time.

- Lucía, Lucía, Lucía - we both spoke together by coincidence.

But at that moment, when we finished our ritual, as if all the weirdness of the night wasn't enough, the place became dark and the lights began to flicker until, suddenly, the lights came back on and we could see that Lucía had materialized - not in her ghost form, but in flesh and blood - inside the chamber where we were.

- Where am I? What happened? - Lucía asked as soon as she saw us.

- Charles, Bill where are we? What happened to my body? - she asked, still looking down at her hands, which were now back to flesh and blood.

Before I could explain, the guy on the stretcher woke up and spoke.

- I remember you, I already killed you once, I'll do it again if I have to. I'm not going to die in this dream - said the assassin, going up to Lucía.

Before I could react, I saw Lucía smiling.

- I've waited so, so long for this - Lucía said, dodging the guy's move and elbowing him right between the eyes, knocking him to the ground.

I looked at Bill and he looked at me, we both stared at each other and went back to admiring the beating that Lucía was giving this guy.

I thought I heard a laugh, but looked to the side and saw no one, I didn't want to get in Lucía's way at that moment, she stepped on the guy's ribs and head.

The assassin remained wrecked on the ground and Lucía was beginning to show signs of fatigue.

- Do you hear laughter? - asked Bill.

- Yes, I thought it was in my head - I answered him.

- What? - asked Lucía, not quite hearing Bill's question.

The laughter started getting louder and louder, and now Lucía seemed to hear it too.

- Oh, the laughter. I can hear it too - Lucía answered.

The guy was passed out on the floor from being beaten so it wasn't coming from him, the TV had been destroyed by Bill so it wasn't coming from that either, the door was slightly open, I approached it, but there was no one around.

Oliver, the top hat! I thought.

And that's exactly where the laughter came from, and it got louder and louder, until in an instant Oliver materialized beside Bill, giving him a shove and taking his top hat and putting it back on his head.

- Congratulations, the deeper you dig, the bigger the grave - Oliver said, finishing his long laugh.

- Take it! - he said, throwing a knife at Lucía, who managed to catch it without any problem, and then plunging it into the chest of her killer.

It was so fast that I could only track their movements and see what happened after she killed him.

With the knife stuck in the man, Lucía fell to the ground and her ghost form came out of her body again.

I looked at Oliver to see if he would do anything, but he was just watching it all happen with his arms crossed and his white, cynical smile.

I turned my attention to Bill and he was just wide-eyed, I didn't know if he was looking at Lucía, Oliver or me.

It all happened so fast a bright blue light began to project from the ceiling of the room and suck in Lucía's ghost form.

I jumped towards her offering my hand for her to hold on to, but she didn't even try to hold on to it, she kept going up the tunnel.

- Lucía - Bill and I yelled.

She continued to climb slowly, she just looked at us and smiled.

- Don't worry guys, it's my grandmother and mother, I will finally see them again. Thanks for getting me out of that endless cycle, I got my revenge and I'll tell you one thing, the feeling is not as I imagined, it is.... a lot Better, JUSTICE! - said Lucía smiling as she disappeared through the ceiling along with the blue light.

The lights in the place went out once more and as soon as they came back on, the whole room was rebuilt.

The guy on the stretcher was "alive" again strapped to his stretcher and the TV was working again while another scene played of the guy on the stretcher waking up again in another nightmare.

Bill and I looked at each other as if we couldn't believe what had happened there, so we both looked at Oliver who started to applaud.

- Now that is an exorcism. I have seen many before, but the way you did this Poltergeist, I have to acknowledge your class. My first exorcism was of a demon, and it wasn't a pretty sight, let alone a pretty sound - said Oliver as he approached the two of us.

I braced myself for a fight if necessary and he, seeing my posture, just said.

- Calm down champ, we're done for the day. I think we've made enough of a mess, and this little excursion, you and your little friend here should earn us a few things in the future - Oliver said, moving even closer to us and throwing us back up.

As this time I was used to it, I just felt light as if I was floating and moments later I managed to land without breaking anything, so the three of us were again in the living room of my house.

Back home

Bill was lying unconscious on the floor, so I went over to check if he was alive.

- He'll be fine, he just needs to get some rest, you don't have to worry anymore - Oliver said regarding Bill.

- By the way, I was just dropping by to congratulate you on the report you did in the Deep Web, people loved your work and even some of the big guys said something like "wow, this is a masterpiece" , "what a unique report", "this is a terrifying portrayal, it will give anyone shivers down their spine" - said Oliver.

- Thank you? - I replied, walking over to Bill, picking him up off the floor and putting him on the couch in the living room.

- Do you want anything else? Haven't you already fucked with us enough for today? - I told Oliver, subtly telling him to get the hell out of my house.

He either didn't understand the subtlety of my words or he just ignored it.

- So, as I was saying, I came by to congratulate you and also to say that you got promoted, it will take a while for the next job to come, so take your time to rest. Oh and about your friend, it will be hard for him to go back to his normal life, our little visit to you know where awakened the supernatural for him too - said Oliver.

I turned to look at Bill - lamenting that I involved him in the whole mess - and when I turned back to Oliver and asked him what it meant to be promoted, he was no longer there, along with his hat.

Son of a b..., I thought to myself.

I left Bill sleeping in the living room couch and went to the suite to take a shower.

I wanted to digest everything that happened and get some rest, my brain felt heavy.

I stepped into the shower and the water was very hot - on purpose - I sat on the floor, because I couldn't stand up anymore, I let the water hit my head and stared at the floor, I started to laugh - a dull laugh - and seconds later the laughter turned into a cry of relief.

I fell asleep under the shower, I don't know for how long, maybe an hour or two under the hot water, when I came out I was wrinkled and red, the pain for me was no longer the same as when I was mortal, so a few hours under the hot water was nothing.

I took the towel and dried myself off even though my skin was burning, I thought I heard a noise coming from the bedroom, I wrapped myself in the towel and ran to see who or what it was. I wished it was Lucía and almost called her name, but when I got to the room it was just a gray cat, it was near a open window, I got closer trying to scare the cat away, but instead of going outside and running away, the cat came in and climbed on my bed.

As I was already tired, I didn't care, so I closed the window and lay down sharing the bed with the feline, in just a few minutes I was already asleep.

I woke up in the middle of the night and the cat was still there, staring at me. I went down to the kitchen to drink some water and to see if Bill was still there and if he was okay. I went through the living room and he was still in the same position as I left him on the couch. I went to the kitchen, drank some water and snacked on something in the fridge, before going back to the bedroom I grabbed a bottle of water, just in case I got thirsty during the night.

I got to the bedroom and noticed the cat was no longer there, the window was closed and so was the bedroom door, so he couldn't have left. I went to the bathroom to pee and he wasn't there either, I didn't really care, so I went back to bed and tried to go back to sleep.

As I was about to fall asleep, I heard a meow, so I opened my eyes to see the damned cat, but there was no cat. I got out of bed, decided to look for the feline a little more, heard the meowing again and this time had the impression that it was coming from under the bed. The room was very dark and once again something was disturbing me in my house - I couldn't have even a single peaceful day in that place.

- Come out kitty cat or whatever you are - I said aloud as I flopped down on the bed, expecting something to jump in my face or rip my head off.

To my surprise there was nothing there, but as soon as I got up again there was someone on my bed.

- What a nice booty you got there, also don't call me kitty, I am a grown cat, can't you tell? - said a woman leaning over my bed as she waited for me to stand up.

For a brief moment I thought about Lucía again, but I knew it wasn't her.

- It's three in the morning, if you had any idea how my night was you wouldn't have come to mess with me today - I told her.

- Good morning then - she chuckled.

I took a good look at her, even though the place was still a bit dark.

She had the most pale skin I had ever seen and also the most beautiful pair of breasts - perfectly round.

She was very similar to the description of the woman who offered Oliver the contract.

- Oliver told me about you - I said.

For a brief second her face changed, but not for long.

- That big mouthed demon talks too much, but I know him like the back of my hand, I bet he told you about his first time, he always tells this story and in the end he says he never had much choice but to accept the contract, he goes around whining, but he loves being immortal and all the benefits it brings - she said as she lit a cigarette near the bedside ashtray.

And that was exactly what Oliver had said and done.

- So it's you, what are you doing here? Are you looking for him? He came by earlier, but he's already gone - I told her, trying to look away from her round breasts.

- What a rude booty, staring at my breasts and trying to kick me out of your house already - she said, glaring at me sexually.

- Can I have a drag? - I asked her, holding out my hand.

- Yes - she answered, approaching me.

I took a long drag and handed the cigarette back to her.

- I have come to meet the newbie that everyone is talking about, I read and saw your Deep Web report, I liked it a lot, although it wasn't enough to bring me here, but I couldn't resist when I heard about your little trip to hell with a mortal, if the feat of leaving hell with a living mortal wasn't enough, the exorcism of a vengeful ghost was the icing on the cake that brought me here to take a good look at your lovely ass - she answered, laughing and taking a last drag on her cigarette.

- That's the reason I don't smoke pot often. I always get horny when I do - she said, taking off her clothes and rolling like a cat on my bed.

- A little giggly and downright naughty - plus those wonderful round breasts.

I wanted it and she knew it, so as she reached out and pulled me into her arms I went in without resisting.

Her smell was different, similar to white roses, her curves and breasts drove me crazy, but I managed, or at least thought I managed, to cover it up.

- HAHAHAHAHA - she laughed at me and meowed like a cat.

She continuously rubbed her breasts against my body, I couldn't handle it and let myself be taken, we kissed and I ran my hands all over that perfect body.

I took off my shorts and with no need to ask she started sucking delightfully, I turned her around with my newly acquired strength and repay the favor with my tongue between her legs - 69 - after a few minutes the room seemed to sweat along with us, we took turns - immortals take their time - she on top, on her side, underneath, upside down. We went all night and everything seemed to go by so fast, when we finished we realized that the sun was already rising.

Finally we just lay in bed, tired, I was exhausted and so I went to sleep soon after.

Hours later I woke up and there was no one beside me, there was only a note on the headboard of my bed.

"Booty, did you sleep well? I didn't want to wake you up, you were asleep so soundly, I suppose the fatigue from your adventure in hell plus our own adventure has left you exhausted, from the looks of it you must have gained even more physical stamina. Yesterday I didn't tell you the main reason why I came over. You have been promoted and we have a new job for you at the agency. Oliver will show you everything, I hope you adjust well and that we see each other soon, kisses." - signed Belatrix Hyssel.

I read that and went back to sleep.

I couldn't sleep for a long time, I kept wondering how Bill was doing and if he was awake yet, I was also very hungry, so I decided to get up and go to the living room to see how Bill was doing. I went downstairs and to my surprise I smelled food, I hurried up and when I got to the kitchen it was Bill, for the first time I saw him cooking.

- I bought some bread, I saw that there was some ham and mozzarella in the fridge, I also fried some eggs and bacon, the coffee is just finishing - said Bill all excited and full of energy.

- What's the matter with you? - I asked him.

- Nothing, I woke up feeling excited. I had a horrible nightmare last night, I don't even remember when I went to sleep, that weed was really strong - he answered.

- Nightmare, I see... Wasn't it the one I told you that I worked for hell and one of the guys who hired me came here and took us there, and we were stuck, barely survived, wasn't it? - I said to him as I walked over to the kitchen and approached him.

- Fuck! It wasn't a dream then? - said Bill disappointed and well aware of the answer.

I approached him and he took the knife that was beside him and stabbed me in the arm.

- What the fuck is this? Are you crazy?! - I told him, slapped his face and took the knife from him.

A little bit of blood came out and since the cut was not big, I regenerated very quickly.

- HAHAHAHAHAHAHAHA - I started to laugh and showed him that there was no more cut.

- Fuck! So it really wasn't a nightmare, what happened? I just remember that monsters started popping up all over the place, something was on my head, we avenged Lucía, and I don't remember much about the rest - Bill said.

I told him everything we did in the cave from hell and how we got out of there, and I also told him how I got involved in the whole thing again, as well as what little I knew about hell.

I didn't mention what happened yesterday in the bedroom, I just said that I was promoted and that Oliver came to tell me about it, but when he arrived and saw that Bill had seen Lucía, he decided to play with us. It was like a joke to him, despite the fact that all the fun was for his amusement.

He remembered Lucía and about hell.

- Man, why did you show me that, now I'm going to be seeing these things and I'm not immortal as you are, you fuck! You're a bitch, you just get me in trouble - Bill said, looking scared and pissed off.

- HAHAHAHAHAHAHA, how many times have you asked me what I was up to, that I could talk to you about anything, that we are brothers - I answered him laughing.

- But not that, you cuckold, you know I'm scared to death about these things - said Bill.

- You will see it makes no difference, they would exist anyway, stop crying and here's what I'll do, I'll hire you as my helper, you'll do most of the research and homework. I pay you seven thousand every month, take it or leave it, the other option is that you don't come back here anymore and we never see each other again - I told him.

- You are a coward, huh, only seven thousand? - said Bill, the opportunist.

- Then you better move out of town to enjoy the supernatural, and being poor - I answered him.

- Deal, research for seven in cash, I already want the first payment - said Bill, the negotiator.

I took my cell phone and transferred the money to his account. He was happy and left me alone to have my breakfast.

- I'm moving out of my parents' house, can I live here with you? I don't want to live in that house, I bet that damn place is filled with ghosts, and since we don't know when Oliver will come, you'll need me

- Bill said, coming up with the perfect excuse to move in and live with me.

I always said no, but that was because he didn't have a job to pay his part of the rent, but now that he had a way to pay with his "job", I didn't object, in fact I really wanted someone to keep me company and no one better than my best friend.

After breakfast Bill went to his house to get his things and when he returned he was now officially living with me.

The Second Job

Five days had passed since Bill moved into my house and no word from Oliver or my next assignment.

Bill spent his whole paycheck in only four days and now on the fifth day was asking me for a raise - for playing video games all day and annoying me - he bought sneakers, clothes, glasses, workout equipment, a laptop and a bunch of other stuff he didn't really need.

He wanted to travel, but seemed afraid to leave me. Considering everything that happened, he could only remember parts of what happened in the cave. A few nights ago I heard a noise that woke me up, it was like a scream, but I wasn't sure if the scream occurred in my dreams or if it happened in my house, so I remained in bed trying to fall asleep again and waiting in case the noise was repeated, since I didn't hear anything else I fell asleep. The next day I asked Bill if he heard anything, he mentioned having horrible nightmares, but said he heard nothing. I asked him what he dreamed about, he shrugged, saying he couldn't remember, but it felt to me like he was hiding something, I didn't insist, I figured it must be normal to have nightmares after experiencing everything we did in the hell cave.

I also would rather he didn't go away on a trip, and leave me alone waiting for Oliver and the second job, especially not knowing what this assignment would be, after all, I was promoted, so I figured the job would be a lot different from the first one.

I showed Bill how to delve deeper into the Deep Web and asked him to do some research, try to find out something about the reports I made about Carlos, or if he could find more information related to hell.

In his research he even found the report I made, but only a part of it, since to access the rest was blocked by a paywall. He did not find anything concrete about hell, that we had not seen before.

It was always like this, a notice that a job would come and an anxious wait that made my days take unpleasantly long. We carried on with our routine, sometimes even going out at night to have some fun.

So far, since the visit to the cave, we hadn't seen anything different, although Bill claimed to have seen a smoky figure with yellow eyes when he was walking home alone during one of the partying nights, he swore he spotted something watching him near the garbage cans, but when he got a better look, it wasn't there anymore.

I made fun of him by saying that I was the booze monster. He got angry and stopped talking about it. I thought that maybe it could be Oliver watching him, but it was better not to say anything, since I wasn't sure.

Bill does not remember being possessed by ITTAN-MOMEN, and I didn't mention it either, but coincidentally or not.

Bill had cut back on drugs and alcohol, and on the day he saw the figure, he exaggerated a lot, but as we didn't know if he had actually seen anything, I thought it was better that Bill remained unaware about the possession.

Almost two months went by.

Bill and I were not talking as much, the anxiety of the upcoming job and being with each other almost all day was wearing on our friendship.

The few times we didn't argue were when we did the things we liked to do together, but we couldn't do the same things over and over again, even though we tried.

There was a new movie on Netflix about the domination and manipulation of big corporations that expand their roots by buying smaller companies, pretending that the free market exists, but in reality it only exists so that the big corporate groups can buy and incorporate them into it, the movie showed how they influence the politics and economy of different countries, spying and controlling everything and everyone through their cell phones and social networks.

Bill and I talked about the movie and decided to order a pizza and watch it together. When the delivery man arrived I went to answer the door and as I opened, who was outside holding the pizza? Oliver.

- Movie and Pizza, Yum yum! - he said walking through the door with the pizza.

I had no reaction and just closed the door after he walked in.

He left the pizza on the kitchen counter and went into the living room without saying anything.

- Your pet is here! Hi Bill - Oliver said teasingly.

Upon seeing him Bill grew tense, but couldn't resist teasing him.

- It wasn't enough to be the errand boy from hell, now he's also a pizza delivery boy? Things are really looking bleak - Bill responded.

Oliver gave a faint laugh and sat down on the other sofa without saying anything else.

- So Oliver, what are you doing here? Did you come to talk about the next assignment? - I asked him.

- Always straight to the point, relax a bit, you still have an eternity ahead of you, yes I have come to give it to you, but let's eat the pizza and watch the movie first, isn't that what you were going to do? Act like I'm not here, it's been so long since I've seen a movie, I still remember the last movie I saw... - said Oliver, taking a cigarette from his pocket and lighting it.

Bill looked at me, as if he didn't want to watch the movie anymore, but since I wanted to avoid any kind of trouble and thought Oliver would be upset and somehow manage to make us behave the way he wanted, so I just shrugged at Bill, as if I couldn't do anything about it.

- What was the last movie you saw? - asked Bill.

- Edward Scissorhands, or "Eduard Mãos de Tesoura" as you may know it - Oliver answered.

- Gee, he speaks English - said Bill, with a childish voice and making a funny face.

I couldn't handle it and laughed along with him, even Oliver couldn't stand the teasing, he put his hands over his mouth for a moment, trying to disguise his laughter.

- I liked the movie, but when I tried to replicate the experiment on a mortal it didn't work very well - Oliver said, staring at Bill, causing him to stop laughing.

- Was this one of your jobs or did you just do it for the sake of curiosity, fun and pleasure? - I asked Oliver, who looked at me as if I was asking the right question.

- Are we going to wait until the pizza gets cold? - said Oliver, changing the subject and going to the kitchen to get the pizza.

I went to get pizza with him, and insisted he answer my question, he said it was time for pizza and a movie.

We watched the movie and it was structured like a documentary, during the movie Oliver would make some exclamations like - "interesting", "it's much worse than this", "oh, if only they knew the truth" - along with some laughter and looks as if he liked what he was seeing.

Bill and I tried to question Oliver about what he was trying to say, but we were ignored, so we ignored him in return. The pizzas were great, and although the movie had many theories, it didn't mention any names, nor did it have any proof, that is, despite being very interesting, I wasn't a big fan of theories.

- What a boring movie! - said Bill as soon as the movie ended.

- I didn't think so - I retorted.

- It's a lot of unchecked information for the poor mortal's head - Oliver teased.

- Maybe if you tell us or show us how it works we might understand it - I said to him.

- Maybe some other time, now it's time to work - said Oliver as he yawned, waved goodbye with his hand and fell face down on the couch already asleep.

We wondered what had happened, but before we could do anything about it, we too began to yawn and fell asleep.

The next thing I knew, I was a specter floating above my body in my living room, and it seemed that I was the last one to regain consciousness, for as I looked to the side I could see Oliver and Bill, who were also conscious specters.

Bill had a worried look on his face and Oliver had his usual smart-ass look on his face.

I moved closer to my body and noticed I was still breathing, so I immediately assumed we were in an astral plane, like in a dream or when people are in a coma.

I always imagined that astral projections would look like ghosts, but I was wrong, we had all our normal colors and wore our normal clothes, the only difference was that we were transparent and floating.

- In the second job I will need you to.... - Oliver was talking but was interrupted by Bill.

- What am I doing here? I'm the research guy - Bill interrupted Oliver.

- I had to add the potion for the second job to the pizza, since you ate it, you're officially on the job, now you have to come with us - said Oliver.

- Bill, what is that on your neck? - I asked him.

There was a sort of handkerchief with yellow eyes floating around Bill's neck.

- What? There's nothing on my neck - answered Bill, looking around.

He couldn't see the scarf that was exactly like ITTAN-MOMEN, he was somehow standing next to Bill and we didn't know why, so in order not to worry him, I just blurted it out and looked at Oliver as if to ask him to explain what it was or at least tell me that he was also seeing the scarf around Bill's neck.

- As I was saying before I was interrupted by you, the second job takes place within the dream world, I don't know how much you know about lucid dreaming, but this practice is becoming more and more known and frequented by mortals, and where there are mortals, you can bet there is confusion. Many of them enter this lucid dream state and don't know the rules, or if they do, they do not give a shit about them. And this has led to more and more confusion, possessions and deaths, so we will have to visit a fraudulent guide who has been leading a group of lucid dreamers to soul-eating and possessive demons, that little by little are getting closer to possessing these people's bodies and sucking their souls - Oliver said while Bill and I looked at each other with wide eyes.

- I've had lucid dreams before, but lately I've been having some serious sleep paralysis and I've seen a yellow-eyed monster watching me in my room - said Bill.

- Is it really sleep paralysis? - asked Oliver sarcastically.

- Are we going to keep talking or are we going to carry on with our work? - I said to change the subject from the yellow eyes that were probably ITTAN-MOMEN watching Bill while he slept.

- Follow me - Oliver said, taking off and crossing through the walls.

We did the same and flew off.

- I should just be the research guy - Bill complained.

- So do the field research, it's better to do it in practice than based on hunches in books and on the Internet. Take advantage of the fact that you are a specter and that you cannot die - I answered him, really hoping that nothing could happen to him.

- He can't die, but depending on the monster we meet, it could be that any one of us could meet an end much worse than death - Oliver interjected.

- Couldn't we handle this with our normal bodies? Is that the easiest and safest way? - I asked Oliver, who again ignored my question and continued talking, without responding.

We continued to follow Oliver and crossed the city by flying past the buildings, lampposts, and cars.

- We will be arriving shortly, as I told you before, there are some rules in the dream world, I will explain to you how they work so you don't get fucked up and also don't cause us any problems, especially this funny mortal who broke in, he is your responsibility Charles. Moving on, the dream world is a place where most mortals visit, however, they usually don't know that they are dreaming, so when they feed the dream world with their imaginations or thoughts of the day there are no consequences, mainly because they don't remember or know that they are dreaming. The dream world is an intermediate world, between the life plane and all the other planes, when humans know they are dreaming they become lucid dreamers and this changes everything, because they begin to use this ability to invade dreams and modify things, thus attracting what they don't know and breaking a lot of the rules I will teach you.

- <u>Rule number one</u>: Don't eat too much or take drugs before a lucid dream. This may make it difficult for you to wake up from sleep, causing your dream to last longer than expected.

- <u>Rule number two</u>: Don't create people, beings, creatures, or anything that you need to have "life", it will only serve as a catalyst for something that may be good, bad, demonic, alien or another being from a different astral plane.

- <u>Rule number three</u>: It is best that you have your Ba, that is, your dream object. You will use it, and it will help you remember that you are dreaming, in case you lose control over your dreams.

- <u>Rule number four</u>: It is best not to invade other people's dreams, especially those of people who have no control over their dreams; you don't want to get into certain fertile minds.

- <u>Rule number five</u>: Don't sleep inside your own dream, or someone else's dream, as this can lead to various inceptions, causing you to get lost and go into the limbo, and when this occurs your body goes into a coma.

After pouring out all this information we had reached the place he wanted to take us to, he didn't give us much time to think and kept talking.

- Sleep paralysis, seeing ghosts, witches while paralyzed is nothing more than people who have had lucid dreams - in some cases unintentionally - and have broken two or more of these rules, attracting some beings and becoming the target of an evil creature.

I have always been suspicious about these monsters that people claim to see when they have sleep paralysis. Bill had sleep paralysis from a young age so this time he listened carefully without mocking Oliver.

I was full of questions, but just as I was about to ask, Oliver spoke up again.

- Here we are, that's the house - he said, pointing to a very large apartment.

It appeared to be a complex where several people lived, the window of the apartment we entered was open, but even if it wasn't we could simply go through the wall.

We entered the place and there were five people lying on the living room floor, they were sleeping on the floor and on top of them was a cloud with spikes connecting the bodies - like a comic book balloon - connecting the five of them to the cloud.

- Before we go into their dream I need to further explain what we are going to do, I will need the help of both of you, so pay close attention. As you may have realized, these five are in a single dream, they are not as we are, between the dream world and the human world, so they are not in spectrum form, they are inside this cloud, already in the dream world, but we do not know what this dream of theirs looks like, nor what was created inside, So we have to be careful, for the possibilities are infinite, so I hope you have understood that when we sleep we can enter a dream or we can stay between worlds, which is how we are now, when we stay between worlds we can explore or we can enter other people's dreams. To become a lucid dreamer, all you need is to be in your own dream and be aware that you are dreaming, in the case of being in someone else's dream, you need permission for other dreamers to alter the dream. This group has been meeting for months, they are keeping this dream active, taking turns between them, one is always sleeping keeping the dream active, if that didn't seem fucked up enough, none of them know the rules, so they are creating and connecting things in the dream that they can't even imagine. They are about to be possessed, so, the situation we have is this, a dream created by five people, as far as I know there are more than one hundred creatures in there and it only increases every hour, I was also informed that these five are trapped in their own dream and can't wake up, they have been sleeping for more than forty-eight hours, the guide and creator of the dream is being manipulated by one of the seven leaders of hell, Beelzebub. Lucifer has been missing for millenniums, it is said that he is looking for his father, just like the angels, and because he is not taking care of hell the seven leaders of hell are each by themselves and all have different plans, Asmodeus who until then is our boss, is coordinating hell's operations on earth, he sent us to stop the plans of Beelzebub - said Oliver talking too much as always.

- Do you know who the seven are? - Bill asked me.

I just nodded negatively and Oliver continued talking.

- The mission is to end this imaginary world by dispersing the creatures without consequences to the mortal world and also to return Beelzebub to hell, where Asmodeus will take care of him - Oliver finished.

- And these five? - I asked him.

- What about them? - questioned Oliver.

- Hey, aren't we going to save them? Take them to a prison or something? - Bill interjected.

- What will happen to them is not important, as long as they don't get in our way, maybe they'll even survive - Oliver replied.

I looked at the five on the floor and four of them appeared to be normal people and even matched the house, so I assumed they were the residents of the apartment, while the guide had a more "expensive" appearance, gold watch and fancy clothes, so looking at them they didn't seem to be bad people, except for the guide who looked like one of those charlatan pimps.

I was going to ask who they were and how they got into this, but Oliver took a piece of paper from his pocket and spoke again.

- The name of the guide, the guy with the gold watch and bald head, is Roberto, the other four are students of Oneirology - those who study dreams - Ana the fat one with blond hair, Claudete the short one with big eyes, Natalia the big nose with a hole in her chin and Felipe the guy with long arms and legs. We don't need more than this information, another thing, remember that they are stuck in the dream, because they lost control, they are in different parts of the dream, Felipe and Claudete are together, Ana and Natalia are alone, Roberto the guide is with Beelzebub, when all his vitality is sucked out Beelzebub will possess Roberto's body so he can put his plan into action in the human world. You can imagine how bad it would be for mortals, and for the business in hell, to have one of the seven leaders free. When we enter we will be trapped like them, the only one who can undo the dream is Roberto, since he is the one who created it, so we have find him and solve this mess, but probably when we enter the dream we will not land in the same place, I have no idea how they created this dream, but I have the information that Roberto is surrounded by monsters and we have to get to him - explained Oliver.

- You mean we are going to enter this place surrounded by monsters that were created by these people and in a place only they are able to create things? And if we die there, what happens? I don't trust you, Oliver - said Bill.

- Exactly that, I'm glad you understood. Now about creating a lucid dreamer, it will depend on the rules that the creator put in place, maybe he didn't put any, he is an amateur that doesn't know what he is doing, besides that he was being manipulated by Beelzebub, who gained his trust by teaching him some tricks. I don't think there are any rules, in this case the only rule in action should be that immortals can't do anything inside, because they would need their souls for that, but in case there is any other, we will only know once we are in - Oliver explained for the last time before jumping into the dream cloud projected by the people on the ground.

As he jumped in he vanished, Bill and I looked at each other and then jumped in as well - I wonder why the hell we did that.

I stepped in and it was like walking into a hurricane, I whirled around and was thrown into the air, I had my flesh and blood body again, I could only see where I was when I stopped whirling, I was in free fall, I noticed I had a parachute on my back that opened itself automatically. The place seemed to be a small town, surrounded by a large valley of mountains.

I could see as I was going down that Bill was also parachuting, and since we didn't know how to handle it properly, we fell in places far from each other, until then, no sign of Oliver who jumped just moments before us.

It appeared to be a small town, a hospital, a church, a movie theater, a square, a tourist spot and a shopping street, at least that's what I could see before landing, a country town with visible alteration, the Christ the Redeemer, a doughnut store with a giant doughnut outside, the main street reformed with LED billboard panels, all of this contrasted with the simple appearance of the rest of the town, although there was a great looking mini casino in the town center, beside the square and the town hall.

I landed where the houses were the most humble, there didn't seem to be anyone there. I was far from the town center and thought that was where we would find everyone. In the fall, I ended up getting caught in a tree and stuck to the parachute wires on the branches of the tree. I yelled for help but without much hope and heard a noise that resembled a door closing, upside down, I turned around and realized that there was a house next to the tree.

- Are you human? I saw three people parachuting like we did when we arrived. Are you human? - asked a trembling woman's voice.

- I am, are you? Who are you? Help me here, I am stuck, we have come to help you, what are your names, oh yes, Roberto, Ana, Claudete, Natalia and Felipe - I answered.

- I am Ana, who are you? And how do you know we are here? - answered Ana while she attempted to climb the tree.

- My name is Charles, the other two who landed are Oliver and Bill, we're going to help you, we need to get to Roberto so we can get everyone out of here safely, you've been asleep for over forty-eight hours, your bodies won't hold out for long - I answered her, trying to assure her I can be trusted.

She didn't answer me and I couldn't see or hear her anymore, I thought that she might have left because she didn't believe what I said, but the parachute ropes that were holding me started to turn into sand and as if by magic, I was free and fell to the ground.

The grass I fell onto was as soft as a mattress, I stood up and could see Ana, the chubby blonde that Oliver had mentioned, she was standing back and appeared to be a little scared.

- How did the ropes turn to sand and why is this grass so soft? - I asked her.

- We can edit this world, at least that's what Roberto explained and taught us, so I just made the changes in the structure of the rope and the grass, but I don't like to use it, because it always draws the attention of monsters - answered Ana.

- Are you Ana? I was given some information about the people we are supposed to rescue - I lied to her about the rescue, as I needed her trust and cooperation.

Until then we talked from a distance, but when I mentioned rescue, she approached me.

- Yes, my name is Ana, so far I am the one who rescued you, right? - Ana questioned, feeling a little more comfortable and closer to me.

- Are you alone here? Where are your friends? We didn't know what it would be like in here and landed far from each other, there are two more people to help us get you all out. Do you know where Roberto is? - I asked her.

She held out her hand so I could get up, since I was still sitting on the floor while we talked.

- We split up, we were creating some objects when they started to come to life, the celebrity-looking mannequins we created got weird and asked us questions, as if they wanted to get to know us better, but actually they were studying us with specific questions, it seemed like they wanted to take over our bodies and lives - Ana said.

- We have to go to the center, I think we can find everyone there. Are we far away? Do we have a vehicle or do we have to walk? - I asked, as we didn't have much time.

- We don't have cars, Roberto made sure not to create vehicles and since we can't create anything from scratch, there is no way to edit something to become a car, if we walk it will take about fifteen minutes to get to the center - Ana answered as we began our walk.

On the way she was telling me about everything, in short, Roberto called himself a spiritual guru who had access to the world of dreams, so he took money from some people saying he would teach them how to be lucid dreamers, but apparently he doesn't know any of the rules and is just a profiteer. Ana told me how strange their second to last session was, in it they asked Roberto to create people for the city so he made mannequins that resembled celebrity figures, only Roberto could create them, until then nothing strange happened, but when we returned for the last session things were different and started to get weirder and weirder, the "celebrities" were acting strange and when Felipe edited one of them to turn it into a motionless statue, the others got aggressive and split up. Ana was left alone and ended up where we met her.

- How many people did you create - I asked her.

- We helped create, not create, that's different, Roberto who created all the celebrity mannequins, I think it was almost a thousand - Ana said.

We were almost arriving at the town center, a few more minutes and we would be at the main avenue, but suddenly a big explosion happened in a building a few meters from where we were - the movie theater building - after the smoke cleared a little I could see Bill running together with three other people, Ana's friends, they were Claudete, Felipe and Natalia. They were running towards us and only afterwards we realized that from the explosion a giant marshmallow - from

Ghostbusters - and some miniature pink heads with arms and legs - from the Bucky anime- had emerged.

- Bill we are here - I yelled at him and the others to come over to us.

I thought it was a good idea to call them, but not only did they all come, but the monsters and the celebrities heard me and came rushing towards us.

Our friends got to us first and Ana was guiding us, showing us where we should go to get away from the monsters.

- It wasn't my fault - said Bill, admitting his guilt.

- What did you do? - I retorted.

Every time he said this, it was because the fault was his.

He couldn't explain it to us, for the celebrities were in good shape and almost catching up to us as we ran like crazy towards a path Ana showed us as a shortcut to avoid them.

Ana guided us towards City Hall through downtown alleys and shortcuts that she probably created. Once we arrived at the city hall the gate was locked, Ana quickly edited the gate and unlocked it, we went through and she edited again so that the gate was locked.

The city hall was large, but still a small town hall. We closed the doors and checked the windows, there were so many rooms that from the inside it didn't appear to be that small. The four who were with us and who had been to the city many times, led us through the rooms until we reached the back of the city hall and jumped over the wall that divided it from the commercial avenue.

As soon as we broke into the ice cream store that was behind the city hall, I asked Ana to explain to her friends what I had told her, who we were and what we were doing there, meanwhile I would talk to Bill and find out what happened and if he seen Oliver.

- What's up kid, is everything okay with you? What did you tell them? How did you find them and what was that explosion? - I asked him.

- Nothing's okay, man, look at all the crazy things you drag me into, I'm glad that at least this time I'm getting paid. I told them that I fell in here with the two of you and we were going to try to end the dream and get them back to the real world, is that what I should have said? This business of creating things is a mess, I was not prepared for it, in fact just thinking about what happened makes me afraid to think too much - answered Bill.

- Afraid to think too much? Don't tell me you created that marshmallow monster and Bucky balls? - I asked him, already figuring out the answer.

- I was not prepared to crash in the movie theater, I fell through the window going straight through the glass and as soon as I landed these three came to meet me, I didn't know if they were the people we were looking for, cause I didn't pay attention to what Oliver said, neither the names nor the appearance, so as soon as I saw that there was something coming my way I ran away and entered a room, there were posters of the Ghostbusters and as soon as I saw the poster with the giant marshmallow doll, I started to imagine how cool it would be if there was one here, and just like that, a miniature appeared in the room and started to move, inflate, expand and grow, I desperately left the room and these three were there, we started to run and during our run I told them that I was looking for some people who lived in a shabby apartment, they told me it was them. The marshmallow was growing and the ceiling was starting to fall on us, so I wished it would explode, and as soon as I thought about it the pink balls from that Bucky anime you showed me started popping up in place, but instead of helping us, they joined the marshmallow chasing us and exploded the whole place, we ran out and saw you guys from afar calling us - explained Bill.

At least our story still fit, as we said we were there to rescue them, even if we didn't arrange it before we were lucky to have said the same speech and managed to gather four of the five, now we needed to find out where Roberto was.

I insisted that Bill should empty his mind and not create anything else which could be possessed and chase after us. We approached the four again and I questioned them if they could create things as Bill had done, but they replied that they could not, so I deduced that the rule that Roberto had created for that world was limiting the four rather than defining him as the only creator of that place, so the four could only edit and not create anything from scratch like Bill did.

For a moment I wondered if immortals could also create something, or at least edit it, but I controlled myself, as I also had a creative mind and did not want to risk it, or change the focus of the mission.

- We need to get out of here, if they surround us we will be doomed - Bill said aloud to everyone.

- You know this place better than we do, we have to find Roberto and our other colleague - Oliver - do you have any idea where they might be? Only the two of them can get us out of this dream, so we have to find them and settle this matter - I told them.

- Roberto is at the church, your friend must be there too, the church is not far from here, but to get there we have to cross the commercial avenue and the central plaza - answered Felipe, with his screechy voice.

- Great, here's what we're going to do, Bill stays here with you while I go check outside to make sure the road is clear, I'll find a safe route to the church, catch your breath and get ready to run to the church if we need to - I told them.

I exited through the back door, for the front door had one of those bells that makes noise when the customers arrive, and by the back door there seemed to be none, so I went on through there, it was a large alley that connected to the corridors of the stores and the avenue. I entered one of the corridors and went around to the entrance of the ice cream parlor on the avenue, very carefully I snuck under a car that was on the street and from there I could see the marshmallow giant and the crowd of Hollywood mannequins, they were about three blocks from us, searching the town hall and the stores nearby.

I went back to the store, being very careful not to be seen, and when I came back everyone was enjoying ice cream.

- Try it, it is better than the real thing - Bill said, offering me an ice cream.

I slapped his hand, the ice cream fell on the floor and everyone looked at me.

- Guys, this is not a joke, you have been lying in your apartment for over 48 hours, without eating, without doing your needs or living in the real world, we can't screw around, we have to take this situation seriously, I may be boring, but you will thank me later. We have to get to the church or you won't be able to go back to your bodies and I don't know what that might mean for you - I said grumpily, bringing a bit of realism to the table and giving Bill his usual scolding.

I explained to them how it looked outside and we decided to do what we agreed before, go to the church, leaving through the back of the ice cream parlor, passing through the corridor and once we got to the front of the ice cream parlor on the commercial avenue, we would cross the avenue, then go through the plaza to the church, where we hoped to find Roberto and Oliver so that we could solve all this bullshit as soon as possible.

They finished their ice cream while I explained the plan to them, just as we were ready to go out the back door, the front door opened - bling bling bling - the bell made a noise and alerted us, we were already in the back ready to leave, we crouched down, I indicated with my hand that they should be quiet and not make any noise. We wouldn't be able to open the back door without being noticed, so I snuck around looking through the door trying to see who entered it.

It was one of the mannequins, but this one was a child with a backwards red cap, she was alone and appeared to be about eight years old, we remained silent, first she peeked to see if there was no one around and soon after making sure she was alone, she opened one of the freezers, grabbed some flavors of ice cream and tasted them, However, as soon as she took a closer look, she noticed that there were a few scrambled ice creams and that there were also several empty ice cream tubs on the counter table, at the instant that the "child" saw the empty tubs, she seemed to have an epiphany and threw the ice cream she was eating on the floor and left the ice cream parlor screaming through the crowd, saying that we passed by. Thankfully, she didn't decide to look in the back where we were, so as soon as the "child" left screaming, I asked everyone to stay together and follow me.

As we went out the back door we could already hear the noise of the crowd coming towards us, the marshmallow giant hearing that fuss and noise was also approaching, he was walking through some houses that were in the way as if they were toys.

While the crowd was hunting us in and around the ice cream parlor, we were already near the avenue, we had passed by some stores and alleys very carefully, I had to change the plan a few times during the trajectory, because some of the stores were locked and another time because of the crowd that was approaching where we were, but even though I had changed the plan, I still followed the original route - to go to the church - and trusted my instincts since everyone else trusted them too.

Before leaving the store I asked one of the four of us to draw on a piece of paper a map of what the town center looked like, so that I could better locate where the church was and in case we needed to detour, as we did, I would be able to improvise and keep knowing where we were going, by always approaching the church.

I was worried about getting all that crowd to the church, so I went around behind the ice cream parlor, along the avenue and store corridor. We kept going until we reached the end of the corridor, which was where the avenue met a street that also went up towards the church.

I followed the little paper map they had made, now instead of crossing the square, I decided that we should go around it by the street on the left and then towards the church. The town center had a central plaza where two streets and two avenues surrounded it, on the upper avenue of the plaza was the church, on the right street was the bars, on the lower avenue of the plaza was our location on the commercial avenue, now we were on the border of this commercial avenue, the street to the left of the plaza, the street with the fancy houses - the noble part of town - forming the drawing on the paper, the town center.

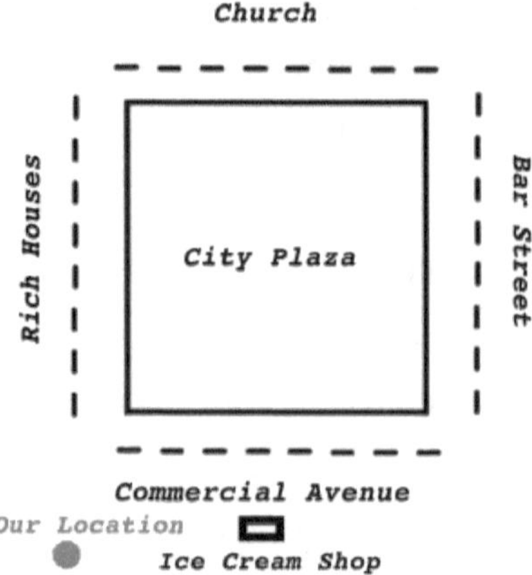

- Which one of you knows this side with the rich houses? - I asked them.

- I know this area a little - answered Felipe.

- Great, I will need you to explain or guide us through this side until we get to the church, we will have to be very careful not to draw any attention from the crowd which is still looking for us, we don't want this group chasing us all the way to the church, this could make things even more difficult - I said to all of them.

Felipe came closer and started to tell me what that side was like and how we could get through without attracting attention, but before he finished explaining, a door opening noise interrupted us, so we all hid.

This time Chuck Norris and Jesus Christ had walked through the door, they were with the crowd that was looking for us, luckily we were able to hide in time, the four dreamers edited the floor of the place and hid in an unnoticeable way, Bill and I were hoping that we wouldn't be seen and that they wouldn't come in our direction.

They passed right by us, but left soon enough to check another store and carry on their rounds looking for us.

- Fuck, that was possessed Chuck Norris - Bill whispered as he got closer to me.

I didn't give Bill much thought, I just made a sign with my fingers in the direction where we should go, but before we continued towards the church on the fancy side, the left side of the square, the four dreamers reappeared from the ground so Felipe could finish explaining to me what that side looked like.

It was a cluster of noble houses that looked like apartment complexes, only this complex had only luxurious houses, so we wouldn't be able to hide like we were hiding in the stores, since there were no buildings there and all the houses kept a certain distance from each other.

We were lucky it was night time and there was a park there with many trees, but in the park there was also a well lit exercise track that could hurt us.

We had to decide whether to go through the trees or through the houses, if we went through the houses we ran the risk of being seen from above by the giant and of someone being in the houses, but if we went through the park we could easily be seen because of the light from the exercise track which illuminated the whole place very well.

I had to decide quickly as the crowd's footsteps were getting closer and closer to us, going through the trees in the park was the fastest way and apparently the safest, so I opted for it, then quickly explained to everyone what we would need to do.

- We need to go through the shadows of the trees, we can't be slow, but we also can't draw attention, the park's exercise track is well lit, if we are careless, we will be noticed easily and will be exposed to the giant and the crowd - I told them quietly, showing them on the map how we were going to do it.

There was a trench next to the park trees, that's where the rainwater would drain off, if we went through there, we would be able to stand slightly lower than if we were standing on the plain above, so, as we had to remain unnoticed, we went through there, despite the fact that it would slow us down.

We walked very carefully, almost a third of the way through. The mob was still at the store avenue, but they were apparently finishing their search there, and now they were going after the giant that was heading in our direction.

Two thirds of the way through, we slowly made our way through the shadows, the crowd now scanning the houses on the way, as the giant came towards the park where we were, I asked them to stop for a moment, I needed to change plans a bit.

- Bill, we will not all make it there, the giant will see us, follow them to the church, I will distract them and lead them in another direction, after that I will meet you there - I told Bill with my serious face, this way he knew I really meant it and did not question my decision.

Bill just looked deep into my eyes to make sure I was not joking, then asked the others to follow him as I headed back towards the houses.

I didn't plan this, although in my subconscious I knew that at some point someone would need to sacrifice himself or herself as bait, I just didn't expect that this person would be me.

I needed at all costs to make sure that the crowd didn't chase us to the church, so as soon as Bill and the others went on, I headed in the opposite direction to where the biggest houses were. I walked for a few minutes until I reached the first houses near the park, all of them had their lights off, which made me believe that they were empty and there was no one inside. I kept walking, passing by several of the same houses and not entering any of them, just circling and running stealthily one by one, another by another, until I was far enough away from the park, so that Bill and the others were further away enough.

All right, I walked a long way and reached the opposite side of the park, now my new plan was to enter one of the houses in the area, go to the stove, open the gas and somehow blow the whole place up, causing the giant and the crowd to go in that direction instead of going towards the church.

I entered the largest house nearby and as soon as I opened the door, all the lights in the place immediately went on, illuminating the entire block that until then remained quiet and dark. I hadn't expected this, and sure enough it had caught their attention, but not enough to get them all coming my way, so I went ahead with the plan and went into the kitchen and opened the gas valve, took some aluminum foil and put it inside the microwave setting it to start in a minute.

I ran away from there and a little while later, two blocks away, I bent down waiting for the explosion, just as I thought it had not worked, a big explosion happened and a little while later I could already see the giant coming in this direction with the crowd.

Mission accomplished. I got out of there before the giant and the crowd arrived and went straight ahead passing by the yards, very carefully so as to not activate the lights in any of the houses.

I was a few meters from the end of the street and I kept going on crossing the houses, I thought it was better to continue this way until the end of the street, than to run the risk of returning to the park path where the others had passed. It was the last houses and I could already see the church, I jumped over the wall of one of the houses and there were some beautiful Marys hanging from the windows, I did not expect them to be alive, they were like talking statues that as soon as they saw me began to scream, but as I was already away from the crowd and the giant, I think they did not hear them, but not to run any risk, I went to the windows, threw them from there and so they fell to the floor breaking and shutting up.

I kept following and finally reached the church, there was no one around, I looked around for any sign, but nothing, so all I had to do was go in.

At the entrance of the church there was a big staircase and the huge doors at the entrance were locked. I went to the side looking for some place that would let me into the church. I looked around the side and the doors there were also locked, I went to the back and there I finally found a door that was not only normal sized, but was also unlocked. I entered and as soon as I passed through the door, I could hear the sound of people running and screaming in my direction.

- Don't close the door - said Bill.

It was already too late, when I turned my attention back to the door, there was no door anymore. Everything happened so fast, as soon as I could discern what was happening, I could only see a giant serpent with a woman's head - very similar to the gorgon in the game God of War - running after Bill and Ana, the other three, Claudete, Natalia and Felipe had been turned into statues by the gorgon, turned into stone, completely still. I ran along with them trying to understand what was happening.

I found some urns, sacks of wheat and bottles of wine along the way and threw them at the gorgon, giving us time to try to outwit the monster or manage to hide.

On the way Ana ended up tripping and falling to the ground, I wondered why she didn't do something, like edit the place, run or even fight, there was no way to save her, so she just looked at the two of us and nodded for us to continue, she used herself as bait, giving us time to run and hide, while she was petrified by the gorgon.

- Bill, what's going on? Did you find Oliver? - I asked him quietly as we both hid in a room with lots of furniture, musical instruments, and statues covered with white cloth.

We were under a ping-pong table as we whispered to each other trying to understand what had happened.

- I wonder how well the priest and the nuns play ping-pong - Bill whispered unnecessarily before getting down to serious business.

- Man, when we got here Oliver's body was lying next to Roberto's, and in Oliver's hand was this note - said Bill.

He handed me the note, and on it was written.

"You took too long, I had to go in without you, stay here and wait for me to come back, you should go in only if my hat makes any noise, but that shouldn't happen, I'll solve everything without you" - said Oliver's note.

- Charles, I screwed up again, man - said Bill.

- What did you do this time? - I asked him worried, since he only called me by name when the shit got really bad.

- That medusa was my fault, after I found the note, we split up to try to find a way out, as when we entered the door was gone and the editing powers of the others no longer worked, I found a mirror with serpents on the edges and when I looked into the mirror I thought I saw something wrapped around me, but immediately the mirror cracked and turned into the first thing that crossed my mind, the medusa from God of War - Bill said explaining and whining until I interrupted him.

- Calm down, it doesn't matter anymore, focus, we have to get rid of her, you should instead of thinking this nonsense, come up with a way to get out of here or defeat her without creating other things that can be possessed, as Oliver explained, that is, lifeless objects, this is a dream, be creative, but in our favor - I answered him.

I don't know how he did it, but for an instant he closed his eyes and a few seconds later a spear with fire at its tip appeared out of nowhere.

- A spear? Years of video games for that? Make a bazooka, you wretch - I told him grumbling and desperate as the fire lance had drawn the medusa's attention.

I took the fire spear, I had never used a spear before, but with the power of despair I threw it at the medusa, it went right through her, her eyes glowed, and she turned to ashes.

- Hey you bastard, take that you bitch! - Bill stomped his foot on the ashes of medusa and spat at it.

- If my immortal power didn't work here we would be fucked, but anyway, next time do a bazooka or a war tank, a spear was a pain in the ass - I told him laughing as we calmed down and went to where Ana and the others were.

They were still petrified and so far there was nothing we could do, I thought about asking Bill to try to do something, but thought it was better not, since so far his skills had only screwed things up.

Bill took me to where Oliver and Roberto's bodies were, above them was another cloud from the dream, this one was darker and there was some thunder coming out of it.

- They are in a dream inside another dream, didn't Oliver say that this is dangerous? I think we have two alternatives... - before I could finish speaking, a thunder interrupted me and the roof of the church where we were standing opened, it was the giant marshmallow creature.

With one hand he was holding the roof of the church, looking for us, when he spotted us he smiled and held out his other hand trying to catch us.

We ran and the doors of the place started to appear, the crowd was banging on the door trying to get in.

- Bill for God's sake, make an inanimate lock for all these doors, if they get in we're fucked - I yelled at Bill.

A divine miracle caused Bill to be able to grant my request and immediately several boards with nails closed the entrance to the doors, although this would not hold them forever.

We were surrounded and out of options, it was the end, I couldn't come up with any more ideas and the giant was getting closer, he was going to get me, but Bill, rising from the ashes, managed to use some of his brain and with a flamethrower, started to melt the marshmallow giant's hand and make him move away from us. The doors didn't look like they were going to hold anymore, the giant realized that he had no need to catch us, he could throw things at us, it was madness, I was about to suggest to Bill that we take the bodies of both of them and try to get out of there, until I noticed that the cloud had cleared and Oliver was getting up and fixing the top hat on his head with his sarcastic white smile and Roberto, the only one who could get us out of there, still remained on the floor without moving.

- Oliver! What happened? What about Roberto? - I asked him quickly.

- Charles and his endless questions... - Oliver said again without answering any of my questions.

It wasn't even necessary, as moments later Roberto moved and regained his senses, opening his eyes little by little, but still unable to get up from the floor.

Oliver, realizing all the confusion, this time not in our favor, held Roberto's body on his back and told us.

- You brought the whole town here? - said Oliver as he seemed to be still recovering from his dream with Roberto.

- We landed far away from here, we found all the others, they are here, but they were petrified by a medusa Bill created by accident, we killed it, but they didn't turn back, they are still petrified, they created a crowd of famous mannequins and a giant marshmallow while they were with Roberto - I told him summarizing and lying at the end about the giant to lighten Bill's load.

- Can you create things? Then why on earth are you creating things to make our lives more difficult? Didn't I already explain how it works? - said Oliver, teasing Bill.

- I, I, I... - Bill was about to answer, but I interrupted him.

- We don't have time for this, he already understood and helped us against the medusa, tell him what we need to do so that he can help us, or you can create things yourself and solve them on your own - I answered Oliver, so that Bill would understand that it wasn't his fault.

- We're lucky that he didn't set any complex rules here, I been in much worse dreams - said Oliver pointing to Roberto who was on his back and making an effort to regain his senses and wake up completely.

We went over to where Roberto's friends were, but they were all shattered, they must have been broken when part of the ceiling collapsed because of the giant.

Oliver said that there was nothing we could do, but that if Roberto woke up, he could free us and also wake up his friends.

- Follow me - Oliver said, going into one of the rooms and finding a secret passage with a staircase leading up to a tower.

We narrowly escaped, for as soon as we started up the stairs we heard the church doors bursting open and the crowd starting to come in looking for us and climbing the stairs behind us.

We arrived at the tower and on the way there we had only one option, to climb up to where the church bell was and that's what we did, we desperately climbed the stairs of the tower while the crowd chased us up the stairs, like a reverse snowball.

- Do something Bill! - I yelled at him.

- I can't think under pressure, what do I do? - asked Bill.

- I don't know, make the steps disappear so that they can't get up the stairs - I said, suggesting impulsively.

He stopped running for a second and just as he was about to be caught, the steps turned into those soapy ramps of children's slides, so the crowd that was about to catch us started to slide down and the scene was so funny that we stopped to laugh as we watched them furiously sliding down the slide.

- Take that you fuckers - Bill yelled.

- It sounds like it was your idea - I retorted.

- And wasn't it? The soap was the magic touch - he said.

- A ten-year-old child would also be familiar with that magic touch - I teased him as we walked back up the stairs.

Roberto, who until then had not spoken and was still being carried by Oliver, was starting to move and manage to stand up, he gave a strange smile as he watched Bill and I picking on each other.

The crowd had not given up, they were squeezing their way through the passage like a sausage being stuffed, so the ones at the back were pushing the ones at the front, and slowly climbing up little by little non-stop.

At that speed they would not be able to reach us so soon, so at that moment our only concern was the marshmallow giant that was also coming towards us.

Our luck was that despite its size, the tower was right in the middle of the church, which meant that the giant couldn't reach us with his arms and also couldn't climb the church roof, since he had destroyed most of it himself.

- What are we waiting for? How do we get out of here? - I asked the question that everyone wanted to know the answer to.

- Roberto is going to get us out of here - Oliver answered.

We all looked at Roberto and he didn't seem to know what was going on, I could see drool at the corner of his mouth and there didn't seem to be any Roberto inside that body.

We reached the top of the tower, the giant had climbed the church and went inside, so he could finally reach us, we were a little above his little hat with STAY PUFT written on it.

- We have no choice, we have to jump on him before he destroys the tower - Oliver said jumping moments before the giant let out a scream and landed the first punch on the tower that wobbled, didn't fall, but clearly couldn't take another strike like that.

Without a second thought, I jumped on the giant's hat, and Bill did the same. Soon after we jumped, the giant took another lunge and the tower was entirely destroyed, turned to dust.

The giant had not seen us, and as soon as he destroyed the tower he stood still while the crowd rose from the rubble and searched the destroyed tower for us.

- What are we going to do? Roberto, end this, take us home and bring your friends back! - I told him, but looking at Oliver.

- I can't do anything, we are depending on Roberto and Bill, since he seems to have a free pass to create things in this dream - Oliver answered.

- Have you tried to wake us up Bill? - I asked him.

- How can I do that? - he answered.

- Him having the permission to create, doesn't mean that he can wake us up, I already said that only Roberto can get us out of here, I said that we are depending on him not to screw up - Oliver replied teasing Bill.

Meanwhile Roberto couldn't answer us, he drooled and only grunted with his mouth.

We began to argue, Oliver and I, about what had happened in the dream and how we were going to get out of there, until the marshmallow giant began to deflate, getting smaller and smaller, deflating like a balloon and with that, we began to approach the ground.

I looked at Bill and he was focused, he was the one doing it, he finally seemed to understand how to use his lucid dreamer power, so, having done that, we hit the ground and soon after we landed his focus was over.

- Suck it, I'm the fucking boss! - Bill said as soon as he finished, ruining his achievement, for I knew that the giant was his fault.

- Get Roberto, I'm going to the house where he is on, there must be some clue that will get us out of here or help us bring him back, hide, I'll be back soon - Oliver said handing Roberto to me and running off at an incredible speed, but much slower than the one he had shown us before.

Roberto couldn't do much, he only moved his eyes and had involuntary movements of his body muscles.

I managed to catch him on my own without any effort and we left near the church in the direction of the square, hiding at the entrance, near the trees.

A few minutes later we heard a noise and it was Oliver.

- I found this note that says that the exit is at the fountain in the center of the square, it's not far from here - Oliver said.

Before we could continue, Roberto started to squirm and so I left him on the floor, where he kept squirming and spasm, we all just stared, no one seemed to know what to do, or what was happening, although Oliver couldn't convince me with the theatrics he was doing with a surprised face.

After a short time Roberto had stopped squirming, he was completely still, I thought he had died, but suddenly he stood up and surprisingly began to act like a normal person, he finally said his first words.

- I put the exit in the town square, the one in front of the church, we have to go to the central part of the square where the water fountain is - Roberto finally said something.

- Are you all right? What happened? Will you bring your friends back? Once there, what do we need to do to get out of this dream? - I asked him, again asking a thousand questions.

- They will come back as soon as we return to the real world - Roberto said, answering only this question.

- Your friends had mentioned zombies in the square, why on earth did they decide to create zombies in a square? Can you get rid of them? - said Bill reminding us of the zombies Ana had mentioned.

- I am still weak because of the other dream Oliver rescued me from, I can't do anything yet, I tried, but nothing happened - answered Roberto.

Now we were facing a square with zombies possessed by who knows what, we still needed to get to the center of it, find the fountain and then get out of there.

We entered the square and right away we found the first zombies coming towards us, but luckily they were slow, like the ones in the old movies.

- Bill, you could help us by creating some weapons to get rid of these zombies - I told him while punching the heads of the approaching zombies.

Bill focused, pushing hard, but nothing was happening.

- I can't make them go away like I did the giant marshmallow - Bill said after giving up, as he was about to give birth or shit with the force he was exerting.

- If you could do that with the marshmallow, then you probably made it - Oliver said.

- Oliver, can't you create anything? - I asked him, changing the subject.

- No, and can you? - Oliver asked me.

Oliver had said that immortals couldn't do anything in the dream world, they lost this ability, so I hadn't tried anything so far, but before I could think of trying anything, we realized that we were again surrounded by zombies, but this time Bill, realizing the real danger, created weapons to get rid of them so we could continue marching towards the center of the square.

Bill still had his flame thrower and was spraying fire everywhere with it. I took the machine gun, but I didn't like it, so I preferred to exchange it for the twelve-gauge, so that the zombies that came near me would be blown out of their brains with accurate shots.

There were about a hundred zombies, and although they were not fast, they were also not dumb like the ones in the traditional movies, they seemed to think normally, they just didn't have the speed to get close enough to offer real danger, so in a few minutes we had gotten rid of the horde and were finally able to advance to the center of the square to get out of there. The square seemed larger from the inside than when we looked at it from the outside, the trees and bushes seemed to get denser and denser as we got closer to the center of the square.

We passed through some bushes and saw glowing eyes and shadows peeking through the darkness.

- What the fuck is that? - Bill asked when he saw the glowing eyes and shadows.

- When we made this square it was supposed to be like a mini enchanted forest, but we didn't know that the things we created could be possessed, now the elves, fairies, spirits, and all the other beings we created are possessed by evil things - answered Roberto, speeding up his pace and leading us along the path.

- We'd better go quickly, are we getting close? Where is the exit? - I asked him.

- Don't worry, we're almost there, follow me fast - said Roberto, running.

We were armed to the teeth, so none of the goblins and fairies dared to cross our path, the shadows were coming towards us, but they didn't have shapes, they were just shadows, so all our attempts to finish them off were in vain, the shots just went through them, nothing could touch them, but they couldn't touch us either.

Suddenly, Bill launched fire at some shadows, but the flames also passed through them, so the fire caught some dry bushes that were around, and in a few seconds, the fire began to spread, making the flames bigger and bigger, thus generating enough light to scare away all the shadows around.

A fire started, we began to run, and before long we reached the center of the square.

As Roberto had said, in the center of the square there was a fountain full of coins.

- Take a coin, throw it on the bridge and you will wake up, but you have to be one at a time, you can go, I will be the last - said Roberto.

We all took a coin and of course Bill was the first to throw it into the fountain and as soon as he threw it, it disappeared completely.

- Next is you, Charles - Oliver said.

I was ready to do the same as Bill, but I had a bad feeling.

- I'll go after you, I insist, after all this is my job, right? - I retorted.

- Don't complicate things or disobey me, just do as I say - Oliver said, raising his voice.

I hadn't seen Oliver like that before and this made me even more suspicious.

- Something happened when you were there in the church in his dream, didn't it? - I asked them both, pointing at Roberto.

Nobody answered me, they just looked at each other.

- Oliver what happened there? Roberto, is your friend Samuel going to be okay? I asked two questions and purposely misspelled the name of Roberto's friend.

- Yes, as soon as I leave here Samuel and the others will be fine - Roberto answered.

Oliver realized what I had done, Roberto had taken the bait, and as soon as he finished speaking, Oliver came at me, with all his incredible speed he threw me away from the fountain with a flying kick and made me drop my coin, then "Roberto" threw his coin on the bridge, instantly disappearing like Bill.

I stood up, but before I could get my coin Oliver was faster and soon after Roberto left, he also threw his coin on the bridge, leaving me behind alone.

I ran to the coin, picked it up, and then threw it over the bridge, but unlike the others, nothing happened to me. In fact, something started happening, the whole city was disappearing, being erased, I could see the outskirts of the city starting to disappear.

I took more coins from the fountain again and tried over and over, nothing happened, the city kept being erased and the void getting closer to where I was. I didn't know if I would be left in a void or if I would also be erased like the city. I didn't have much time, I had to find some way out of there.

I couldn't think why the hell Oliver had done it, and I was very regretful that I hadn't left when I had my chance. There were no more mountains, no more houses farther from the center, in place of what was there before, there was only darkness, which grew bigger and bigger by the moment.

- Oliver! Bill! - I shouted for them, but there was no answer.

I thought about what Bill would do if he were there, and remembered his ability to create things in the dream world, and that I had not yet tested whether I could do anything.

I wasn't sure where to start or what I needed to do, so once again I remembered Bill, his screw-ups, his achievements, and the look on his face when he was trying to create something. He would close his eyes, force himself to look like he was going to shit and then something would happen, so I did the same, closed my eyes, took a deep breath, thought of a red door - I don't know why that color - and thought that as soon as I opened my eyes there would be a door that could get me out of there and back to the real world.

I opened my eyes, because I knew I didn't have much time left. When I opened them I saw the red door, but I also saw that if I didn't run to it immediately I would be erased together with the whole city in the dream.

I ran to the red door that was a few meters in front of me, opened it and walked through, it was like stepping into a light, for a moment I couldn't see anything, until it started to disperse and when I could see again I realized that I was lying down, bound and gagged in what looked like the trunk of a moving car.

I was relieved that I had managed to get out of the dream, but apparently I had already gotten myself into another jam.

I tried to free myself from the ropes that bound my legs or the chains that bound my hands, but I was unsuccessful, whoever had done this had done it in a very professional way.

I closed my eyes again trying to do as in the dream and create something with the power of my mind, but since it was not a dream, nothing happened. I felt good on one hand, since this meant that I was back in the real world.

Oliver's betrayal

There wasn't much I could do but wait for the car to stop, even though I was in a trunk barely able to breathe properly the question of what had happened to Roberto and Oliver kept hammering in my head.

"Why did they leave me behind alone?".

I kept trying to free myself, after moving a lot I managed to push the back seat of the car forward a little, so I could open a gap where I could see inside the car.

With some difficulty I found a position where I could see through the gap.

There was only one person in the car and from the black top hat and shoulder length hair it was definitely Oliver. I tried to squirm and knock and get his attention, but I couldn't, the radio was loud and he was driving like a lunatic. I don't know exactly how much time passed, but we stayed on the road for a long time, until suddenly the car stopped, Oliver's door opened and he went towards the trunk.

I waited in silence and as soon as he opened the trunk, I could confirm that it really was Oliver.

Without any finesse he easily pulled me out of there due to his immortal strength and threw me chest and mouth to the ground. The fall hurt like hell, I was in doubt if I still had immortality, but when my broken nose started to heal, I realized that it still worked.

We were on a road in the middle of nowhere, it was night, and Oliver had thrown me in front of the car, with the headlights pointing to my face.

I tried once more to free myself from the restraints, squirming and trying to make noise, but Oliver just looked at me and got back into the car.

He pulled out a black box that looked a lot like a coffin and threw it on the ground next to me.

He walked back to where I was standing and when he got very close to me, he started to count the steps out loud in one direction.

- One, two, three... - Oliver counted step by step until he disappeared into the darkness.

- One hundred and seven steps - Oliver yelled from where I could only hear him, as I couldn't see him anymore.

Shortly after that he came back, without his top hat on, he looked down at me, laughed, approached the black box, opened it, took out a shovel and walked back in the direction he had shouted before.

At first I couldn't hear any more noise for a while, but after my ears got used to the silence I started to hear something and I could identify what that noise was, it was Oliver digging, he was digging a hole and deep down I knew that hole was for me.

Before long the shovel sound ceased, and a while later he came out of the darkness walking quietly toward me, passing me and walking back to the car to leave the shovel in the trunk.

Then, after closing the door, he reached into his pockets, took out a cigarette, lit it, and slowly walked back towards me as he smoked.

- Charles, Charles, Charles . - said Oliver, bending down beside me and blowing smoke in my face.

- We're in the middle of nowhere, please don't go screaming at me when I take off your gag, I just want to talk to you and try to explain your mistake - Oliver said calmly as he helped me sit down on the ground and removed my gag.

- You son of a bitch, you bastard, what are you doing? Why did you leave me there all alone? - I didn't lose my mind, but I couldn't help but get pissed off when he took off the gag.

- I told you, there's no point in yelling - Oliver said as he waited for me to stop my yelling and cursing.

I didn't keep at it for long, I knew it wouldn't do any good, so I tried to calm down so he could talk again.

- Has anyone given you any information about Beelzebub? Or did you notice something during the mission? Answer me, how did you know that wasn't Roberto? - asked Oliver, telling me something I still didn't know.

- I realized what? I just felt a suspicious sensation and said it on the spot, I didn't know anything, that's why I tested Roberto about his friend's name - I answered him.

- Ha Ha Ha Ha Ha... - Oliver began to laugh with his hands over his face.

- What? - I asked, but he wouldn't stop laughing.

- You had to open your damn mouth, everything was already settled, you could have gone home, but no, you had to butt in - Oliver said, stopping laughing and making a very serious face.

- Where's Bill? Are the students all right? So that was Beelzebub? What happened to Roberto? Tell me. In fact, don't tell me, pretend that I didn't do it, let's pretend that nothing happened, I don't know anything - I told him, asking the questions that were pounding in my head, but aware that the more I knew, the worse it would be.

- You are always full of questions, this time I will answer some of them, since you will not pose any danger to me anymore - said Oliver.

- What do you mean? Are you going to bury me in that box? - again I asked questions.

- Good thing you already understand part of it - said Oliver, putting out his cigarette and bending down to pick me up and put me in the coffin.

- I don't want anything to do with Bill, so rest assured, he is fine, when I got back I only knocked him out, he will probably be asleep for a few days, but he will be fine. The students were left behind in the dream, you saw what happened right? They are erased and now they are in a coma without their spirits. Roberto surrendered to Beelzebub, so since my Immortality contract was about to end I made a deal with him. Roberto no longer exists, or rather, he exists, but he is so deep in Beelzebub's consciousness that he will never wake up again. Is that what you wanted to know? Because I wanted to tell you some more things, but I will only go on until you interrupt me, when that happens I won't say anything more and you know what I will have to do - Oliver said, answering for the first time all the questions I had asked.

He waited for a brief moment to see if I would interrupt him, but since I didn't, he spoke again.

- Great, let's get down to business. I don't want you to hate me, I like Bill and you, but it's the law of the wild, survival baby. My days in Hell inc were numbered, Belz made me an offer I couldn't refuse, I thought you would never notice anything but when you got suspicious and did tested Roberto about his friend's name I figured you had received some secret mission from hell about Beelzebub's escape, but as it turned out it was just you being you, we left you behind and I never thought you would make it back from the dream, if I had more time I would make you talk about how you managed that, but as it doesn't matter now, not much will change. Your body should be in the same condition as Roberto's friends, it would be easier for me to get rid of your comatose body, but you are insistent, although this doesn't change anything, it will only be more unpleasant for you to be conscious, there is not much point in explaining myself since you would never understand my motives, so take this last lesson, the best way to get rid of an immortal is this, no dismembering, sea or any other nonsense that is out there, I have been killed these ways countless times, but the only one that really held me was being trapped in a coffin, not even a nuclear bomb can kill an immortal, I was in Nagasaki and the only consequence that bomb had on me was a ringing in my ears for years. But back to the point, you must think that my plan will not work out, because after all, someone will look for you, or even there is a job in hell to be done and they will find you, this last option may even be true, but what do you think of this story? I'll be in charge of doing your jobs and I'll involve Bill in the simplest ones, telling him that you asked and that you'll get immortality for him and of course you won't forget to pay him, so he'll think that you keep sending him money, maybe I'll even become his friend - Oliver said with a broad smile on his face.

- Bill would never betray me - I interrupted him, as I could not resist the things he was saying.

- Who said anything about betrayal? What if I told him that you were sent to work in another country? Will he remember you as the years go by and he gets older? What about the letters "you" will send him saying that you won't be coming back and that he should forget about that friendship - Oliver said.

He thought of everything, I knew that at this point the only thing keeping me out of that black coffin was Oliver getting tired of saying all this shit to my face, I looked around once more trying to find something that would help me identify where I was, but the only thing I could see before Oliver threw me into the coffin was the starry sky.

Whatever that place was, there was only bushes, stars, dust, and no sound of cars passing by.

- Oliver, we can make a deal, why are you going to leave me buried in the middle of nowhere? No one gains anything from this, I will not stand in your way, nor will I talk about Beelzebub with anyone, in fact I don't even remember what happened, see? Don't do this, it was you who got me into this mess, dragged me into this and I thought I could always trust you, even when you wanted to have fun with us I knew you were trying to be like a mentor to me - I appealed to the sensible side and thought I had managed to convince him.

- In a way you are right, I see a lot of myself in you. I think that in the last three hundred years Bill and you were the people who managed to make me feel human again, for a few moments I even considered some things, but take this as my last mentorship for you, never trust anyone - Oliver said, making me faint with a kick to the head and finishing the job.

I blacked out, as the kick he gave me probably broke my neck and by the time my immortality revived me there was nothing I could do. I was tied up, with no space and no air in a black coffin who knows where.

I was still immortal and that meant I was still working for hell, but it also meant that Oliver and Beelzebub were working alone.

I couldn't do anything, the harder I tried, the more out of breath I became. Dying of suffocation is not a good thing and not a very quick thing, it was strange the first time I went out without air, I thought that this time I had really died for good.

For a long time I didn't feel anything, no sensation, but little by little I started to feel something and as soon as the sensation of non-existence started to pass I started to feel peace, a peace so deep that as I realized this feeling, the other feelings started to appear, so now I started to feel alive, to think, to feel and to question again.

- Where Am I? Who am I? - I thought I asked out loud, but there was no sound.

I had no body, there was only my consciousness, silence and a dark emptiness. I started to remember who I was and the last moments with Oliver, but I still didn't know where I was.

When I realized that I didn't have a body, I realized that I couldn't do anything because of it, so almost immediately I started to feel like I had a body and was floating. Now having a body I could hear, talk, touch, and smell again, but I still couldn't see anything.

I also couldn't move, I could only feel that I was floating, as I could now stretch out, both my arms and legs, but I couldn't touch anything but myself, floating in a deep darkness.

- "It was like one of the crazy dreams I have" - I spoke quietly, forcing myself to remember my last memory, trapped inside the black coffin.

I was in the coffin!

- "But what was that place?" - I asked myself.

Surely it wasn't the cramped coffin.

I thought a lot and came to the conclusion that possibly when an immortal runs out of oxygen, instead of dying, "we" dream, or maybe we go straight into the dream world.

As soon as I came to this conclusion, the darkness began to disappear and turn completely white, like an unpainted picture.

I could see myself floating naked on an empty white.

I was in the dream world and when I discovered this, I became the lucid dreamer of that place, so, knowing this I could do like Roberto and the others, build my own place in the dream world, since in the real world I was buried, stuck and without oxygen.

And that's exactly what I did, even without any experience in this, I focused on closing my eyes and imagined slowly descending until I touched the ground. I started to feel that I was descending slowly until my feet touched the ground, I opened my eyes and I was still in an eternal white, but now I could touch, walk, jump and move normally on an invisible ground, being afraid to fall, since I couldn't see what I was stepping on, because except for me, everything was pure white.

This was my dream world, by the looks of it I could create anything, I just needed to use my imagination, but I didn't know how far this power went. Did I need to use only my creativity and imagination or were there limitations?

Since I was stuck in the real world, I had plenty of time to test all these theories, seeing as there was no hope of anyone finding me anytime soon.

Before I tried anything else, I remembered the rules that Oliver explained to me before, as this was my world, I could add some rules that were different from the world Roberto had created, so I went over them again in my head trying to remember them all.

- Rule number one: Don't eat too much or take drugs before a lucid dream. This may make it difficult for you to wake up from sleep, causing your dream to last longer than expected.

- Rule number two: Don't create people, beings, creatures, or anything that you need to have "life", it will only serve as a catalyst for something that may be good, bad, demonic, alien or another being from a different astral plane.

- Rule number three: It is best that you have your Ba, that is, your dream object. You will use it, and it will help you remember that you are dreaming, in case you lose control over your dreams.

- <u>Rule number four</u>: It is best not to invade other people's dreams, especially those of people who have no control over their dreams; you don't want to get into certain fertile minds.

- <u>Rule number five</u>: Don't sleep inside your own dream, or someone else's dream, as this can lead to various inceptions, causing you to get lost and go into the limbo, and when this occurs your body goes into a coma.

I could remember all the rules.

I didn't have any Ba yet, so I was thinking about what I could use to be aware that I was in a dream and not in real life. Before long I decided to create a cigarette that would not burn me if pressed it against my skin, so that every time it didn't burn me I would know that I was still in the dream world.

All right, I created the cigarette and a lighter, lit it and pressed it on my skin, nothing happened. The other rules didn't help me as much, they were too vague and there still seemed to be a lot behind the dream world.

I carried on trying other things, the infinite white was starting to hurt my brain, so I closed my eyes and imagined a world scenario, sky, clouds, sun, moon and stars, so when I opened my eyes the eternal white was no longer there, now I was stepping on real ground, solid earth, the sky was blue and everything seemed so real that it was impossible to distinguish from the real world.

The day looked beautiful, I now wanted to see it at night, so I moved the time forward with my eyes closed, when I opened it the night was out. The stars were spaced out, so I decided to try something else, this time without closing my eyes, I thought about dragging them with my hands, I made the movement in the air, as if I was picking them up with my fingers and dragging them to where I wanted, I had trouble with the first one, but as soon as I managed, the others were easy. I also drew more stars with my finger and then I left the moon with a more yellowish color, not much, but it looked like a giant cheese, as I slightly increased its size.

Now the place had sky, earth, day, night, sun, moon, and many stars. I sat down on the floor, creating tired me out, but I continued anyway. Now I needed to think how to create a way that would automatically alternate between day, night, cloudy, rainy, storm, and other creative ways to control the time and climate of that place.

As much as I thought I could not think of anything different than a computer, my idea was to have in this computer a way to control the whole place, and at the same time I could create rules and restrictions so that only I would be the creator of the place, so perhaps after getting everything under control, I could try to communicate with Charles or someone who could get me out of there and find me in the real world.

Before creating the computer I tried to modify the place, I needed electricity, water, and the basic sanitation for the city I was going to build.

I shouldn't really know what to do, but amazingly my years of SimCity building places and managing them helped me create the water canals, sewage, light stations, garbage and water treatment plants, and everything else a city would need to maintain itself.

Before I even built the computer, I designed a house, the basic furniture, and then, when everything was ready, I finally built the computer.

I no longer needed to close my eyes to create things, I was getting better and better at it. The computer I created came with a keyboard, mouse, and even a desk, but I had to create the chair to sit down and start working.

I plugged it in, pressed the Power button and voila, the Windows computer started to open in my dream world. When it started there was a screen where it asked me for the name of the "city", I found it strange, I even tried to skip it, but I was only allowed to continue after deciding on the name, I thought of Dream City, but I found it a little corny, so after considering others and also not being satisfied, I decided to just change the name a little, so I named the city DreamNopolis.

I typed in the name of the city and now I could proceed.

After this screen the desktop was open and it was identical to the Windows start screen, there was no application on the desktop, but as I was thinking about how to control the city's climate, an application came up, it had a picture of a sun, I double clicked on it and seconds later a window appeared and in it were several options to change and control the city's climate, exactly the way I wanted it to be.

I could choose the duration schedule for morning, afternoon and evening. There were sub options for choices such as what color the sky would be at certain times. As I was testing the colors, I could immediately see from the window that the sky outside was changing in real time, and that was the coolest thing ever.

There were also options for nighttime, when I selected it they opened the sub options for dusk and dawn and just like so I could also set colors for those times.

Until then it was all very simple, nothing difficult, I even found it strange, I thought I would have more trouble with all that, I explored the application more and found an option written "advanced" unchecked, I clicked to check it and as soon as I did that other options appeared, they were so many that I think that until this day I don't know them all, but I will mention some like, control the clouds, choose season, temperature and weather condition, cloudy, rainy, angry or stormy.

There were settings for natural disasters, volcanic eruptions, earthquakes, tornadoes, hurricanes, tsunamis, and avalanches. And also apocalyptic settings, such as asteroid collision, rain of fire, zombies, machine takeover, flood, and Jesus coming back - I never had the courage to use the Jesus coming back setting.

I finished setting up and stopped playing with the weather part of DreamNopolis, it was time to start building the place, but before I could continue something happened and out of nowhere, I was pulled from DreamNopolis back to the real world, I woke up inside the coffin.

The ropes that bound me had loosened and worn out, I managed to get rid of them easily and was free in the coffin, my eyes were blurred and I saw some things moving, but they weren't exactly in front of me, they were right in front of my face, worms that wiggled around eating my skin as it regenerate and thus becoming a banquet for all those disgusting bugs, getting fat from consuming so much eternal flesh.

As my hands were untied, I immediately tried to get them all off my face - very disgusted - I also realized that there was a part of the coffin that had been cracked, I tried to force myself to get out of there, but I was many feet off the ground and no matter how hard I tried, the most I could do was to get more earth into the coffin, returning the trouble to breathe.

Gasping for breath, my vision began to dim and before I blacked out again from lack of air, I realized that my clothes were also in rags and falling apart and seeing this I came to the conclusion that time passes differently in the real world when one is in the dream world.

I blacked out!

DreamNopolis the city of dreams

It was dark again, I had no body, exactly the same as before, but this time I knew where I was and what I needed to do.

I wished I had come back to where I left off, I wondered where DreamNopolis was and why everything had gone back to the same way it started, I had lost all my previous "work", I was back to square one, but my skills as a creator had improved so much that it took no time at all for DreamNopolis to be back to where I had left it.

The city was exactly the same and the weather settings were also ready, but I didn't want to risk losing the settings and all the work I had done, so I needed to think about how to solve this problem, I needed to make a backup of DreamNopolis so that if something happened and I woke up, I wouldn't have to create everything from scratch again when I came back. So I decided to try something, but I wasn't sure if it would work, since I would have to wake up to test it. I accessed the computer and imagined an application on the desktop with the design of a floppy disk, immediately the application appeared on the computer, I opened it and there was an option, save backup every time you change DreamNopolis, without blinking I checked this option and hoped that it was that simple and that it would work, this way every time I woke up the city would always remain active.

I proceeded to design the place, the ground was all flat, so I added some elevations, peaks, ridges and mountains.

It was daytime in DreamNopolis, a cold morning with a bright orange sun, but still weak, I created some archipelagos near the sea coast, it was not easy to create things from scratch and if I continued like this it would take a long time to finish everything, so I thought I would use parts of cities I liked and knew, so I tried first taking some natural beauties, the flowered fields of Amsterdam, the beautiful castle cliffs of Ireland, the frozen Alps of Switzerland and the Brazilian seaside beaches. I was creating and strategically spreading them around the city.

I could now feel some life in DreamNopolis, I still needed to create a lot of things, but by taking whole parts of places I wanted and fitting them into the city, everything was getting ready much faster.

I created the houses, the neighborhoods, the businesses, now DreamNopolis was a full city - or a mix of several cities in one place - it had a lagoon, a beach, mountains, shopping malls, outdoor parks, amusement parks, playhouses, stadiums, bridges, monuments, and everything a city needs to be complete and fun.

I had no idea how much time had passed, I was beginning to think that I was there forever, I felt alone and this was beginning to bother me and stir up some of my curiosity and craziness to test how it would be to create something alive, something that could be possessed by something, like what happened in Roberto and his friends' dream.

The rule said not to create animate things, they could be possessed by some creature and come to life, but I knew that breaking this rule would be a matter of time since I couldn't live there alone forever - neither could Adam - yet the fear of what might possess things and appear there, kept me restrained enough to not create things right away and think it over.

I went back to the computer and this time "created" an application and the icon design was a silhouette of two people - which reminded me a lot of the MSN icon - I double-clicked it to open it.

My intention was to try to create an application to communicate with people who were in the dream world. The application opened and there was not much on the screen, it showed the message "you have no contacts added", it had a very similar interface to MSN and SKYPE, I clicked the button, search and typed Bill's name and after searching for a moment the name appeared with three options available, send connection invitation, send message and invade.

I tried the first option "send connection invitation", but after I clicked, I got the message "the user is not online". What did this mean? I interpreted it as Bill not being asleep.

I then clicked on the second option "send message", when I did this the computer's webcam turned on and started recording. I assumed that somehow this message would appear in Bill's dreams so I started talking.

"Bill, Oliver kidnapped me and buried me somewhere many palms underground in an old black wooden box, I am somehow in the dream world and able to communicate with you, I need you to help me, search for me, somehow there must be cameras from when Oliver kidnapped me, try to follow the tracks and find me!" - I said while recording the message.

There was still the last option left, even with the other rule against entering other people's dreams, but since it was Bill and I trusted him, I clicked, but just like the first option the message "the user is not online" appeared.

I looked for other names on the list and found them all, I even thought of sending a message to some of them, but besides the fact that they wouldn't take a message in a dream seriously, I also didn't want to involve anyone else in all this madness from hell.

I put the name Belatrix Hyssel and made an attempt to connect, but without success, so I wrote a message very similar to the one I had sent to Bill explaining roughly what had happened and hoping this would work.

I remembered the Oneirology students, Ana the fat one with blonde hair, Claudete the short one with the big eyes, Natalia the big nose with the hole in her chin and Felipe the guy with long arms and legs, Oliver had told me that they were trapped in Roberto's dream - who was now Beelzebub - their names were very common and I didn't know everyone's full name, except Ana, because we had more time to talk than I had with the others, since we met earlier on the way we ended up introducing ourselves and so I knew her full name - Ana Amélia de Souza.

In her name there was only an enable option, so I clicked on it "send connection invitation" and this time the message that appeared was "connecting...". I waited a bit and then I noticed that a portal appeared like a big door, there were strange symbols on it and it started to glow, before I could understand what was happening Ana went through it coming and appearing in front of me.

She looked exactly the same as the last time we had seen each other, as soon as she saw me she ran towards me crying and tried to hug me, but she had no body, she was just a specter like a ghost, so she passed right through me.

- Charles, what happened? Where did you go? I thought you abandoned us, you have no idea what I've been through - Ana said, crying and looking at her body without understanding.

- It's a long story, I was also deceived and you were trapped in Roberto's dream, Beelzebub took over his body and returned alone to the real world, calm down you'll be fine, what happened to you? - I asked her, trying to calm her down a little.

She didn't say anything for a while, just trembled and stared uncomprehendingly at her ghost form. Little by little she was recovering, I didn't want to rush her.

- I don't really know where I was, it was an infinite darkness and I only had my own thoughts, from time to time I could hear some whispers, they offered me things, they wanted to make pacts in exchange for information, stories and salvation, but most of them wanted my soul in exchange - Ana said confirming my suspicions about where she was.

- Calm down, I will try to explain to you what happened, but I am not sure if I understand correctly, most of the things I will tell you are theories - I told her explaining the whole story.

I explained to her the whole story, from my involvement to hell, immortality, supernatural, dream world, rules, what had happened after she was petrified, and how I was betrayed, buried, and now in the dream world trying to communicate with the real world to be rescued.

She asked a few more questions and I answered what I knew - telling it the same way I am telling you.

Now that she was calmer, she said she didn't want to go back to where she was, asked me to let her stay there, and started asking me about the place I was building.

I took her on a tour around DreamNopolis and introduced her to everything I had created, explained my ideas for the place, but made it clear that what she really wanted was to return to the real world.

- Wow, this place looks amazing, did you do this all by yourself? - asked Ana.

- Yes, I've been here for so long I don't even know anymore - I answered her.

- Our group couldn't do many of these things, maybe because we didn't know the rules, but this place is much more real than our town. Did you notice that in Roberto's dream there was no wind? We couldn't breathe? The body weight didn't seem the same as in the real world and so on? So here, even without having a body I can feel the temperature, the breeze, it even feels like I'm breathing. Wow! The others, how could I forget them, Charles we have to bring them here, Claudete, Natalia and Felipe, they must be in the same place I was, please do the same as you did with me and bring them here - Ana said remembering her friends who had also been left behind.

- I just didn't bring them because I don't know their full names, do you? I forgot that, we need it to rescue them - I told her.

- Yes I know, we have studied together for a long time - answered Ana while we went back home to use the computer.

We went back to the computer, opened the application and she told me the full names of her friends to bring them to DreamNopolis the same way I had done with her.

One by one they were leaving the portal, arriving as shaken as Ana, each one had the same reaction, as soon as they left the door with the strange symbols, they ran crying towards Ana to hug her and as they were also specters, they could touch each other.

After everyone was gathered and had calmed down I told them once again the whole story from the beginning just as I had done with Ana. I also talked about my theories and that I wasn't sure about them, only suspicious.

- Thank you Charles for saving us - they all thanked me.

- Don't thank me yet, you are in a coma in the hospital and I am stuck buried somewhere, we still need to figure this out - I told them not letting them get soft.

We talked some more while I introduced them to DreamNopolis.

- Wow, how did you do this all by yourself? Are you going to leave us here? If you wake up, what happens to us? - asked Natalia.

- I honestly don't know, but I created some rules in this world, theoretically the computer will keep a backup of DreamNopolis, so even if I wake up everything should continue to exist and work, but I haven't tested this rule yet, we need to see if it will work, I can try to keep you here yes, but my idea was to try to make you wake up, so you could help me get out of the coffin in the real world - I answered her explaining my plan to everyone.

They seemed apprehensive because they didn't want to go back to where they were, but since they were not sure what would happen if I woke them up, they agreed that we should try to wake them up somehow.

Back to the computer, I "created" another application, this one had the icon design of a house, I double clicked and opened it, the idea of this application was to manage the inhabitants of DreamNopolis, being able to classify them as one of three categories, visitors, residents or administrators.

I classified all of them as residents which is the classification that allows them to stay in the city even when I am not there.

There was a tab in the application called "invitations received", I clicked on it and there were several requests to access DreamNopolis, there were so many invitations and so many different names that I couldn't look them all up and they would probably be from creatures, monsters, demons and other bad things, so of course I didn't accept any.

Seeing the invitations tab and that I needed to accept them made me a little more relaxed about who could come to DreamNopolis and this gave me the idea for another application, this time with the brick and lock icon design, this application would work as a firewall for the city, so I opened it to see what security settings it would be possible to set up in that application.

There were some options already checked and some unchecked.

I realized that the marked options were the ones I considered essential when I was creating the city.

Options checked:

- Entry allowed only if invited.
- Allow residents to stay in the city even after the host disconnects.
- Alert trespassing attempts.

Options unchecked:

- Allow visitors to make invitations (I didn't check it)
- Allow Residents to make invitations (I didn't check it)
- Allow administrators to make invitations (Checked)
- Allow visitors to stay in the city even after the host disconnects (Not checked)
- Allow admins to stay in town even after the host disconnects (Checked)
- Revoke admin permission when host is not logged in (Checked)

Ana, Claudete, Natalia and Felipe simply watched without questions and I believe without understanding anything.

- There you go. I made some more configurations to guarantee that you are safe in case I wake up, I also made sure to include new rules that avoid invasions and people who are not invited," I explained to them.

- Just being here together is already something, I don't want to ever go back to where we were - said Felipe, looking in the bright side.

Since I was on the computer I went back to the application that searched for people, I went again to search for Bill's name, I wanted to see if this time he was "online".

I already knew what the "send invitation" and "send message" buttons did, so this time I decided to click on the "invasion" button, but before clicking I explained to the people that this could already be one of the tests if they would stay there when I left, if it worked, I would probably invade the dream that Bill was having, so when I came back if they were still there great, but if not they could rest assured that I would bring them back as soon as possible.

They were too afraid to go back to where they were, so they asked me not to do this test at that moment, to wait for them to rest a little more and try this the next day, I was understanding of their request and ended up accepting, after all I didn't know anything about where they were, but I could tell when they arrived that it didn't seem pleasant at all.

I showed them which houses they could stay in while they were there, all of them would be my neighbors, but none of them wanted to leave the house where I was, the most they could do was walk around town together, but it didn't take long for one of them to come back to the house and see if I was still there on the computer.

I remained at the computer creating another application, this one with a clock icon design, I wanted to use it to understand how time passes in DreamNopolis in comparison to the real world. I opened the application and there were no settings to be made in it, the only thing on the screen was the following message.

"Six seconds in the world goes by within a second"

I looked for other things, but that was it, there was nothing I could change, no matter what I did, every time I opened the app the same message would appear.

I came to the conclusion that a second in DreamNopolis was six seconds in the real world, meaning that a minute would be six minutes, an hour would be six hours, a month would be six months, and a year would be six years.

This makes sense, since the average person sleeps eight hours, and there are dreams that seem like they have been going on for days.

I didn't know how much time had passed in DreamNopolis, but with new settings, I set a date and calendar for the city, so from that moment on I would know how much time was passing in the real world.

There was nothing else to do on the computer, I was out of ideas for rules and settings for DreamNopolis, so I decided to find the others and tell them that it was time for us to test the settings and go after Bill. But before I could find them, my vision darkened again and once more I woke up inside the coffin.

We were going to test how the backup settings would work in a different way than I had planned, but at least we would know if all that work in DreamNopolis had been of any use.

There was really no way out of the coffin, I got rid of the bugs that were eating my flesh again and tried my best to get out of there, but the only thing I could do was to break the rest of the weak wood of the coffin, which caused all the earth above to invade the coffin suffocating me and leaving no room this time for any oxygen to be formed.

Unlike the other times, as soon as I became aware there was no darkness, there was DreamNopolis, the city was exactly the way it was before I left, I was in the computer room and left immediately to see if the others were still there.

I went next door to the house where they had settled in after feeling safer. I rang the doorbell and before long I heard quick footsteps on the other side of the door and then the door opened.

- Charles, are you okay? Where did you go? You said you would let us know, did you get ahold of Bill? - Claudete questioned.

- Are you all okay? I'm fine, yes, I didn't go to Bill, I just woke up in the coffin all of a sudden - I explained to her, entering the house and going over to the others.

I explained to everyone how it had happened and we were all happy that the rules and settings were working. Everyone seemed to have a huge weight off their backs, at last they seemed to actually feel safe now.

With the backup and their safety secured, it was no longer a problem to go visit Bill.

I spent days in front of the computer trying to connect to Bill, but without success, meanwhile the city seemed more and more gigantic for only the five of us living in it.

I hardly ever left the room, while the others used the city and brought ideas to be implemented, new neighborhoods, bridges, summer camps, caves, lost cities at the bottom of the sea to be visited while diving, mini-golf parks, water parks, horse racing parks, and everything else they could imagine when they started to feel bored.

A few more days went by and just as I was about to give up, I was losing patience and thinking that the "invasion" button doesn't work, so I clicked it one last time and finally, the bloody button worked so the portal with the doorway full of strange symbols appeared and I stepped through the bright light coming from within it to another place.

I was definitely in one of Bill's dreams, I wasn't surprised when I saw that I was in a nudist harem of marijuana cultivators, it was exactly what I expected from a dream of his.

We were the only men there, I was amazed at the amount of detail he had created, not even I could think of so much beauty in one place, there were redheads taking care of the Purple Haze, blondes taking care of the OG Kush, brunettes taking care of the Pink Mangoes and other types of marijuana that were classified by the type of women who took care of them. Bill was sitting on a throne and he had a cigarette the size of an arm by his side, I approached him slowly so that he couldn't see me and when I was very close I gave him a scare, but I shouldn't have done that, because as soon as I scared him I woke him up, so at the same moment I was thrown back into DreamNopolis.

When I realized that I had returned, I understood the mistake I had made, so at the same moment I ran to the computer to try again to invade his dream, but as time passed differently in the dream world I could not find him awake again, so I had to wait a few more days until I could find Bill sleeping again.

Six days later, one hundred and forty-four hours in DreamNopolis, and twenty-four hours in the real world, this way I was able to predict when Bill would be sleeping and I could again invade his dream.

It was another dream, now I seemed to be inside a shooting game (FPS), it looked a lot like Counter Strike in the slums of Rio de Janeiro, but much more real than the games we played. This time I approached Bill when he could see me coming, but since I was wearing a helmet and vest covering most of my body, he without hesitating gave me several shots before I took off my helmet and identified myself.

- It's me, dammit! Are you playing in your dream? Crazy bastard... - I told him after taking a few more shots before he approached.

- Charles? Is that really you? Man, I got scared in a dream last night and I could have sworn it was you who scared me - said Bill.

- Yes it's me, don't shoot - I said raising my hands.

- This is the third time I've seen you in my dreams, a long time ago you appeared out of nowhere like a hologram and left a strange message about being buried somewhere and that Oliver had betrayed you - Bill said confirming that the message had arrived, although he didn't believe it.

- So you got my message. I don't know where to begin to tell you about everything that happened, by the way, yesterday in your nudist harem dream it was me yes, I'm sorry for the scare, I didn't know you would wake up from that - I told Bill with a smile on my face for being able to talk to him again.

- I got it, but I didn't know what to do. I even asked Oliver about where you were and if it would be long before you got back, but he just told me that you were doing some work and that you didn't have time to get back - said Bill.

- I don't know how long it has been, let me explain to you what happened so you can help me. Oliver buried me in a coffin somewhere, when you came out of Roberto's dream world I accidentally found out that it was Beelzebub who was in Roberto's body, Oliver allied with him and as soon as he realized I found out that it wasn't Roberto he knocked me out leaving me behind, when I managed to come out of the dream world I woke up inside the car minutes before he buried me somewhere - I explained the essential part to him.

- What? He had told me that you were sent to another job, only this time in another country. The bastard has been coming to the house and handing me some papers that needed to be posted on the Deep Web - replied Bill.

- He told me that if you started asking too many questions he would forge a goodbye message from me, telling you that I was going to live in another country and that I no longer wanted to be your friend, since I was now immortal - I told him before continuing.

- I would be suspicious, but maybe I would believe him eventually if he kept in touch - Bill answered sincerely.

- When I woke up I was already buried in the coffin and it didn't take long for me to black out again due to the lack of oxygen, I didn't die because I was immortal, but when I realized that I existed again I found out that I was in the dream world and the strangest of all was that even being immortal I could create and shape the world the way I wanted, for some reason that rule Oliver had told us about immortals not being able to be lucid dreamers doesn't apply to me - I told Bill, explaining about DreamNopolis.

- Or was what he said a lie? - Bill pointed out.

- Yeah, that could be it. So I could edit the place the way I wanted, and since I didn't have much to do, I ended up doing like Roberto and the students, but I was careful to create rules that required an invitation to go in. I created an entire city called DreamNopolis, and I also managed to rescue the souls of the students who had been left behind, the ones who are in a coma since that mission - I explained to him.

- Oliver told me that the students had returned and were fine - said Bill.

- That son of a bitch betrayed us, made a deal with Beelzebub, and Hell probably doesn't even know what happened since he's doing the job I was supposed to do - I told him.

- And he even brought me papers of reports from hell to be sent to the Deep Web saying that it was you who had sent them so I could help - said Bill.

- That's why I need your help more than ever Bill, I can't stay in the dream world forever, you have to find me - I told him.

- I'll find someone who can help us find out where you are and get you out of there - Bill reassured me.

- Time in the real world is different from time in the dream world, I don't know when you will wake up and when we will be able to talk to each other again, so I need you to get some information about Roberto/Beelzebub and the students, maybe we can help them wake up -

I told him, passing him the names of the students so that he could remember to look them up.

We were still in Bill's shooter dream and sometimes while we were talking, soldiers would appear and we would shoot them as if we were in a video game, only much more real.

- If you run into Oliver, don't say anything and for God's sake, don't let him know that we had this conversation, don't tell him that you found out that he betrayed us and are planning my rescue... - I was telling him when suddenly, the dream shattered and again I was thrown back to DreamNopolis.

I woke up on the floor of my room, the four students were wide-eyed, anxious and waiting for me.

- Are you okay? How was it? What happened? - asked Ana.

I told them everything that happened in Bill's dream and they realized we hadn't made much progress, but that we would have news the next time.

I sensed that everyone seemed upset that they couldn't do anything, but the truth was that there really wasn't much they could do, unless by some miracle one of them woke up and joined Bill in my search.

So I decided that during the next few days I would try to create a way to make them wake up in the real world and I would also take some inspiration from Bill's last dream to create some new things in the city.

I created an application on the computer with the intention of making them wake up, but this time, unlike the other applications that worked exactly the way I wanted, this one didn't work, every time I started it I would get the message "the application does not meet the requirements to start".

I had no idea what those requirements were and even though I kept pushing and trying other things the message remained and there was nothing I could do to move forward, so I gave up trying that and spent the rest of the time doing the alteration in DreamNopolis that Bill's dream had inspired me to do.

When I wasn't working on trying to wake them up or finding the place where Oliver had buried me, I was out with the students around town. We would go out and implement new ideas around DreamNopolis to pass the time, and when I finished the modification that Bill's dream had inspired me to make, I called them to test it out with me.

I designed a way in which we could select an area of the city to play and what would be the objective we would fight for, so, as soon as we selected what the mission would be - territory domination, capture the flag, bomb deployment, hostage rescue, and more - we entered the cabins that were scattered throughout the city and were teleported to the place in the city we had chosen, thus, we went out collecting weapons, vests, and various other equipment. Every scenario was equippable and interactive, we could use chairs, hammers, glasses, bottles and bombs to accomplish the defined objective, we could also shoot in several ways with the various weapons we found during the mission, it created all the immersion and freedom that I always felt missing in video games, everything was so real that it was as if we were in the real world, but we were still safe in DreamNopolis and no matter what happened during the mission, all the places we destroyed were restored as soon as the mission was over, then the neighborhood was rebuilt and we woke up in the cabins back in the regular city.

The test was a success, the students loved using the cabins and they were like escape valves for them, as when they entered the game they regained their bodies from being a floating spectrum and this made them feel alive again.

A few more days passed in DreamNopolis and I had managed to connect a few more times in Bill's dream, he was passing me information and updating me on how things were out there.

He hired a detective named H. Chinaski, the detective managed to access some cameras close to our house and found the moment that Oliver put me in the trunk of the car, now he was trying to access other cameras and follow the path that the car had taken, his main objective was to trace the route and find the place that Oliver buried me.

Bill also got information about the students; they were in a coma in a clinic that their families paid for, were kept alive by machines, and there was a date when the machines would be turned off if there was no progress in their clinical condition.

I was worried when I heard this, because we did not know what would happen to Ana, Claudete, Natália and Felipe when the apparatus was turned off.

There were only two weeks left in the real world before the shutdown date, that is, three months left in DreamNopolis. Bill had consulted a kind of saint/wizard and he said he could help us if he could go to the hospital in the dark the night before the apparatus was shut off, so that he could perform a ritual that according to him would open the portal back from the dream world to the real world for a brief moment for the lost dreamers.

At first I didn't want to tell the students anything, since there was nothing they could do, but with a few days left for them to turn off their devices in the real world I decided to tell them, I told them as if Bill had just found out, I also told them about the plan of the wizard's ritual and they agreed to perform it even though they were quite worried about what would happen to them if the plan didn't work out.

During the two months in DreamNopolis we implemented new neighborhoods, I spread missions that didn't require cabins around the city, and more and more the city became large and complete. Many of the ideas that we had included in the last week needed to be tested, but we no longer had the focus for it after the news about the shutdown, I hoped that the plan would work, but being alone made me afraid.

The ritual would start at ten P.M. o'clock and the wizard said that it would end between eleven hours and fifty-nine minutes and midnight, we didn't have much to do except keep pushing the button on the computer program during this period to send the students back to their bodies.

I talked them all through calming them down and asked that if the ritual worked, they would help Bill find me and if possible visit me from time to time in DreamNopolis.

From what we knew the ritual was happening at the moment, I opened the application that before returned the message "the application does not meet the requirements to start" and this time, it showed a spinning circle with the word "loading". This was a good sign, so now the application met the requirement. When the application started loading the students in front of me started blinking, I was worried, but it was a sign that something was happening.

Finally the program loaded, it now showed the names of the four students and in front of each name there were buttons written "wake up", as soon as I clicked on the first one - Felipe's - he immediately disappeared from our view and when this happened the other three who were left also yelled.

- Go! Go! Go!

So immediately after I pressed the three buttons, they also disappeared.

I stood in front of the computer for a while not knowing what to do and not even sure if the ritual succeeded, the only thing I could do was hope that everything was working out until I heard from Bill.

I was once again alone in DreamNopolis, but I didn't want to think about it too much, so I stayed for a few days waiting for Bill to sleep so that I could again invade his dream and get news about what had happened, if the students were all right and returned to their bodies.

I insisted for several days until I succeeded.

In this other dream of Bill's, he was in my house, I missed that place so much that as soon as I entered I knew exactly where to look for him, in the living room, on the sofa as usual.

- So, did it work out? - I immediately asked him, referring to the students.

- It seems like it, I was there with the wizard and they were waking up one by one, we had to leave because the nurses showed up and started asking questions, they were surprised by what had happened, the students were very thin and awful looking, weak and malnourished, I hope they recover well soon - said Bill.

- Good, did you manage to talk to them? Do you have any news about Oliver or my rescue? - I asked more questions.

- The detective said he will do some digging, but after the previous ones I'm not putting much faith, he keeps asking for more money, Oliver hasn't showed up for some time - replied Bill.

- You should see DreamNopolis sometime, next time I will send you an invitation so that you can go there, I need to show you the city and tell you about some ideas I had - I told Bill.

We chatted for a while until he woke up and I went back to DreamNopolis.

There, now I was all alone in DreamNopolis, just when I had gotten used to the students and the town was full of things to do, but now no one was there but me.

A few more days passed, I spent my time alone testing some missions that we had spread around the city and hadn't tested yet. I also created a tracking application for the city, in this application I could follow by a radar where the guests of DreamNopolis would be.

A few days passed in the real world and weeks in the dream world, it seemed like an eternity and I still hadn't managed to connect in Bill's dream and neither had he come to the city. I sent messages to the students and also invitations for them to visit me, but none of them had shown up either.

I began to get paranoid, thinking that maybe it was all a work of imagination, or maybe it was all just torture in hell.

It was torturing to think about it and have no information or person there, but suddenly, the computer starts to glow and the portal that I used to go to Bill's dream appeared, but this time he came out of it.

- You really did come - I said to him, smiling with happiness.

- Man, what a trip, I knew you were the culprit - I said looking around curiously.

- Trip? What do you mean, trip? - I asked him.

- Getting here at this portal felt a bit like when we went on the mission, as soon as I fell asleep my projection left my body and there was a strong golden light, far away that attracted me, I flew there and when I arrived there was this portal waiting for me. I'm sorry I didn't come sooner, but I wasn't sure if it was you and also, after the deal with the wizard things got very creepy, I have some things to tell you - said Bill with a worried face.

- Creepy? What do you mean? - I asked him.

- The students are back in their bodies, but they don't remember anything that happened, in fact they don't even remember who they are, besides, Oliver seemed to be monitoring the students, we stole the videos from the clinic, but some nurses told us that a man with his descriptions went there to ask some questions, I bribed them not to tell anything and to call me if someone strange showed up - said Bill.

- Did he look for you? - I asked him.

- Yes. He came to my house and asked me some questions, he had the nerve to ask if you came back and if I had heard from you, he gave me another report from hell for the Deep Web, he said he would be back in a few days to check it out - replied Bill.

- He didn't expect the students to come back, I bet he will check to see if they remember anything or if they will recover their memories, maybe it's better that they don't remember anything - I told him.

- Yeah, but man, tell me how are you doing? Where are we? - Bill asked me.

- I'm fed up, here it seems like years have passed, while over there only months have gone by, I want my life back, help me Bill - I begged him.

- Calm down, hold on, we'll find you - Bill said, putting his hand on my shoulder.

- I'll show you DreamNopolis, I need to tell you an idea - I told him as we left the house.

As we left the house Bill could see how big and beautiful the city had become.

- Man, it feels like we are in the real world, only prettier, how strange. Did you and the students create all this? - asked Bill.

- Mostly me, but they helped me, even you helped a little - I told him.

- Me? - asked Bill.

- Yes, thanks to your dream I had the idea to include missions within the city where we use the reality of appearing to be in the real world, to do video game things or things that we would only do in the dream world. We created several missions inside the city and do whatever we want here - I explained to him.

- What do you mean? - Bill asked, not even trying to understand.

- Think about the game GTA or any other game where the map is a city, did you? - I asked him.

- Yes, I will think of GTA San Andreas, which is my favorite - answered Bill.

- So, DreamNopolis is the city with several missions with several styles within it, just like in GTA, only we have the reality of the real world and don't have the limitations of video games, are you beginning to understand? - I questioned him again.

- Hum... I think I understand - replied Bill, looking as if he didn't quite understand yet.

- The students and I create several games within the city, but we don't need a television, a computer, or a controller, we are the players - I told him, finishing the explanation with a slap on his forehead.

- But there are only the two of us here - replied Bill, breaking all my enthusiasm.

- Thanks for reminding me - I retorted.

- That's not what I meant, I just wondered why there were no inhabitants. Didn't you say that the city is protected? Isn't it only by invitation that we get here? - Bill asked, asking the right questions.

- I didn't think about that, I was just following the rule of not creating creatures, beings and anything that is animated so as not to be possessed, so I didn't create characters and NPC's (non-playable character) - I answered him.

You could tell he was interested after he understood what we had done.

- Show me one of these missions - Bill asked.

I knew exactly where to take him. We walked for some time until we reached a stadium that was a little different from what Bill had seen in person. This was one of those stadiums from the Harry Potter movie, where we could play Quidditch with flying brooms.

Bill, like any fan, freaked out. We stayed there until he woke up, I couldn't show him any more missions since his excitement wouldn't let me, but on the other hand I was happy that he liked it.

We were in the middle of a competition when he simply disappeared, it scared me a little, but for the amount of hours he spent there, I figured he woke up, I just wasn't sure how it would be.

I felt less lonely for the rest of the days and used the time to enable Bill's permanent invitation and so he started to visit me regularly, every time he slept he would show up here wanting to know about the other missions and giving feedback on changes and new ideas.

It was almost as if when he was not in DreamNopolis I was working on the missions, and when he was, we were testing them together and catching up.

So much time had passed in the dream world, I could no longer tell how much time had passed in the real world. The detective's investigations came to nothing, and every time Bill talked about him, it was bad news about another failed dig.

I was beginning to get the feeling that I would never leave and that they would never find me. Bill's visits were no longer enough to bring me peace, nor did they help me forget about the real world.

There was an idea hammering in my head and the more time I spent alone in DreamNopolis the stronger the idea became.

I was thinking of trying to somehow free up DreamNopolis for lucid dreamers, that's right, I wanted to bring in people from the real world, but not all of them, only those who could control their dreams, so that I could include this rule in DreamNopolis and people would be able to come and visit the city as Bill did and with that, they would enjoy the reality that the dream world offered and the missions we had created to have fun in the city. It would be like an online game in the dream world, where lucid dreamers from all over the world would interact and make friends.

I told Bill the idea and he went nuts about it, it seemed like everything he had ever wanted was being told to him, but he still said something I hadn't thought of yet.

- But how are we going to free this world without NPCs? Some missions will need a guide, the city needs puppets to take the place of the inhabitants so that we can have even more realism. The missions will need more life, the city needs inhabitants, gangs, mafia and people who will tell us what to do, where to go and what to look for - said Bill.

I had already thought about this, but always came back to the limitation of creating other beings since they could be possessed, as in the students' dream. If I created NPCs, they would probably be possessed by something, and these things would probably never obey me or willingly participate in DreamNopolis missions.

I took more time to think about this while Bill kept insisting on bringing his friends, with each new mission he got more and more excited and talked about a session introducing DreamNopolis as the city of dreams for some people. He also insisted that I give him more power and administrator privileges, he wanted to be able to make even more changes besides the ones he was previously authorized, but I decided it was better to leave him with the same privileges that the students had.

I agreed to test with his friends if it was possible to bring other people to the city, but first I asked him to wait until I finished some missions that we were creating, then, when everything was ready we would call them.

At least that was the excuse I made up for Bill, what I really wanted was to check on the invitation application a new configuration I had made, I included in the application a filter that listed only names of people I had already met in my life, but there was a name there that I had never met, only heard of.

Asmodeus.

This was the name of my "boss" and I knew it, because Oliver in one of his long conversations told me the names of the leaders of hell and which of them were our "bosses".

Hell, Purgatory and Paradise

The only strange name in that whole list was the name that only contained one word, that is, had no last name - Asmodeus - I had never seen him or been in the same place as him, at least that's what I thought.

In the application, the same options appeared as for the other names, "send connection invitation", "send message" and "invasion". I pressed the send message button and the message "impossible to send messages to this user" appeared. As Asmodeus was not in the dream world but in hell, I really imagined that this was going to happen, so right away without thinking much I pressed the "invasion" button, but as soon as I pressed it a portal full of symbols just like the ones that appeared when I visited Bill's dreams appeared. I went through it and in the same instant I arrived in a village, it was night and it looked very old, there was a big wall surrounding the whole place and everything there seemed to be made of stone, just like the Flintstones' houses, I observed the place and spotted a location that seemed to have its lights on, I headed towards this place and as I got closer that part of the village seemed to be the commercial part, I kept walking until I arrived in front of the lighted place and as soon as I entered I realized that it was was a tavern.

I could tell it was a tavern because of the large counter with drinks, the chairs and tables scattered around the room near the piano. There was a person in the tavern, he seemed to be the waiter, but he wasn't serving drinks behind the counter, he was playing the piano, but as soon as he noticed my presence, he stopped.

- Charles? What are you doing here? - asked the waiter after he stopped playing the piano, yet still remained seated with his back turned.

- Do you know me? Who are you? I'm looking for Asmodeus - I asked him.

- Do you really think I wouldn't know my own employees? - replied Asmodeus.

I was surprised to find out that this was Asmodeus, but I didn't let it intimidate me, I kept my posture and continued.

- So it is you! I thought that the leaders of hell would be different, but anyway it's a pleasure to meet you in person - I told him trying to be cordial, since I would need his help.

- Different how? You know what, forget that question, what are you doing here? Or rather, how did you get here? - Asmodeus asked.

- I had to invade your dream - I started to explain, but was interrupted.

- Dream? This is Hell, I just created a replica of Sodom, the village I grew up in, did you like it? - Asmodeus interrupted me and explained that we were in hell.

- Sodom! Cool, so this is somewhere in hell? I thought I couldn't get here through the dream world, I thought DreamNopolis could only invade dreams - I told him, while thinking out loud.

- DreamNopolis? What is it? Answer me now, what are you doing here? - said Asmodeus.

- I came to ask for your help - I answered him.

- My help? Shouldn't it be the other way around? After all, it is you who work for me - Asmodeus asked ironically.

- Yes, but Oliver betrayed me and left me buried somewhere that I can't get out, so I ended up going to the dream world and creating DreamNopolis the city of dreams - I answered him, saying the damned slogan that Bill made.

- You what? Then who is doing your work? An immortal managing to manipulate the dream world? Interesting - Asmodeus asked, but before I could answer, he started playing the piano again.

It was a sensational melody that I had never heard before, I didn't interrupt him - I didn't have the courage - until he finished the song, standing up and speaking again.

- Let me get this straight. Oliver betrayed you, has been doing your job with that little friend of yours, and you, who should be seven feet under the ground, have discovered that you possess the power of a lucid dreamer, so during your time imprisoned you have created an entire city in the dream world and can also invade people's dreams and even hell? - Asmodeus asked as he walked towards the bar counter.

- Yes, but... - I said, but was interrupted again by him.

- And now you want my help to rescue you, but what's in it for me? - Asmodeus asked, deducing everything that had happened with great ease.

- I don't know what else I can offer after signing that contract - I answered him.

- There are countless things you can offer, but let's talk a little more about this city in the dream world, what's its name again? - Asmodeus asked, pouring us a drink on the glasses he had just picked up.

- DreamNopolis - I answered.

- Take me there, I want to see this city created in the world of dreams by an immortal, I still can't believe you have this ability - Asmodeus said, taking a sip of his drink and pointing with his head to the other glass for me to drink.

I finished my drink and stood up, before I could say anything, the portal with the symbols appeared, so, we entered it and I went back to DreamNopolis, but now with an unexpected visitor.

Asmodeus looked dazzled when he arrived in the city and saw all that, his eyes had the same look as when a person from the countryside arrives for the first time in the big city.

- Did you build this all by yourself? - Asmodeus asked.

- Yes - I told him, hiding the truth about the help from the students.

- Wow, such a depth of detail makes me feel like I'm in the real world, and it's been millennia since I've been there. I can feel that this place has very solid rules, just that we from hell don't know about such a big place in the dream world is already a great demonstration of that, so it looks like we can't invade either. Come on, introduce me to the place and don't leave out the details - Asmodeus demanded.

I introduced the whole city to him in the same way I had done with the students and with Bill, I also showed him some of the missions and explained that I wouldn't show him the others, because there were hundreds of them, but even so he insisted that I explained some of the details of the missions to him.

- Who have you brought here? Some of these missions are impossible to do alone, they need one more person - said Asmodeus.

- I brought my friend Bill, some other missions are incomplete because of missing people and also because of missing NPCs - I told him, explaining again what NPCs were, because he did not know what it meant.

- You see how you have so many things to offer! I'll rescue you from wherever you are, but I'll want a few things in return - said Asmodeus.

- So you know where I am? - I asked him.

- No, but I know someone who can find out and find you. You just have to do the things I say, and maybe then I can even give you another promotion - said Asmodeus.

- I'd rather know what these things are! - I retorted.

- We can help each other, I have some souls in hell that should no longer be there. Since Lucifer left hell saying that he was going to look for God, purgatory has become the only place that keeps the order of the world working, since Lucifer didn't teach us how, hell can no longer make the souls that have served their sentences reincarnate and follow their cycles, so some of these souls have been corrupted by standing still for centuries waiting for another opportunity, they are turning into creatures and some of them become so strong that they can escape to the real world with their new form. You could see some of these creatures trying to escape from hell when you briefly visited that part of the caves with your friend, when Oliver took you there. We could try to make the souls that have not yet transformed and have already served their sentences to be these DreamNopolis NPCs, so we would gain time until we solve the issue of making them follow their cycles in the real world, maybe then they will stop transforming into creatures, maybe you can solve the problem of their reincarnation here, it would be a great achievement not only for hell, but also for humanity - Asmodeus said explaining his idea.

I didn't really understand how we would do it, but it seemed like a good idea since I couldn't stand being buried and alone in DreamNopolis anymore.

- If you rescue me I'm up for it - I answered him.

- But we need to do a test first, let me show you a soul, send us back to Sodom - Asmodeus said.

I did as he asked, again the portal appeared and we went through it.

I was finding it all too easy and too good to be true, but in the end it would help me get out of the coffin, and it would also help the souls that needed to get out of hell.

We returned to Sodom and Asmodeus spoke again.

- Many people think that souls are still being created, but they are not, what exists is a system of souls created by God where all the souls that have existed and will exist have already been created by the almighty, what happens is that some souls are still waiting for their time to start their cycle, while others have already started and even gone through some of their cycles. Each soul has twelve reincarnation cycles, very few have managed to go through these twelve cycles without going through hell, and even fewer have managed to complete the twelve cycles to finally go to paradise, that is, the souls that have finished their cycle have the following destination, the purgatory to wait for their reincarnation time or to hell, the souls that finish the twelve cycles go to paradise. But as I told you before, God and Lucifer are missing and with that things are not working as they should, the souls are stuck in hell after serving their sentences, and in addition, the souls in purgatory are reincarnating faster than they should since the souls in hell are stuck, so if we don't solve this problem before the souls in purgatory finish there will be an apocalypse, because before God disappeared, he had programmed that there would be a final apocalypse when all the souls arrived in paradise or when they stopped reincarnating - said Asmodeus explaining to me all the confusion and the urgency of the plan.

- What do you mean? - I asked, still not quite understanding everything he just told me.

- Are you stupid? Think of it this way, we could populate, what's the name of the city again? - Asmodeus asked.

- DreamNopolis - I answered.

- Yes, we could populate DreamNopolis with the souls who have already paid their sentences and thus make the city more lively and interesting - said Asmodeus.

I was dying to get back to the real world, but I was still afraid to bring these souls from hell, it was something much more miraculous than what I planned to do with DreamNopolis, although if it worked out, it would be extraordinary to have living NPCs when I bring in the lucid dreamers.

- But how do we know it will work out? And how do we know which souls have already served their sentences? - I asked him.

Asmodeus laughed and snapped his fingers, and thousands and thousands of cabinets with huge drawers that looked almost like buildings, began to descend from the sky until nearly everywhere was filled with them.

- Choose one, it will be your first test - Asmodeus said, pointing to the various cabinets that were full of folders with papers that looked like the documents I had been given in the first work with the summary of the soul's life.

I looked at the cabinets and noticed that there were several labels with Roman numerals that seemed to identify the century of the folders inside, there were so many cabinets and labels that it seemed impossible to decide which one to choose.

- Come on, make your choice - said Asmodeus.

- Once I pick one, what will happen? - I asked him.

- I will summon that soul, but it will remember only its last cycle, that is, its last life on earth, it will also remember the torture it went through in hell, for only at the moment of reincarnation are the memories hidden - said Asmodeus.

- So what am I going to tell this soul? How will I convince him to participate in the mission and have a role in DreamNopolis? - I asked him.

- I still don't know how it will work, that's why we need to test it, I don't know what will happen when we do something like this, in fact I don't even know how we will do it, I just suggested this idea because it seemed to fit the solution to the problem we need to solve. How to do it, that part I leave to you, we from hell have tried almost everything to make these souls reincarnate or go to purgatory - said Asmodeus.

While Asmodeus was talking, I kept looking through the cupboards until I accidentally found a folder with the name F. Nietzsche.

- I never thought he would be here - I said aloud.

- It seems that this whole "God is dead" thing didn't go down too well in heaven - Asmodeus replied with a ironic chuckle.

So it was Nietzsche, without much patience to look at the others, I chose that soul.

- Interesting, so let's go, if you succeed with this one I think the others will be a piece of cake - said Asmodeus taking the folder and proceeding to conjure the soul.

He threw the folder on the floor and with his fingernails scratched some symbols around it, when he finished he said some strange words and moments later Nietzsche's soul had appeared above the folder, floating, transparent with blue lights around it.

- What do I do now? - I asked.

- Now it's up to you, get the folder and the soul will follow you, it may take a while for him to come to his senses and start talking, take him to DreamNopolis, as soon as you hear from him come back to get more souls and tell me about your progress, you still have a lot of work to do - Asmodeus said.

I bent down, picked up the folder and Nietzsche's soul followed me, just as Asmodeus said it would, the portal with the symbols reappeared and then I returned to DreamNopolis, but this time with a soul.

I returned to DreamNopolis with one of the greatest thinkers mankind had ever had, he had gone through hell, served his sentence and still withstood all the years of waiting to continue his cycle by reincarnating.

- Mr. Nietzsche, welcome to DreamNopolis - I told him, trying to get that soul to show some reaction.

Nothing!

I put the folder on top of the sofa and then he sat down, I continued.

- As I understand, you were in hell and served your entire sentence, you were supposed to reincarnate, but for some reason those condemned to hell stopped reincarnating - I said, explaining to him what had happened.

It didn't seem to have an effect, but seconds later for the first time I saw him making a different expression, his eyebrows raised and for a brief moment his head tilted slightly to the side, as if my words had brought him back.

- You don't need to explain something I already know - Nietzsche said, still sitting without directly looking at me.

- I'm not trying to explain, in fact I would like explanations - I answered him, and this time, for the first time, he turned around and really looked at me.

- Are we still in hell? I can't even remember the last time I talked to someone, are you really real? - said Nietzsche, still rambling and coming to his senses.

I didn't interrupt him.

- It's interesting how they say that when we reincarnate we will lose the memory of this self, which until then is the self I remember always being. Why do we lose our memory after going through a sentence and serving it? Does this make any sense to you? I don't think it matters anymore, "GOD IS NOT DEAD" - said Nietzsche starting to shout.

- "GOD IS NOT DEAD" - he said.

- "GOD IS NOT DEAD" - he said.

- GOD IS NOT DEAD" - he said.

I tried to calm him down and when he stopped screaming I said the last thing before he went back to his previous vegetative state.

- God is not dead and we need to find him - I said, closing Nietzsche.

I tried to interact and get him out of that state again, but the most I could do was to waste my time, as he continued to stare vacantly into the distance.

Even being in that state I managed to get him to follow me wherever I wanted, I took him to see the city and during our walks he sometimes started to mumble and say some of his famous phrases.

He didn't seem to hear me and I didn't even know if he spoke during the walks because of me, I couldn't wake him up in any way, but

I could feel that as the days went by he seemed to begin to recover in DreamNopolis.

A few more days passed and then Bill came back to visit me.

I told him everything that had happened in my visit to Asmodeus and also showed him Nietzsche, he loved Asmodeus' idea to populate DreamNopolis using the souls from hell that should have been reincarnated and already paid for their sins - Bill wanted to turn the city into his perfect RPG.

Between Bill's comings and goings the days went by in DreamNopolis and finally Nietzsche seemed to improve, so it was time to test how Nietzsche would react to having a real body leaving his ghost form the same way the students did in the missions we created around town.

I put the folder in the cabin the students used and moments later Nietzsche and I were teleported to the location we selected from the mission and he had a body.

Nietzsche looked down at his hands, filling his lungs with air as if he hadn't taken a breath in a long time.

- Are you all right? Nietzsche? Do you remember me? - I asked him.

He didn't answer right away, he looked around, he watched as if he didn't quite understand what had happened.

- Am I alive? - asked Nietzsche.

I thought hard about what to tell him, but there was no easy answer.

- You are in the dream world, in the city DreamNopolis, remember we talked about this before? I took you out of hell, I'm trying to help you come to your senses so that you don't become a creature from hell - I told him without getting closer.

- It is much easier to reason when you have your five senses again - said Nietzsche.

- We are on a mission I created inside the city, which allows you to stop being just a soul. Glad it's working, are you feeling better? - I asked him again.

- A little. I don't want to go back to being a spirit, I don't want to go back to hell - Nietzsche said, a little agitated.

- You are not going back there, but when the mission is over you will go back to being a soul, but you will be able to return to the mission whenever you want, meanwhile I will try to create a definitive form so that you will have your body when you are in the city.

I resumed talking to him for a while longer as the mission was ending. I just wanted to calm him down and show him that he could trust me.

After the mission was over, I returned to the cabin to pick him up and he was a soul again, but unlike before, Nietzsche was now aware of what was happening around him.

- I want a body - Nietzsche repeated as soon as he saw me.

I was happy to see him improving, conscious, and asking for a body, so I immediately picked up his folder and took him to the house where the computer that controlled DreamNopolis was.

On the way I tried to explain to him about the rules, missions and the programs I had developed in the computer to control the city, after talking a lot and assuming he understood what I was explaining, we arrived home and he asked me.

- What is a computer? - asked Nietzsche, tearing away my famous smile.

I forgot that I was talking to an ancient soul who, besides not knowing much about the present world, was still recovering from a long season in hell.

I explained to him in a simpler way so that he would understand what that machine - the computer - was doing or could do in the city.

Nietzsche after having a body again and feeling alive was very agitated, he no longer needed me to get around and now conscious, he could take his own folder and go wherever he wanted, so I left him free to walk while I concentrated again on the computer.

I spent several days in front of the computer until I created a new application, but when I clicked to start it the following message appeared, "The 3D printer must be connected to the device for the application to run.

Of course, for the program that would create the bodies for souls from hell to work, it was going to need a way to do so.

I started immediately after the message to build this 3D printer as well, it had to be very big, because the bodies of the residents of DreamNopolis would come out of it.

There, after finishing the construction of the printer, which was almost three meters high and looked like one of those machines from Star Trek, I started the application again on the computer.

This time when the printer connected to the computer was recognized, the application launched, but another message appeared on the screen, "Please insert the soul in the indicated place on the printer to configure the body creation settings.

I asked Nietzsche to go up with his folder to the printer and as soon as he stood in the indicated place the application message disappeared and some lights came on in the printer.

Now on the application screen there was information about Nietzsche and also settings for creating his body, it was like those games that when you start a new game and have to create a character.

I could change both physical attributes, personality traits, and even Nietzsche's life story, but I had agreed with him that I would not change any of this, I would only change the request Nietzsche had made, to be a little taller, nothing exaggerated, he just wanted to feel taller, so I agreed and gave him an extra ten centimeters of height.

I fulfilled our agreement even though I had in my hands the opportunity to erase his memory and mold him the way I wanted. I went through the settings screens for history, missions, personality, and physique without making any changes, except for the height. It was the last screen of the application before starting the creation of the body for Nietzsche, on this screen it was necessary to define the permission that that body would have in DreamNopolis, having the permissions visitor, resident, master and administrator, I defined that he would have the resident permission and after selecting it, the button called "start creation" that was disabled was enabled and then I finally clicked on it.

On the computer screen the message "Creation started, estimated time to finish: undetermined" appeared and moments later the printer started making noise while working.

The printing would take longer than I imagined, while Nietzsche was at the printer Bill visited us, but he woke up again returning to the real world before the printing was finished.

Two days had passed and nothing, I looked at the computer screen again and this time the message read "Creation started, estimated time for completion: twenty-four hours".

Although now at least I knew the estimated time to finish, I couldn't stand waiting there any longer, so I decided that while the printer was finishing Nietzsche, I would go to Asmodeus to give him some information, ask how my rescue was going and get other souls for new tests.

I went back to hell, but this time Asmodeus was not in Sodom, it was another place, some kind of mountain or hill with a long stairway to reach the small cathedral at the top.

I started to climb the stairs until I reached the top and as soon as I reached the last step I could see Asmodeus, he seemed to be meditating, I approached him and as soon as I got close he opened his eyes.

- I was waiting for you to come back, do we have news? - Asmodeus asked.

- I need more souls to test some things - I told him.

- More souls? And the last one you took? What happened to it?
- Asmodeus asked again.

- He is getting a body right now, I managed to create a way to create a body for the souls that have already passed their sentences in hell and make them residents of DreamNopolis - I answered him.

- Um... Very good, you can get some more souls - Asmodeus said, invoking again the thousands of folders with souls.

This time I chose the folders of five hippies from the sixties who had been given the most lenient sentence in hell for driving after consuming prohibited substances and being responsible for a big car accident that killed innocent people and themselves.

After selecting the souls, I questioned Asmodeus about my rescue in the real world, but he just said that first I should do my part and then he would do his part. I returned his unwillingness not telling him any details about what I could do with the souls, I just said that I had managed to create a body for them.

I returned to DreamNopolis and immediately went to see how Nietzsche was doing, if the application was finished and he now had a body.

I went to the computer room and the application had already finished, but there was no one there, I looked at the printer and there was nothing there but the folder with papers, I went back to the computer, opened the DreamNopolis radar application to see if I could find anything, for a brief moment I was afraid that something had gone wrong and had destroyed Nietzsche's soul, but when I saw on the radar application three markings around the city, I was calmer.

Two markings were nearby and another a little further away, the solo marking was mine, the others that were nearby were Bill's and Nietzsche's.

I went there and found Bill outside the clothing store, he said that Nietzsche was talking, excited and choosing new clothes.

- These current clothes are very different from how I imagined them to be - said Nietzsche, wearing sneakers and brand-name clothes that didn't suit him at all.

- Are you feeling well?

- I am, although the size of my foot is a little strange with this new height, but I think I can live with it - said Nietzsche laughing and making us laugh.

We continued all afternoon in the shopping mall walking around the stores and trying to introduce things that Nietzsche didn't know until Bill returned to the real world.

We went back to the computer room and the souls of the hippies were still standing there, motionless without saying anything.

I told Nietzsche about the plan to populate DreamNopolis by giving new life to the souls that were trapped in hell, and explained to him that it would be easier if they didn't remember their past life or what they had gone through in hell, that is, they would have memories and motivations created so that they would not know that this was the world of dreams. He didn't say anything, just reaffirmed his will to stay the way he was and where he was.

Before creating the five new residents, I created what would be the basic story of DreamNopolis to create the stories, missions, memories and motivations of its inhabitants, the five would be like rulers of certain regions of the city, they would have a story and from this they would follow the path they decided, but at the same time they would be participating in the city's missions as NPCs without even knowing it.

The base story of DreamNopolis for the residents would be:

A city started by seven families that after banished from their homeland, wandered lost at sea for a long time until they landed by accident on the island of DreamNopolis, these families upon arriving on the island decided to stay there, thus dividing the territories where each family would be responsible for a certain resource production, these productions would be used as trade / barter between families to survive, prosper and evolve the island, so they can live harmoniously among themselves. Initially there would also be no currency, no politics, no government and no police, but as time went by and with the development of DreamNopolis, some families ended up having their productions considered more important than the productions of other families and this led to conflicts and envy causing wars between them, which caused two of the seven families to become extinct and their less important productions to be taken over by all families and later traded with foreigners who also formed new families and ended up staying in DreamNopolis. Today the city is well developed and most of its inhabitants know about the division of territories of the city's matriarch families, who built the city by warring, conspiring and trying to dominate each other's territories over the years.

With the base story of DreamNopolis done, I now needed to use the five souls from hell to create the last descendants of the city's matriarch families who would officially be the first residents made from scratch in DreamNopolis.

I placed the first soul in the giant 3D printer, opened the program to create that soul's body, personality and missions. It was the same program I had used with Nietzsche, but this time I would reset the memories and personality from the last cycle of these souls and then create the citizens of DreamNopolis.

The first decision would be which gender - male or female - to set for that soul, after defining the gender, the next choices would be about size, ethnicity and details of the eyes, face, hands, legs, feet and everything else you can imagine being possible to do in a character creation.

I defined the first one to be an old, Italian-looking man with a big nose and an enviable beer belly, I moved on to the part of giving him a name and defining the personality of this new DreamNopolis inhabitant.

Thomas Camorra, the mafioso responsible for the commercial part of the city center, descendant of the Camorra family, also inherited the wine fields located to the southwest. If someone wanted to open any commerce in the city center it was necessary that the Camorras knew about it and that the partnership fee was duly paid every month, in addition the family produced the best wines in the city.

I wouldn't control them or tell them what they would do, I just gave them a base story since they wouldn't be a newborn to get their story from the beginning, so I created their bodies, personalities and included the missions they would participate in or know details of to inform the participants of the missions, from then on, when the bodies were created their souls would be on their own, they had free will although their decisions were based on the stories they received, but they could still live and choose what they wanted and were no longer trapped in hell.

I created the other four profiles (other heads of family):

Samanta Groudet or Madam Groudet, which is the way she likes to be called the most, ever since she was a little girl she followed her family in the famous Petals brothel located in the southern part of the city, she learned from her grandmother Margaret Groudet, one of the most powerful women in DreamNopolis, how to manage both the issues related to the mercenaries in her brothel, that go in search of any type of work, as well as controlling the show houses in the south zone that the family owned, besides owning an old gold mine where they extracted everything from gold to precious gems, although nowadays the mine is inactive and hardly explored.

Alder Lopes is a farmer, owner of the biggest meat processing plant and butcher shop in town, his farms and business are located further north in DreamNopolis, during his education he studied in the same school as some other heirs of the other families, Alder had an affair with Samanta Groudet, but it didn't end very well, this affair makes the two hate each other to this day generating unnecessary disputes between them in business, although some say that whenever disputes meet a dead end for both sides, the two get together and from there a temporary peace is sealed until the next conflict occurs.

Silvano Dantas, heir to the Dantas family, like the others, was guided by his family to take responsibility for running the family's lumber, carpentry and joinery business, the Dantas are responsible for most of the deforestation in the eastern territory of DreamNopolis, but Silvano, the youngest of the Dantas, is a little more environmentally conscious than his predecessors, He had to convince the other heirs to make small areas of their territory available for him to use, so that he could keep the city's production going while he recovered his land, and then return to logging with more awareness this time.

Tarcisio Mendes, the last of his lineage and who, besides inheriting the genes of intelligence, ingenuity and capabilities of the Mendes, could build and produce in bulk anything that was proposed to him. For this reason, when he inherited the factories on the west side of DreamNopolis from his family he guaranteed to put these factories in motion at maximum capacity, guaranteeing everything from textile production to the technological productions necessary for the city.

With all five profiles ready it was now time to finalize the physical details of the bodies before starting the printing of all five, but before that I decided to make the simple population of DreamNopolis before releasing the bosses around the city, so once again I decided to go to Asmodeus to get more souls.

I explained to Asmodeus what I had done with the souls and what I planned to do with the inhabitants and the history of the city, he seemed excited about the idea and so he didn't make it difficult for me to bring more souls, so this time I took lockers full of souls that were enough to create the initial population of DreamNopolis.

Back in DreamNopolis now was the task of creating inhabitant by inhabitant, one by one, this was necessary so that the city would really be diverse and have a life of its own, unlike the other generic worlds that existed in games and in the other dream worlds.

I would need to create from the most complex inhabitant to the simplest inhabitant, so I started first by creating a priest.

<u>Father Miguel</u>, responsible for taking care of the church and also the cemetery in the back of the property, grew up in DreamNopolis and is the first priest in his family, he was raised by a very strict father and a mother who loved him very much, but who was not strong enough to go against her husband the times he came home drunk and attacked the child, for many times his father did not understand why his son was a quiet child and preferred to stay at home with his mother instead of going out with his father.

I created the past and the very detailed personality for Father Miguel, it was only left to create his body and leave it around town for a while to see how that soul would react after having its memories erased and now having a new personality. After the creation of the body was finished, he was still unconscious, so before he woke up I took his body to his room which was attached to the church next to the cemetery.

I didn't know how long it would take for him to wake up, so I stayed inside the church sitting on the back bench while I waited until he woke up.

I waited for so many hours that I thought I should go home and make new inhabitants, then suddenly I felt a tap on my shoulder, the priest had appeared, he was standing next to me with his hand on my shoulder.

- Good morning my son, is there something I can do for you? - said Father Miguel.

- Good morning Father, I'm fine, thank God, I just dropped by to have a chat with the Almighty - I said to him pretending to be in prayer for God.

- There is no one better to talk to than the Lord - answered the priest, staring at me as if he was hoping to get an amen.

- Amen - I told him after realizing that this was what he wanted.

- Amen! - said the priest as well.

- Stay as long as you like my son, I have some work to do in the church garden and I can't find the sisters or the gravedigger. I'll leave you in peace now, if you need to go to confession I'll be in the confessional early tomorrow morning - said Father Miguel leaving towards the back of the church.

I still had a lot of things to check, but I decided not to force the situation since so far the priest seemed perfectly normal, his personality was like that of a priest like any other, even nicer than usual. So I went back to the computer and spent the next few days creating the other DreamNopolis residents.

I used the priest as a central point of the inhabitants I was creating, that is, I added the sisters who helped him take care of the church, the gravedigger who took care of the cemetery, the new worshipers who attended the church, the merchants, and all the other inhabitants of the town.

Whenever an inhabitant was ready and woke up, the other inhabitants that had already been created got memories about that inhabitant, it was as if the history that the inhabitants had lived through together was automatically inserted into everyone, so that when they met in the city they remembered the stories that shaped their personalities as if they were memories they had already lived through, thus all the inhabitants alike had links that shaped their personalities - memories - remembered each other even though they had never seen each other before. In this way every new inhabitant made sense of the history of the other residents of DreamNopolis.

I created Bakers, Teachers, Doctors, Firemen, Policemen, Shopkeepers, and all the rest of the normal citizens that every town needs. Between the creation of one and another Bill appeared sometimes, when he found out what I was doing he also wanted to give some tips on the personalities of the new inhabitants, he wanted as always to give his eccentric touch here and there, he suggested that the butcher Marcio, better known as Marcinho, was a cuckold and there was a mission that if some conditions were met his wife would cheat on him and when he found out he would freak out and become the city' s serial butcher killer.

I continued to create each of the residents in detail, with no sloppiness, giving life, sincerity and personality to everyone in DreamNopolis.

I lost track of time and no longer knew how much time had passed since I started creating them. With each new resident it became evident that what I was doing had its price, I was getting tired, opening my mouth and at one point I nearly let myself sleep, but I couldn't do that, I was already in the dream world and I couldn't sleep inside another dream, that would be too dangerous according to the rules, even more so sleeping inside a dream as complex as DreamNopolis had become, that would surely be the end for me.

The creation needed some time, so I stopped for a while and went out to see how the city was doing, to my surprise, as I left the house and walked a few blocks through the streets, I could see that the place no longer seemed as lonely as before, DreamNopolis had now come to life and everything was better than I had imagined.

The city was in full swing, I went into one of the barbershops and trimmed my hair and beard, besides the customers there were also old men reading newspapers, the barbers and hairdressers. I also passed by the market and everything was also working perfectly, the inhabitants were shopping, the vendors were selling, the beggars were begging and the children were having fun with their parents while shopping.

I visited all the territories and confirmed the workings of the city and the people, there were still three things I needed to do, to enable the lucid dreamers - living people - to visit the city, I also needed to release the five heirs - heads of territories - and bring Asmodeus so that he could see all that advance in the city.

I went back to the computer again and the first thing I did was to enable the real world lucid dreamers to get to DreamNopolis, but I inserted a lock so that initially only three people could enter, after doing this, I left the bodies of the five heirs being printed and went to Asmodeus to tell him about all my progress and invite him to check out the city.

I went back to hell and this time Asmodeus was again at the bar in Sodom, I approached him and again he seemed to be waiting for me.

- You look excited - said Asmodeus.

- Do I? - I retorted.

- Excited, but also exhausted - insisted Asmodeus.

- Maybe it's because my immortal body has been buried somewhere for so long - I answered him.

- Yes, maybe it is. Are you here to chat? Tell me what you want this time? - Asmodeus asked.

- The city is working, I created the inhabitants with the Souls, and they seem very normal and happy. They think they are living in the real world - I told him.

He didn't show any reaction and continued to drink whatever he was drinking, so I kept talking.

- I am about to do another test, Bill and I are thinking about releasing the city to the real world lucid dreamers as well. If they succeed the city is full of quests and possibilities that most people won't have the opportunity to do in real life but could do in DreamNopolis - I continued talking to him.

This time he changed his facial expression a little, but still remained silent.

- Would you like to come and see how everything is? This was my part of the deal, now it's your turn to fulfill your part, you have to meet me in the real world before my energy runs out and I end up sleeping inside my own dream - I put my cards on the table telling him the truth and playing all my last chips.

- I was beginning to think that you wouldn't invite me to see how everything had turned out, if everything is really fine I will do my part, but don't think that your work is over, this is just the tip of the iceberg - said Asmodeus, getting up to go to DreamNopolis.

I got up and the portal appeared again so we could go back to the city.

We arrived in DreamNopolis and this time seeing the living city Asmodeus couldn't hide his excitement, but I didn't want to provoke him, so I kept quiet.

- So what do you want to do? - I asked him.

- I don't need a babysitter, go do whatever you want to do and let me see how faithful to the real world we managed to get in DreamNopolis - Asmodeus said, flagging down a taxi and asking the driver to start driving, as he needed a tour of the city.

It wasn't quite what I expected, but I didn't see a problem with Asmodeus walking around the city, after all, the city now had life, and he had also contributed a little to it.

Back in the computer room, the bodies of the five heirs were no longer there, I had no idea how they had wandered off on their own, so I went out into the city looking for where they might be. I couldn't find them on the block, so I built one of those Jetpack backpacks that you can fly around with, I went up and headed north, since I was in the south of the city, while going up and forward I could see a cloud of smoke and a path of destruction through the city street heading north, using binoculars - which I also built at the time - I could see the firemen in their car trying to put out the flames that were spreading through the gas station on the way.

I approached the place dodging the cloud of smoke and trying to find out what had happened there, but before I landed I could see from a distance a car also on fire desperately fleeing. I gave up going down to the gas station, so I quickly moved up again and headed towards the car that was fleeing.

I was not the only one chasing the car, the police officers had begun their pursuit as well, due to the proportion of all that mess it was very likely that a helicopter would show up there in a few minutes, so I continued towards them trying to stop all that mess and solve that problem, but I could not catch them at that speed, I had to follow the trajectory they were taking - still heading north - and take some shortcuts to get close to the car. The route they were taking would take them through the Amsterdam neighborhood where the large trees would help them hide, making air pursuit by me or the police impossible.

I finally approached the car and as I did so I could see that there were six people inside the car, they were the five heirs and next to them was Bill. As soon as they saw me, Thomas Camorra tried to throw the car at me, but it didn't work and they almost lost control of the car with the maneuver he attempted. I signaled for them to pull the car over, but I was ignored and Thomas accelerated the car even more causing me to fall behind again.

I went up a little further, kept going as they made a few turns until I caught up with them once again.

- Pull the car over Bill - I shouted at him.

- They don't want to stop, we're going to Alder's farm, meet us there - Bill shouted as the car slowed down and another of the heirs pulled out a gun and pointed it at me.

I backed away so as not to get shot and stopped chasing them, after all, now I knew where they were going.

I didn't expect Bill to be there with them, although that didn't surprise me, so I set a new course through the air and continued north towards the farm where they were headed, so I could beat them to it.

After a few minutes of waiting, their car arrived and as soon as they saw me standing in front of the house, they parked the car and got out taking a hostage, it was Bill, who seemed to be enjoying being the hostage, even though he had a gun pointed at his head.

- Who are you? Don't come any closer or we'll shoot him - said Tarcísio, getting out of the car with Bill as a hostage.

- I'm not after you, I just want my friend - I answered them.

- You haven't answered our question - said Madam Groudet.

- My name is Charles, I've been living in town for a short time and I don't want any trouble - I answered them again.

- Kill these two sons of bitches - shouted Thomas Camorra to Tarcísio and Alder, who were the ones with guns.

Bill seemed to enjoy the whole thing and before I could think of anything to say, the son of a bitch headbutted back and started his escape based on the Hollywood movies he had seen, but it didn't work, as soon as he got rid of Tarcísio, he tried to get the gun by rolling on the ground, but as soon as he rolled he was shot several times and thus disappeared, that is, he woke up.

The heirs were perplexed when they saw Bill had disappeared in front of their eyes and were paralyzed in disbelief not understanding what was happening.

Seeing them paralyzed and unable to understand, I decided to try something.

- Guys, I can try to explain what happened, but I need you to calm down and talk to me - I said to the heirs.

Alder dropped his gun and everyone approached me.

- How many people from somewhere other than DreamNopolis do you know? - I started by asking them.

They stood there for a while thinking and didn't say anything until Madam Groudet spoke up.

- Just you and your friend - said Madam Groudet.

- What does this have to do with the five most important people in DreamNopolis waking up naked in that house? None of us remember getting there - said Camorra.

- Let him talk, don't you want to know what happened to the guy who was shot and evaporated in front of us? Be quiet! Let's at least hear what he has to say - said Madam Groudet asking me to continue.

- DreamNopolis is a city in the world of dreams, you are souls that have served their sentence in hell, but cannot reincarnate because Lucifer is no longer in charge of hell. I work for hell and I am the creator of this place, you are living here because the souls that wait too long in hell end up becoming monsters - I told them the whole truth knowing they would not believe me.

- Ha Ha Ha Ha! This guy must be pulling our leg - said Alder as he picked up the gun from the ground and pointed it at me again.

Since just talking wouldn't help, as soon as Alder picked up the gun, I made it turn into a baseball, which scared everyone immediately and made Alder drop the ball.

- But how... how did you do that? - asked Alder.

- I am trying to tell you something that no one else in town knows, will you listen to me or will I have to reset your memory? - I told them, already out of patience for all of this, because I was exhausted.

They fell silent again, so I spoke.

- Nobody in the city is controlled, you can do whatever you want, but the tourists when they are killed go back to the real world, because they are living people who can control their dreams, so they visit DreamNopolis to do the things they can't do in the real world - I continued explaining.

- Are you saying that we are not real? That all our memories are false? That this is not the real world? - asked Tarcísio Mendes.

- What I am trying to tell you is that we are in the dream world, but as far as I know that doesn't stop you from feeling alive as if you were in the real world. And I can assure you that this is much better than being in hell waiting and becoming a monster. For us who live in DreamNopolis everything here is real, especially for you who only remember this life and don't remember the torture you suffered in hell - I answered them.

- But that doesn't explain how we woke up naked in that house and who this guy is who disappeared when he was shot - Camorra insisted.

- You just woke up in DreamNopolis, until yesterday you were in hell. That house is where I'm living, the guy who disappeared is a friend of mine who comes here all the time - I explained to him so that he would stop insisting on this subject.

- You mean that all that we remember living and who we are is a lie? - asked Tarcísio again.

I knew that most people would not stand for the truth, so I just lied about that.

- No, you really lived through all that, only before DreamNopolis was in a physical state, because while I was creating the city you were living all that you experienced in a reality that was not physical - I said, deceiving them.

- My head hurts, after all what does it all mean? - asked Silvano Dantas looking confused and unable to understand much of anything.

- Nothing has changed, you can live and still do whatever you want, I just told you this because of the confusion that ended up happening due to Bill having woken you up in the wrong way. If you want I can erase this from your memory in case... - I was talking when I was interrupted.

- I don't know about you, but I've had enough of all this. I'm going back to my house, I hope to continue my life as if this day never happened and I don't want to see you ever again - said Camorra, taking the car and leaving immediately.

After Camorra left the others also dispersed, but before they all left, Madam Groudet asked me a few questions.

- So you work for hell and created this world as a quieter waiting room so that the souls who have served their sentences don't turn into monsters with the eternal wait that has been. Can you tell when we will actually be reincarnated into the real world? And what are you getting out of all this? - asked Madam Groudet.

- We are still working on this part about reincarnation, and concerning getting something, when I agreed to work for hell, I signed a contract, so I have to fulfill it - I answered them without going into too much detail.

After my answers the others left, I had the feeling that this should not have happened, but I thought it was better not to erase their memory.

Once again Bill had caused trouble where he shouldn't have and left without any remorse or consequence to him, for a moment I even forgot that Asmodeus was in town, but when I remembered I decided to go home and check the computer to see what he was doing, but I was surprised by him when I opened the door.

- So this is where the magic happens? - Asmodeus asked, already feeling at home.

- What are you doing here? - I asked, surprised, not imagining that he would be there.

- This city is on fire, and when I say this I mean it in the literal and figurative sense - said Asmodeus laughing as he mentioned the fact that the city was burning and pursues were everywhere.

- The city is alive! Isn't that what you wanted or what you imagined? - I answered him.

- I don't want you to get too full of yourself, but my friend, it is much better here than I could have imagined, and that is why I came to your house, to ask you for another, even stronger dose of reality - Asmodeus said, walking around like a crackhead - he didn't seem to understand how it all worked and didn't know what questions to ask.

- A stronger dose of reality? What do you mean by that? - I asked not understanding.

- Seeing you dictating what all people should do makes me a little paranoid, and also, when you are near, things seem even more real. I want to test the influx of people from the real world - Asmodeus said, confirming that he understood almost nothing about the city.

- You are wrong, I am not controlling them, I mean, I just programmed the inhabitants to do what they want, they are free and have unique personalities, I spent a lot of time creating all of them, I can imagine what they will do based on the life story I gave them, but the choices are theirs to make for themselves, the whole reality and life of DreamNopolis depends on it - I answered him.

- Interesting, I really wanted to confirm that this is how it works, but it doesn't change my order, let's now test the entrance of the dreamers from the real world - Asmodeus said in a different voice tone.

I didn't like his tone very much, but I let it go since in the end I depended on him keeping his word and taking me back to the real world to find where my body was buried.

- The access to DreamNopolis by invitation we already know works, but I have not yet been able to test what it would be like to activate DreamNopolis for any dreamer - I answered Asmodeus.

- But you said the inhabitants were ready, so why don't we test that part now and see what happens? If nothing happens I'll give you more time, but as soon as you get the city on the radar so that people start showing up our agreement will be enough for now for me, so I'll fulfill my part by doing what you want so much - Asmodeus said, playing his card.

In other situations I wouldn't agree to blackmail, but in this case I was feeling that I needed to recharge my batteries in the real world, and every moment there made me feel more and more exhausted. So I agreed with Asmodeus and went back to the computer to make some changes to DreamNopolis.

I opened the application again where I controlled some of the city settings and made a point of demanding that Asmodeus not stay so close, peeking at what I was doing, after much insistence, he agreed, but even so he continued watching from afar what I was doing, even though he didn't seem to understand anything.

I included in the program of the city a specific place, as an arrival point where the lucid dreamers would arrive, I limited it so that only one person from the real world would access for the test and I adjusted it so that this person would be a lucid dreamer, so when he/she got here he/she wouldn't be so easily scared.

Once the settings were done I clicked on the button that was written "Connect DreamNopolis to Morpheus directive" and after that nothing really that different happened.

We needed to wait and see if the setup for a lucid dreamer from the real world to find DreamNopolis uninvited worked.

We went to the place I had set for the dreamer to arrive, it was a few blocks from where we were and when we got there it didn't take long before a bright light appeared from the sky and fell towards us like a giant arrow. The light landed next to us, right where I had defined the arrival point. As soon as the light dissipated we could see who had arrived, it was a woman.

She was wearing what looked like Asian clothes, white with colorful flower prints, and she had very straight black hair and of course slanted eyes.

I swore I heard the first word in Mandarin or Japanese, but as soon as she came closer and spoke again, I could understand everything she said, even though she didn't speak my language and I knew nothing of her language.

- Where am I? - she said, coming closer and asking surprised where I was.

- Welcome to DreamNopolis, the city of lucid dreamers - Asmodeus said, flashing a wide smile.

- DreamNopolis? What's this? Another attempt of the dream demons to try to possess lucid dreamers? - said the Asian woman who seemed to know some about the dream world and the demons that try to possess the dreamers.

- Don't worry, demons don't enter here, it's a place never before seen in the dream world, after all you may never have heard of a city with real people living in it. DreamNopolis is like a video game in the dream world, feel free to visit, ask questions, explore, and even leave - said Asmodeus introducing the visitor.

- What is your name - I asked her.

- Sumi Nishiyama and what are your names? - asked Sumi.

- I am Leo and this is Charles - said Asmodeus before I could answer.

- Nice to meet you. Are you dreamers too? - said Sumi.

- Yes, but he is the creator of DreamNopolis - Asmodeus said, pointing at me.

- Wow, that's cool, I've met someone who could also create worlds inside dreams, but nothing like here, this place is incredibly real, if you had told me this was the real world, maybe I would have believed - said Sumi.

- Where are you from? - I asked her.

- I am from the city of Wakayama in Japan, and I am a yoga and martial arts instructor - answered Sumi.

- I bet she would like that martial arts championship mission you created, Charles - Asmodes told her.

- No spoilers, don't tell her about the missions yet, don't influence her choice, let her explore and choose the mission she wants - I told them.

- True, I was also hoping for some company to get to know the city better, since it's not so fun to get to know the city with the creator, Sumi, would you like to explore the city with me? - said Asmodeus to her.

- Sure, I'd love to see the place - said Sumi, looking excited and no longer as suspicious as before.

Asmodeus managed to get rid of me again. I wanted to accompany them, but he was very convincing and ended up getting her to agree to explore only the two of them.

Hours later, while I was following them on the computer radar, I noticed that the little yellow balls that represented the normal residents of the city, began to cluster around the little blue ball that represented Asmodeus, along with the green one that represented the lucid dreamers of the real world on the radar.

From the radar I couldn't tell what was going on and so once again I put on my Jetpack and went over there. They were in the martial arts mission arena and there was a huge Asian party going on around the arena and all around the place. I went down there and asked one of the people enjoying the event what was going on, so I found out that the final of the martial arts tournament was about to happen and the most surprising thing was that the final fight was between Sumi, versus the last winner of the tournament, Jin Lee.

I entered the arena and there weren't many seats available, so since I couldn't find any place to sit I disguised myself as a referee of the fight to watch it as closely as I could.

It was a great fight and the decision was defined by the referees - WINK - in the end Sumi's narrow victory made it even more delightful for her. The new DreamNopolis martial arts champion couldn't hide her happiness.

At the end of the fight I left the arena taking off my disguise and went to where Asmodeus was.

We waited in the backstage until Sumi reappeared with a broad smile on her face.

- I won, I won - she said, running up to us with the trophy and medal in her hand.

- Congratulations, you deserved to win with more lead on points - Asmodeus said and gave me a look as if to say that he realized I was one of the referees.

- Congratulations Sumi, it was a great fight - I told her.

She was very excited, we went to celebrate at a snack bar nearby, when Sumi said she was starving.

- I didn't think I would feel hungry in a dream, nor that I would lose track of time, how long has it been since I arrived? - asked Sumi as we sat down at the table and waited for the waitress.

The waitress arrived and took our orders, but before she could bring our food, Sumi disappeared, probably waking up in her bed.

- Oh! Pity, I was beginning to like her, but I'm glad it happened, I was also wondering how long it would take or if it would take a bullet for her to leave - said Asmodeus with his normal tone of voice and look back.

I preferred not to answer him since the waitress had just returned with our order.

- Since we're here, I don't see why we should waste this afternoon snack - Asmodeus continued while enjoying our snack.

I hadn't eaten in a long time, so I decided to join him for a meal, and just as we were about to finish, Asmodeus spoke again.

- The details of your city are amazing, even the taste of the food is strikingly the same as the real world. Now that we have tested the arrival of dreamers from the real world, you can release it for others to see, we can turn DreamNopolis into whatever we want, it will be crazy ... - Asmodeus said, when he realized he was speaking out loud, and pulled himself together.

- But before we release it we need to make adjustments, the dreamers can't keep evaporating around, it would be better if they were killed their bodies stayed dead on the ground and if they just woke up, their bodies didn't disappear instantly - Asmodeus said.

- I was already thinking about this, I need to make some adjustments and do some more tests. I need to solve the problem of some souls that disappeared, when Bill shot some souls they vanished, I even tried to see if the souls returned to the folder or if I could use them to create other people, but the souls that die in DreamNopolis by real world mortals disappear? - I was saying, when I was interrupted.

- What! The souls haven't returned to the folder and you don't know where they are? When were you going to tell me this? Just tell me the names of the missing folders - Asmodeus said.

- It's a big city, with only a few days of operation many souls have died and been born - I answered him.

- Born? - asked Asmodeus, looking perplexed.

- Yes, I left the souls that were not yet used to be born as blank souls in DreamNopolis, so that I would not have so much trouble writing the next stories and personalities, these souls would have a unique story and their personalities would be formed by their parents and with the passage of years in the city - I answered him.

- I need to know the name of one of the souls that disappeared - Asmodeus insisted.

We had to go back to my house to get the folders with the names of the people who died, and as soon as we arrived I took the folders of the souls that died in DreamNopolis and gave them to him.

- I only need one - Asmodeus said, getting rid of the others and taking one in his hand.

With the folder in his hand he spoke a few words and repeated them over and over, but nothing happened.

- Damn, I can't use any magic in DreamNopolis, we have to go back to hell and you come with me - said Asmodeus.

I called the gate to get us back to hell, and as we went through, we returned to Sodom.

Asmodeus went back to reciting the words and performing the magic he said.

- I can't believe it, you're a genius - Asmodeus stood up, his eyes sparkling after reciting the magic words on his knees.

- What happened? - I asked him in surprise.

- The soul is in purgatory, it is no longer our responsibility and probably now it will be able to follow its normal cycle - said Asmodeus smiling.

- But why is taking these souls out of hell so important? - I asked him.

- I thought you were smart enough to figure out the answer - Asmodeus said without answering my question and frowning again.

- I have my suspicions, but I wanted to hear them from you - I questioned him again.

- You saw some of the monsters with your own eyes, but you haven't seen any of the monsters that manage to escape into the real world, these are much stronger and more evolved, the problems they cause not only for humanity but for both sides of the coin (heaven and hell) are incalculable - Asmodeus answered.

- How so? - I asked again.

- No more questions, you never answered what would happen to DreamNopolis if you woke up - Asmodeus said.

- DreamNopolis doesn't need me to be asleep to exist, if that's your concern, to continue existing and in order, I just need to be well, and that's increasingly getting out of reach, I feel like my sanity is hanging by a thread and I'm almost asleep inside DreamNopolis and if that happened, I couldn't tell you what would become of the city - I answered him.

Asmodeus walked back and forth thoughtfully, and just as I was about to ask him about our deal, he spoke again.

- I think it's time I fulfilled my part of the bargain, give me a few days and I will see to it that you are found, go back to DreamNopolis and don't try too hard, don't even think about falling asleep, I imagine this is happening because you need to recharge your energy in the real world. All the effort you have been making in the city must be sucking your energy, after all, staying only in the dream world has its price. Try to think about how to resolve those points I told you, close the connection to the city until you hear from me, come back here in two weeks from the time of DreamNopolis, I believe that by then I will have news about your rescue - said Asmodeus practically sending me away and turning his back while leaving.

I returned to DreamNopolis a bit more excited about the promise that Asmodeus would finally locate my body, in the meantime I needed to find the solution to the lucid dreamers' bodies that vanish when they die or when they return to the real world after waking up.

Back in front of the computer I made some changes, but I needed another lucid dreamer to run tests on - where was Bill when you needed him - I waited for some time until he appeared again.

- You didn't tell me that if I got shot I would wake up - said Bill, complaining as usual.

- I need to test something - I told him, shooting him with no explanation as I knew he would ask a lot of stupid questions.

I shot him in the middle of his forehead and now yes, there was a way to test the adjustments I had made and they looked great.

Bill's body was scattered all over the room with his brain, and everything seemed too real to be worth the trouble it would take to clean it all up.

While he didn't return to DreamNopolis I started to clean the place up and just before I finished Bill returned and when he saw that I was wiping his brains off on the floor, he ran into the bathroom and vomited.

- Ha Ha Ha Ha! Are you grossed out? - I debauched him for throwing up on something from the dream world.

- It's not that, it's not every day you find yourself blown up on the floor. Are you done yet? - asked Bill from the bathroom.

- I'm done, all that's left to do is dispose of the body - I told him as I dragged the body to the back yard of the house to bury it.

Having solved the problem of the body when he was killed, I now needed to test what would happen when he woke up, so we stayed around town talking for hours, I even had to tell him in detail what happened to the heirs after he was shot and woke up.

I was telling him about Sumi, when out of the blue his head suddenly bobbed up and down as if he were taking a nap, so he got up and said he was going to the bathroom and didn't come back from there, when I went to look for him he had disappeared, in other words, I was also able to test the setting for when the dreamers woke up, in case this happened their bodies would stay materialized for some time and would only disappear when there was no one around watching.

The few days that Asmodeus requested to learn of my rescue had passed, and since I had managed to solve the problems he had pointed out, I went to him again.

I went through the portal one more time and returned to hell, it was not Sodom, I had returned to the corridor full of doors, the place where souls were tortured. The previous times I was teleported to where Asmodeus was, but this time I couldn't see him, and besides, there were thousands of doors where he could be, but before I could open any door to look for him, one of the next doors opened and Asmodeus came out of it.

- Well, well, well, I was waiting for you, come with me, let's talk somewhere else - Asmodeus said as he exited the door and walked straight ahead through the corridor of infinite doors.

I considered saying something, but decided to wait and just accompany him so that we could talk in this other place.

We walked and walked and walked, until I lost my patience and said.

- Where are we going? Are we never going to get there? - I said irritated.

- Calm down, we are almost there - answered Asmodeus calmly.

As we walked, the doors that were left behind seemed to be the same ones that appeared in front of us, the infinite corridor seemed endless and the more we walked, the more it seemed that it wasn't us who were going fast but the doors that were now passing us moving backwards. I could no longer see the doors on our side, they were just shadows that kept speeding past us down the hall. At one point, I could no longer tell if it was us who were walking or if we were just falling into an endless hole of door shadows, but suddenly these shadows started to rotate and merged into a single shape of a door shimmering in front of us.

- Aren't you coming? - said Asmodeus before opening the door and walking through it.

I entered right behind him.

We had arrived in a super fancy room with leather furniture, pool table, bar, but with some people's heads hanging on the walls, just like the animal heads that hunters put in their rooms. I kept looking at them and the heads looked static, like stuffed animals, I didn't recognize any of them and when Asmodeus said something, I didn't hear him properly, because I was too astonished by the amount of heads hanging on the walls of that room, so he said it again.

- Charles! Hey, Charles - Asmodeus yelled so that I could finally hear him.

- What? - I told him, turning to look at whatever he wanted to show me.

In his hands were two draft beers that he had just poured from the kettle at his private bar. I refused the beer and then turned my attention back to the heads, although they were all in the same place, they were no longer looking the same as before, it was as if they only remained static when someone was looking, so to confirm this, I quickly looked to the side and back at the heads, and then I realized that the heads moved when we weren't looking at them.

- Are those heads alive? - I asked him.

- Ignore them, they're not important - Asmodeus replied as he brought the beer, even though I refused.

I sat down in one of the armchairs as Asmodeus asked and drank the draft beer that he insisted upon.

- The draft is very good - I told him, who seemed to expect some comment.

- I knew you would like it, I make it myself - said Asmodeus, revealing himself to be a brewer in his spare time in hell.

I went straight to the point.

- I have finished the adjustments, when the lucid dreamers are killed their bodies will stay the way they were killed and the police or someone will have to fix them, and when they wake up their bodies will only disappear when they are alone - I explained to him.

- Excellent, I never doubted that you could solve these details. I also have news for you from me, I already have the right person taking care of your problem, it shouldn't take long for us to find you - said Asmodeus as he opened his desk drawer to get two Cuban cigars.

- I also closed the passage of the dreamers from the real world as you requested - I answered as I picked up a cigar and joined him to smoke.

- That's what I wanted to talk to you about, correct me if I'm wrong, once we enable it, dreamers from anywhere in the world will be able to enter the city, correct? - Asmodeus said, confirming that he understood correctly.

- Only lucid dreamers from the real world, if the person cannot control their dream, in other words, is not a lucid dreamer, they will not be able to reach DreamNopolis on their own - I answered him.

- Great, but could this "normal" person make it to DreamNopolis with another lucid dreamer? - Asmodeus asked.

- I don't know if it would work, but I can test or configure it so that lucid dreamers can be guides for non-lucid dreamers in DreamNopolis - I told him.

- Excellent! Let's finish these cigars and go to DreamNopolis - Asmodeus said, taking a big drag on his cigar and then a good swig on his beer.

- Are you going back to DreamNopolis? - I asked him.

- Yes, I'm going to spend a few days there and I also need to be there when they find you, after all, the city will still be active, won't it? Or were you lying to me? - Asmodeus questioned.

- I did not lie, the city will continue to function, yes - I confirmed to him.

We finished our drink and cigar and headed back to DreamNopolis, once again Asmodeus asked me to let him enjoy the city alone while I made the final arrangements for the release of the city to the lucid dreamers, he said he would be back in the morning and that this time it would be fun to see the interaction of the dreamers with the souls from hell that lived in the city.

The hours went by and I felt more and more exhausted, Bill had not shown up and was probably at some party instead of sleeping.

I left everything prepared for the lucid dreamers when Asmodeus arrived in the morning, all that was left to do was to define the limit number of dreamers who would arrive, the more I thought about this number, the greater the doubt.

I created arrival points in all the city's neighborhoods and initially set a limit of two thousand people as the limit of visitors. I went to the kitchen to prepare some coffee, even though I knew it would not have the desired effect, and as soon as the coffee was ready, someone knocked on the door.

Of course it was Asmodeus, who came right over, took a cup of my coffee and went to the computer room.

I walked him there and even though I drank enough coffee to make my hands shake, I was still sleepy.

Asmodeus noticed.

- You look terrible, I just don't tell you to sleep, because if you did you'd probably never wake up - Asmodeus said.

- I know that and if that happens, bye-bye DreamNopolis - I answered him, opening my mouth and letting out a yawn.

I guess he wasn't expecting this, as for a brief moment he moved his eyes to where the computer was and went back to drinking his coffee.

- I have set up arrival points in all the neighborhoods so that the dreamers arrive in different parts of the city, I have also set the initial maximum limit at two thousand people, so in case there are already more than two thousand dreamers in the city, no one else will be able to find DreamNopolis.

- I should have more employees like you - Asmodeus praised.

- Can I turn it on? - I asked him.

- Wait, what if it drains your last strength and you enter another dream? Have you thought about this possibility? - said Asmodeus.

- Yes, I have, so what do we do? - I asked him.

- I would come in the morning and ask you to do exactly what you have already done, although I would only release a thousand people, but who am I to say how many people your city can hold, right? - said Asmodeus.

- Right - I answered him without bringing up the subject, as my exhaustion was only increasing.

- We better do it this way, I'm going back to Hell and speed up your search, by no means release the dreamers before we find you - said Asmodeus, saying goodbye and asking me to invoke the portal for him to return to Hell.

I really didn't seem to have much time left, I couldn't stand up anymore because of sleep, I rubbed my eyes all the time trying to stay awake, but with each passing minute it became more difficult to control and not fall asleep. I couldn't stand it anymore, my thoughts were being taken by exhaustion, it seemed that the moment to face the consequence of sleeping inside DreamNopolis had arrived, but before closing my eyes again, I began to feel the sensation as if I was suffocating, it was as if my lungs could no longer pull air, is almost like I was drowning despite there being no water, still not knowing what was happening I kept fighting with all my strength to breathe or stay awake, since I didn't know what was happening anymore, I couldn't see anything and as soon as I could regain my sight and see the light again, the air started coming back into my lungs and suddenly I heard a familiar voice.

- So this is where you've been hiding all this time - Belatrix Hyssel said.

I had woken up, finally Asmodeus had kept his part of the bargain, and what I thought was the end, because I was falling asleep, was actually my rescue taking place.

- Take this water - Belatrix said, handing me a large bottle of water.

I remained lying down without much strength, I took the bottle and took a few sips of water and also splashed some on my head, with each sip I began to feel as if life was returning to that body of mine that stank of rotting skin and bugs everywhere.

I took some more water and poured it on my head again, and as I did this the bugs began to shed my skin, which was beginning to regenerate back.

- Get me out of here - I told her when I finally managed to say something.

With her unusual strength she lifted me onto her back and carried me to the car.

- You must be starving, your house is far away, shall we stop somewhere for you to take a shower and get something to eat? - asked Belatrix.

- No, straight to my place - I insisted.

- We are very far away, I'll have to stop at a gas station, take advantage and use the bathroom, there are clothes, towel, soap, shampoo, and money in the back seat - insisted Belatrix.

- Okay - I answered, since I didn't have the strength to argue.

She drove for a few hours until we reached a gas station, on the way she helped me get rid of the rest of the bugs on my skin so that when I got out of the car and went to the gas station bathroom no one would be scared.

I was feeling better and better and when I got to the gas station I reconsidered the idea of taking a shower, with some difficulty I managed to get up and go to the bathroom by myself.

It was only when I saw myself in the bathroom mirror after showering that I realized how badly I was looking, my skin had regenerated, but achieved a rather grayish color, I also had to shave my hair since being buried for so long had made it look horrible. I put on the clothes that Belatrix gave me, they were baggy which showed that I had also lost some weight while being buried, before leaving the bathroom I looked at myself once more in the mirror and although I started to feel good, the image that I reflected was of a person whose appearance seemed to be terminally ill and about to die.

I went to the cafeteria and Belatrix was waiting for me there, sitting at a table full of food stuff. I didn't complain, I sat down and tasted a little bit of everything, until I decided what was best and ordered more.

My recovery seemed to be speeding up, although it was not yet reflected physically, I could feel it.

I found out that we were a days drive from home, so I thought I would go to the phone booth at the gas station and call Bill, let him know that I had been rescued and was on my way home, I went to the phone booth, but when I got there I found out that it didn't work.

I went back to the car where Belatrix was waiting for me.

- Do you have a cell phone, I want to call Bill - I told her.

- I do - replied Belatrix handing me her cell phone.

I tried to call several times, but every time it went to voicemail.

During the trip Belatrix insisted on stopping several times and even tried to seduce me by suggesting we relive the moment in my room, but I had no head for that, I just wanted to get home soon.

- If you're tired I can drive while you rest - I told her.

- You'll figure it out later, but the longer you remain immortal, the less often you will need to sleep or feel tired - replied Belatrix.

- So that's why you didn't answer the message I sent you from the dream world? - I asked her.

- Probably, because I haven't slept in over fifty years - answered Belatrix.

We were near the city and after four days awake and inside that car, sleep was starting to hit, even so I resisted until we arrived home.

When we finally arrived, I got out of the car, almost running.

- Calm down cowboy, what's the hurry? - said Belatrix.

I didn't pay attention, I found the key in the usual secret place and as soon as I entered the house my suspicions were confirmed, Bill had turned my house into a pigsty and moved several things around.

- Holy shit ... - I exclaimed upon seeing the condition of the house.

Besides the house being dirty, it was also empty, there was no one there besides Belatrix and me, there was also no sign of Bill.

I went to my room and at least this he had respected, it seemed a separate place to the house, the only clean place and it was exactly as I had left it.

While I was cleaning the house, Belatrix asked for permission to use my bathroom and take a shower to recover from the trip, I agreed and then cleaned the house returning my things to their place while she bathed.

- Wow, you are quite a cleaner. - said Belatrix teasing me as she came out of the bathroom wrapped in her towel.

- Tell me it hasn't gotten much better and more habitable? - I retorted.

- Yes, it has, aren't you tired? - asked Belatrix.

- Why? You keep asking me if I'm tired all the time, what if I don't sleep? - I asked her.

- You know why, silly, you just prefer to play dumb - replied Belatrix in a different tone.

- Asmodeus thinks you've already managed to recover, he's looking forward to your return, he said you need to continue the work you were doing - Belatrix continued, now speaking again in her serious tone.

- Got it, I forgot that time passes differently there, these sleepless days here were weeks there. But I can't sleep yet, I need some more time before going back - I answered her.

- Okay, but I'll have to stay here until you talk to Asmodeus, those are orders, and I intend to follow them - Belatrix said.

The mood between us had faded, she went back to the bedroom and got dressed, now I realized that she was there only as my babysitter, and Asmodeus was waiting for me eagerly.

- I'm going to my room, you can stay in Bill's room or on the couch - I told her, not caring about chivalry.

I got to my bedroom, went to the bathroom to take another bath to relax and try to get sleepy while I was in the tub. The bathtub was full and hot, before getting in I remembered that I had some marijuana cigarettes in my secret hiding place, I went there and for my joy, they were still there, I left the lighter and the joint next to the bathtub, I got in and finally after so long I smoked the green one from the real world.

The joint and the hot water did their job, I dozed off right there in the tub and as soon as I fell asleep I went straight back to DreamNopolis.

The city was just as I had left it, functioning perfectly even after spending a few days in the real world. The exhaustion and tiredness I had felt before was also gone, I felt even stronger and more composed than the first time in DreamNopolis.

I didn't stay long in DreamNopolis, I needed to find Asmodeus in hell to continue the release of the city to the lucid dreamers and I also needed to thank him for fulfilling his part of our deal, freeing me.

I went back to hell and again Asmodeus was in Sodom.

- What took you so long? - Asmodeus asked, looking very impatient.

- Not even a "Hi Charles, how are you?" Or anything like that? I'm fine, thank you for asking. After being asleep for so long, it's not surprising that it takes a few days to get sleepy, is it? The important thing is that I'm here and DreamNopolis continued to work as I told you it would - I told him.

- I'm glad you're alright, but knowing that I was waiting for you to put phase two into action, you could have come quicker - Asmodeus said.

- So I did come. Shall we go to DreamNopolis then? - I asked him.

He agreed, and then we went back to the city and respectively in front of the computer.

It was time to release the lucid dreamers, everything was prepared, all that was missing was to "flip" the switch that connected the real world lucid dreamers to DreamNopolis, so they would start arriving and there would be the limit of two thousand people, which would be easily reached since it would be open to the whole world.

That was not exactly what happened, when it was activated, we watched the radar that showed the colors of the little balls identifying the lucid dreamers and the inhabitants of the city, only minutes after the dreamers began to appear, the little balls that identified the lucid dreamers were gradually appearing on the radar, which were distributed at the arrival points that I had scattered around the city.

- Is something wrong? - Asmodeus asked.

- Not that I know of - I answered him.

- Only a few are arriving - Asmodeus pointed out.

I checked again on the computer and could not figure out what was going on, so there was only one thing we could do to try to understand what was going on, go to one of the dreamers and ask how he had gotten to DreamNopolis, so we would know what could be going on and why so few people were getting there.

We went to the nearest arrival point of the dreamers and there we found a group of three people, Weverton, Thiago and Flora.

They had just arrived from different places in the world and were talking to each other, although they did not speak the same language they managed to understand each other and of course they did not know how it happened or where they were.

We approached them and introduced ourselves, taking the role of "game master" giving them a short introduction and explaining where they were and how DreamNopolis worked. Since they were lucid dreamers, they knew we were telling the truth and that they were dreaming, only this time it was a dream totally different from anything they had ever experienced.

We questioned how they arrived in DreamNopolis and the only one who remembered details was Thiago, so while the others were talking to Asmodeus, I was talking to him.

I didn't even know what questions to ask, but nevertheless managed to find a way to ask them anyway.

- You said you remembered your dream before you came here, could you tell us a little about how it went and what you remember? - I asked him.

- Of course, I don't remember much, but after falling into deep sleep, what usually happens occurred, I entered the astral projection, in this state I can see my own body sleeping and can wander through the real world as if I were a spirit, but this time I could see a huge and strong yellow light on the horizon and this aroused my curiosity, I went towards the light, but in a blink I was already here - answered Thiago, basically telling us everything we wanted to hear.

- I think you have helped enough, I won't keep you any longer, go and enjoy DreamNopolis with your new friends - I told him.

- Thank you, see you around - Thiago said, leaving in the direction of the others.

- Have you found out what you need? - Asmodeus asked soon after letting the dreamers leave to the city.

- Yes, let's get back to the computer - I told him walking towards my house.

- What are you going to do? - Asmodeus asked on the way home.

- Not all people will risk following a giant beam of light, I believe that is why the numbers are not so high, I will try to change this entrance and make it more interesting to attract and pique the curiosity of dreamers - I answered him as we arrived home.

I went straight to the computer, I don't know how but I seemed to know exactly where to go and what to do, I changed the way the entrance would be, now the strong light would write in the sky the following phrase "DreamNopolis the city made for lucid dreamers, come see it, you will be surprised", as soon as they followed the light they would arrive in the city.

I told Asmodeus about the change I had made, he just looked thoughtful and said nothing, so I activated this new configuration. With it active I checked the radar and this time we had the expected result, the maximum capacity of DreamNopolis had already been reached and the radar showed us the several little balls in the colors that represented the lucid dreamers scattered around the city and as soon as one dreamer left, another one took their place.

- It's working - I told him.

- It's perfect! - exclaimed Asmodeus.

Before I could say anything more, I ended up waking up in the real world, for it was already daylight and Belatrix had put on some loud music in the kitchen while she prepared breakfast.

I took a shower, brushed my teeth and got dressed for breakfast.

- Good morning - I told her when I arrived in the kitchen.

- Good morning, sunshine, from what I see you are more cheerful and with a better expression on your face, did you have good dreams? - asked Belatrix as she grabbed a cup and poured me some coffee.

- I managed to solve some issues that were missing in DreamNopolis and what made me happiest was waking up like a normal person does and coming back to the real world - I told her as I took some slices of bread and put them in the toaster.

- On my next nap I will try to get to know this city of yours - said Belatrix.

- What is your issue with sleeping? - I asked her again.

- Basically it's like I explained to you before in the car, the longer you're immortal the less you can sleep, Asmodeus thinks this is a way to make immortals suffer even more for being alive, when they shouldn't be - Belatrix said as she took my toast out of the toaster.

- And how do you feel not sleeping? Do you have any side effects? May I ask how long you have been alive? - I asked her.

- How rude, asking a lady her age - deflected Belatrix.

- Really? Do immortals have such frills too? - I said ironically.

- HA HA HA HA! You really don't mess around, now I know why Oliver liked you so much. I don't mind telling you my age, I just don't want to say it, and about how I feel not sleeping, sweetie one day you'll start to feel the same way, be patient that your turn will come - said Belatrix still drinking her coffee casually.

- I get it, Asmodeus doesn't let you say everything you want to - I provoked her.

- I prefer to corrupt the purity and innocence of people, sarcasm and cleverness don't usually appeal to me, and apparently you came back full of it from where you were - Belatrix said in a cryptic tone and left, telling me she was going to take a shower.

I finished my breakfast and found it strange that there was still no sign of Bill, so I decided to go out and look for him in the places he usually stayed, even though I knew he wasn't supposed to be there.

I went to all the places he could be, but I couldn't find him in any of them, I also tried to call him again on his cell phone, but to no avail, there seemed to be something wrong, something was bothering me and that usual feeling of distrust - a flea behind the ear - was beginning to alarm me.

I went back home and there was no one there, I went to my room and decided to go to sleep, I needed to talk to Asmodeus and ask him about Bill.

I fell asleep and went back to DreamNopolis, I went to where the city configuration computer was, but to my surprise when I got there, Asmodeus and Bill were there.

I managed to get into the room so the two of them couldn't see me, I kept peeking around trying to understand what was going on there.

- You've been messing with this computer for days, what have you got? - Asmodeus asked Bill.

- I have already told you, Charles has given me limited permission, they don't allow me to access the computer programs, that is, I can only change structures in the city, I can also create missions, but for them to be activated, we need Charles - answered Bill.

- Then we'll have to convince him to give you this permission - Asmodeus said.

- Why isn't Charles here? Surely he would know what to do - said Bill.

- The poor guy has already worked too hard, let's say that you would be the copilot while he is not here, there is also the issue that with time immortals lose the ability to sleep and to access the dream world, he shouldn't even be able to create something in the dream world, before him no immortal had managed this - said Asmodeus.

- So this is where you were all the time, Bill? And how is DreamNopolis going, Asmodeus, are you enjoying it? - I asked, suddenly interrupting both of them, who were startled.

- Charles, you arrived just in time, we didn't want to disturb you so soon, since you have just returned to the real world, and while you were there, Bill was helping me to better understand how all this works, but according to him, you didn't give him the necessary permission - Asmodeus said, taking the lead and as usual lying.

- It is not possible for another person to make settings on the computer, the most I can do is give permission to create objects, missions and the bodies of souls, if necessary - I told Asmodeus.

- Are you sure? - Asmodeus asked again.

- Yes, I have tried to open up some functions on the computer for testing purposes, but it never worked - I answered him.

- But what exactly can Bill do? If something happens in DreamNopolis when you are not there and we need to do something, what do we do? - Asmodeus asked, while Bill just watched attentively as we talked.

- When I give Bill maximum permission, he will be able to create buildings, houses and entire missions in DreamNopolis, and he will also be able to create the bodies and personalities for the new souls, that's all - I answered him.

- You could grant the same permissions to me - Asmodeus said.

- I can't grant any creation permissions to immortals, nor to the inhabitants of the city, I tried to grant basic functions to Nietzsche and you, but I couldn't - I answered him.

- We have to make some changes in the city, you have no idea how successful it's been, Bill has been here full time for a while making some adjustments to missions and changing a bit what he could of the city - said Asmodeus.

- You could have waited for me, Asmodeus, don't you have to go back to hell? And how come Bill has been here so long without waking up? - I asked them.

- Bill took some medicine to stay asleep for a few days, about going back to hell, it was you who left me here, there was no way I could go back - said Asmodeus.

I forgot about that, but when Asmodeus mentioned the way back to hell was through the portal and didn't talk about the other way, by dying, I immediately thought about him being afraid of dying in DreamNopolis and like the other souls, going to purgatory instead of back to hell.

- You know you could have killed yourself or had Bill kill you, right? Then you would go back there - I told him.

- I'm still not sure what would happen, would I go back to hell or would this restart my cycle? So the next time I go back I will bring some monsters and Belfegor, one of hell's leaders, to do this test, after he gets to know the city we will kill him and see if this will return him to hell or purgatory - said Asmodeus revealing his concern and plan.

Before he went back to hell Asmodeus asked me to increase the amount of dreamers in the city, he said he wanted around one hundred thousand lucid dreamers in the city at a time and to leave the portal open for him to return from hell with the guinea pigs so we could test what would happen if the monsters and a leader from hell were killed in DreamNopolis.

I opened the portal and kept it open until Asmodeus returned.

- So you are working with Asmodeus behind my back? - said Bill.

- No! I didn't even know you would be here, and don't forget, you're the one who got dragged me into this shitty mess, remember? - said Bill.

- You'll never forget that, will you? - I retorted.

- We're still on the same side, right? - I asked him.

- Of course, why are you asking me that? - said Bill.

- I'm suspicious of Asmodeus, I think he's looking for someone to replace me or someone he can control more easily, I'm sure he's up to something - I told him.

- But it's only you who can control the city, he told me something about the souls that were stuck in hell and turning into monsters, that are now residents of DreamNopolis and if they are killed by lucid dreamers they can follow their cycle to purgatory - said Bill.

- Yes, but there are still some things that Asmodeus is not telling us, so we have to be careful not to be taken by surprise. Speaking of surprises, where are you? Why aren't you at home? - I said to him.

- I'm in a kind of infirmary, it's like I'm in an induced coma that lasts a few days - answered Bill.

- How long have you been here? - I asked him.

- I don't know, I think ten days of DreamNopolis - answered Bill.

- Um... Have you been monitoring the lucid dreamers? Tell me what you were doing - I asked him.

- When I arrived there was no one here in the house and apparently Asmodeus didn't know exactly where or when I would arrive, so I had to look for him. There was no sign of him, so I went back home and sat down at the computer to see if I could find him on the radar - said Bill.

- Can you use radar? - I asked, interrupting him.

- Yes, I can see the little colored circles that identify who is in DreamNopolis, I found a little ball with a different color - gray - and deduced that it was Asmodeus, he was together with several other city dwellers in the casino that is located in the Munique neighborhood, even though it was far away I went there and only managed to find him after bribing some security guards and find that he was in one of the secret rooms of the casino with the heirs of DreamNopolis, I tried to enter or approach to hear what they were talking about, but as soon as I approached Asmodeus opened the door as if something had warned him that I arrived. After he saw me he did the usual fake ceremony, greeted me and introduced me to the other heirs, even though they already knew me, after that we came here after I told him I had found him using the radar - explained Bill.

- And that's all you know? - I asked him again.

- Yes, so far that's all I know - answered Bill.

I had no idea what Asmodeus was up to, and it seemed that Bill didn't know much either, so everything in DreamNopolis was news to us, to the immortals, and to the leaders of Hell.

Bill and I continued talking, I gave him some instructions in case something happened to me and also asked him to go home when he woke up.

Before we could agree on more things, the portal made a small noise and out of it came Asmodeus, Belfegor, a monster and a person, the last two of whom were tied up and wearing collars around their necks.

- Look at Belfegor and admire everything that my words could not explain - said Asmodeus.

I thought Belfegor would say something, but he just filled his lungs with air and then sighed, while looking to the side, observing DreamNopolis.

- Who are these two? - I asked them.

- Ah yes, this is Charles the Immortal who created all of this, he's the promising employee I told you about, precocious at everything, job promotion, immortal power, being betrayed by his guardian, and he's also a great questioner - Asmodeus said with a laugh as he introduced me to Belfegor.

Once again Belfegor just looked at me and didn't say a word.

- You still don't believe what I have told you, huh? I'll show you - Asmodeus said as he walked towards a car that was passing by on the street.

The car came closer and closer and slowed down to avoid driving over Asmodeus, until it stopped completely.

- Buddy we have a problem here, can you help us? - said Asmodeus to the driver.

- Problem? - asked the driver.

- Yes, my wife is having our baby and she can't wait for the cab to arrive. Could you help us take her to the hospital? - Asmodeus asked.

- Gee, sure, where is she? - asked the driver.

- I will need your help to carry her, she is over there in our house - said Asmodeus pointing to my house.

Gladly the driver parked in front of the garage and went down to help Asmodeus, but as soon as the driver got inside he was hit on the head and fell to the ground unconscious.

- Do you have any weapons here? - Asmodeus asked.

- No, but... - I was answering him, but was interrupted.

- Bill, create a weapon with a silencer, Charles, go to the computer and find out the name of this soul, I will demonstrate to Belfegor that the souls that have served their sentence in hell when killed in DreamNopolis by lucid dreamers follow their cycles, I also brought these two, a monster and this soul that has not yet served its sentence in hell to find out what happens when we do the same thing to them - Asmodeus said.

I did as he asked, found out the name of the resident that Asmodeus had kidnapped, went back to the room where they were and Bill had fashioned a nine millimeter revolver with a silencer.

- Very good Bill. Did Charles find the name of this soul? - Asmodeus asked.

- Yes, I did. His name in DreamNopolis is Danúbio Soares, but the soul's name is Ayumi Watanabi - I told Asmodeus, handing him the folder with Ayumi's data.

Asmodeus looked through the folder and once he had checked a few things, he asked Bill to shoot.

Bill took his time, but after a while he shot Danube in the head.

- There! Belfegor, look for yourself where this soul who had already served his sentence in hell went - said Asmodeus handing him the folder.

Belfegor and Asmodeus went through the portal to hell again, a few minutes later they came back, and for the first time I heard Belfegor speaking.

- This soul is indeed in purgatory waiting to continue its cycle, impressive - said Belfegor.

- And that's why I brought these two, a soul that is still serving its sentence and this monster that was once a soul that served its punishment in hell - said Asmodeus pointing to the two collared men and telling Bill to shoot again.

Again, after hesitating for a while, Bill shot them both.

Once again Belfegor and Asmodeus returned to hell, and just like the first time, they came back talking.

- I'm not buying it, the monster's soul reincarnated instantly without going through purgatory and the waiting line. Moreover, that soul's cycle, which was the fifth, was reset to the first - said Belfegor with an astonished face.

- Are you sure? That can't be possible - said Asmodeus.

- What does this mean? Why are you so surprised? - I asked them.

They did not answer me, but returned to their previous neutral posture when they realized that they had said too much.

- The soul that did not fulfill its sentence went back to hell - Asmodeus said, confirming the fate of the other test.

Asmodeus had already agreed with Bill that as soon as we knew what had happened with the first two tests, he would shoot Belfegor, and that's exactly what he did.

- Why did you do this? - I asked, surprised to see Belfegor dead.

- Stop your crying. We need to do this one more test, he would never accept it gladly, and also he was on Beelzebub's side, plotting behind my back all this time - Asmodeus said.

- What is Beelzebub up to? I forgot that he is out there in the human world - I told him.

- I'll tell you later, I need to find out the result of the last test now - Asmodeus said, entering the portal and returning to hell.

Before I could talk more with Bill about what had happened, I woke up again in the real world.

After a few hours playing video games and thinking about what was happening, the front door opened and Bill finally arrived.

- Turn on the TV, have you seen the news about DreamNopolis? - said Bill, coming in all agitated.

- News about DreamNopolis? What do you mean? - I asked him as I immediately picked up the remote and put it on the news channel.

On the news channel the headline was, "DreamNopolis - the city of dreams - they were talking about reports from all over the world of people who during their dreams arrived in this city, they were making friends with people from other places in the world and when they woke up they came into contact with each other in the real world as well, thus discovering that DreamNopolis is much more than just a dream. There were also reports and interviews on other TV channels, in them the dreamers continued to tell more about the city and everyone was amazed at what they could do in the city of dreams.

- What the fuck is this? - I asked Bill.

- They took me out of the induced coma a few hours ago and while coming here by Uber this news started playing on the car radio - Bill said.

- I hadn't thought about this possibility, people spreading it to the world about DreamNopolis and I didn't expect other people to believe it either - I told him.

- I wonder what Asmodeus and hell will think about this? - asked Bill.

- I don't know - I answered.

We continued watching TV, the reports were all over the world and several people believed and wanted to know, some others thought it was some kind of collective outbreak.

We went away from the TV and searched the internet for information about DreamNopolis where we found people offering tourism services and even excursions to visit the city.

In such a short time this had taken on proportions I would never have imagined, as we read about the incredible things people reported having experienced in DreamNopolis, I grew more afraid, for I did not know what hell's reaction would be and the impact on the natural order of things.

As night fell, I didn't want to sleep, but at the same time I wanted to put an end to the anguish and find out what Asmodeus thought about DreamNopolis being popular among humans, so I accepted the sleeping medicine Bill offered me and minutes later slumber finally came. As soon as I fell asleep I returned to DreamNopolis and minutes later Bill also appeared there, before I brought Asmodeus back from hell I decided to check the city and the inhabitants, everything was all right, I took the opportunity to increase the limit for lucid dreamers, because I noticed that it was more crowded than ever and after this I called the portal for Asmodeus, who didn't take long to go through it, showing how eager he was.

- At last the sleeping uglies are back - Asmodeus said, referring to both of us as he passed through the portal.

- Welcome back, I didn't even have to go all the way to hell to pick you up this time, were you eager? - I asked him in an ironic tone.

- Actually I saw the portal, so I decided to save time and come here - said Asmodeus.

- We have news - said Bill.

- I also have news about our tests, but first, tell me your news - said Asmodeus.

- The lucid dreamers are telling the real world about DreamNopolis, some of them are even offering services to bring normal people to the city - said Asmodeus, explaining him very directly about our news.

- Oh, is that so? I imagined this would happen when we enabled the humans to enter, I don't see any problem, in fact, this seems to me even better than just the lucid dreamers coming, now the rich will also be able to experiment and donate their fortunes to our dream agents - said Asmodeus, who seemed to be planning things steps ahead of us.

- I don't see a problem either - said Bill.

- And why would you see anything? - I asked Bill, but before he could answer Asmodeus spoke again.

- Later you two can have your little couple's fight, but first let me tell you about what happened with our experiments - said Asmodeus excitedly.

- Okay - we agreed, so he continued.

- You won't believe what happened to Belfegor when we killed him in DreamNopolis - said Asmodeus in a mysterious manner.

- Belfegor turned into an angel - I told him, guessing.

- But how do you know? - Asmodeus asked, surprised.

- Is that really what happened? - I said, until I was interrupted

- Of course not! Shut up and let me talk. Belfegor completed all his cycles and went to heaven - said Asmodeus.

- Completed all his cycles? What do you mean? - asked Bill.

- That's it! We the seven leaders of hell, are souls who were missing one of the twelve cycles to finish our journey and go to paradise, but Lucifer told us that paradise is a place where all who go never come back, he also told us that it is a place where we become one with God, so there is only the eternal feeling of satisfaction and happiness, that is, none of the carnal and mundane feelings reach there, so we the seven leaders of hell accepted the proposal of freezing our cycle and with that, turning into the demons we are today - said Asmodeus explaining the origin of the leaders of hell.

- And this is good? - I asked him.

- Yes, we can use this as an option for Beelzebub and in case some other leader messes with us, but we can't lose this advantage, so don't tell anyone else about this - Asmodeus said, asking for secrecy among the three of us.

- We could have an event in DreamNopolis where the dreamers and residents would kill the monsters we release from hell, so that these souls could be purified - said Bill.

- Good idea, but we'll think about it later, now Charles needs to adjust a few things before you two wake up. Charles, increase the number of lucid dreamers, limit entry by country, and also do something about the tour guides who will bring people who aren't lucid dreamers, I'm not sure what to do, but I think you will know - Asmodeus said.

I went to the computer and adjusted the proportion of lucid dreamers to be the same among the countries, and when one country did not meet the minimum quantity that proportion would be distributed again to the other countries, but I did not know exactly what to do about the guides who would take normal people to DreamNopolis, even so I added some conditions, if the guide left the city the tourists would leave along with them, after the dreamers who were not lucid dreamers entered the city for the first time, they would not need to have a guide again, because after this they would be able to return alone the next time.

I explained the adjustments to Asmodeus and explained how it would work, although we did not agree on the amount of lucid dreamers and on giving the ability to normal people to return alone, we came to an agreement to try it this way at the beginning.

We sent Asmodeus back down to Hell, so that he wouldn't be loose in DreamNopolis and although he didn't want to go, I was firm and said that if he didn't go I would expel him, so with a frown he went through the portal and after a while Bill and I woke up, returning to the real world.

But as soon as I opened my eyes I was surprised by Belatrix watching me morbidly with a needle in my neck, which caused me to black out again, only this time I didn't stop in DreamNopolis, I was somewhere in the dream world, but in a dark room and no matter how hard I tried or how hard I pushed, I couldn't do anything to get out of there.

Just as I was beginning to lose hope, a small beam of light appeared and as soon as I looked into it, I was pulled out, waking up in a kind of hospital bed with my hands and feet tied together.

With my eyes still a little blurry and my vision returning little by little, I could see that there was someone waiting for me to wake up, it was Belatrix, she settled on the chair as soon as she realized that I had woken up.

- Apparently you're not happy to be stuck in the limbo, you don't have to look at me like that - said Belatrix.

- Limbo? Why did you do that? - I asked her.

- You shouldn't underestimate all the years of knowledge we have in front of you, we have potions and spells you can't even imagine, one of these potions doesn't allow you to dream while unconscious, in other words, limbo. You have something valuable and it needs to be controlled, in addition to being very stubborn you like to do things your way - replied Belatrix.

- I get it, I've learned my lesson, you can get me out of here - I told her.

- No, you won't get out of there so soon, you better get used to it because things are going to start getting even more intense, but only in the next story - said Belatrix introducing another syringe and throwing me into limbo again.

Back in the limbo, the place I am at the moment, I write this story in an attempt to keep my mind sane, waiting for an opportunity to share it with someone and maybe even getting some help.

CONTINUES IN THE NEXT BOOK...

www.ingramcontent.com/pod-product-compliance
Lightning Source LLC
LaVergne TN
LVHW041458170726
843492LV00005B/1290